Troth

E. H. Lupton

Winnowing Fan Press, Madison, WI

For Bryan,
because of the curse tablets,
and for other reasons he can probably guess.

Chapter 1

ULYSSES FINALLY, OFFICIALLY, LEGALLY moved in with Sam ten days after someone blew up the physics building. It felt like ten days into a new future he wasn't too sure he liked or understood. One man had been killed; the city was still on edge. The physics building was also known as Sterling Hall, and although there was no relation as far as they knew to Sam's grandfather, who was arguably evil and definitely a biology professor, it felt like an ill omen. Everyone with an office on the west side of campus was still picking up broken glass.

Ulysses had just set down a box of books on the living room floor when there was a knock behind him. He turned, thinking he'd accidentally shut the door all the way and left Sam or Obe stranded in the hall, but no. It was wide open, and there was a tall, thin Indian man standing at the threshold, one hand raised in greeting.

Ulysses mirrored the gesture. "Can I help you?"

"I'm your neighbor," the man said. He gestured nervously over his shoulder at the door across the hall, apartment 4B, the only other one on the top floor of the

Baskerville building. "This is going to sound rather odd, but—are you Ulysses Lenkov?"

Ulysses confirmed that he was. "Have we met?"

The man shook his head. "My name is Vikram Ranganathan. I met your sister earlier today." Vikram was dressed neatly despite the heat, in a short-sleeved collared shirt and slacks. No tie, but he did have a couple of pens stuck in a pocket protector in his breast pocket. Almost certainly a professor.

"Celeste?" Ulysses asked, mostly in an attempt to keep the conversation going, since Vikram had fallen silent.

"Yes," Vikram said. "Oh, excuse me."

Sam had come out of the stairwell carrying a box labeled *Records* and was hovering awkwardly behind Vikram. The other man shuffled sideways; Ulysses flattened himself to the wall to let Sam get past.

"You met Celeste," Ulysses prompted. "At her shop?"

"Yes."

"And she sent you here to talk to me."

"Yes," Vikram said. He was watching Sam over Ulysses's shoulder as he set down his box and then straightened up and stretched. Ulysses glanced back at Vikram, and waited. Sam was a lot to look at, sometimes: rangy, curly dark hair, olive skin, light green eyes the color of grass in the spring. Vikram was married, to judge by the ring on his finger, and his interest in Sam seemed half curious, half uncomfortable. Ulysses realized after a moment that his visitor was waiting some kind of reassurance that it was okay to talk about whatever was bothering him in front of Sam.

Ulysses exhaled. "Was there a problem that led you to Celeste's shop?"

"Yes," Vikram said again. "We have a ghost." Ulysses waited, eyebrows raised, and finally the dam burst. "My mother passed away six months ago, and she has been haunting our apartment ever since, causing a ruckus and keeping us up all night. My wife has said she will leave me if I don't figure out how to get rid of her. Someone at work suggested I go to your sister's shop, because it seemed like the kind of place to find things to deal with ghosts. But when she found out what was going on and where I lived, she said I should come talk to you instead." He eyed Ulysses. "I realize this probably sounds very strange. Do you deal with ghosts?"

"I do." Ulysses noticed abruptly how sweaty and grimy he was from carrying boxes and cleaning all day. Obe appeared through the door to the stairs carrying yet another box, and Ulysses decided to move the conversation. "Come in," he said to Vikram, who followed him through the living room, past Sam's curious gaze, and into the kitchen. It was a nice space, with golden yellow counters and a large east-facing window over the sink. They'd shoved a small vinyl and chrome table from Sam's previous apartment into the breakfast nook. Ulysses waved Vikram to a chair and went over to the sink. "What does she want?" he asked. "The ghost, I mean. Did she tell you?"

3

Behind them, Obe announced, "I think there's one more down there." Sam groaned.

"Flip you for it."

"Fuck you, man. Go get it yourself. I'm sitting down."

"Come on, I'll get you a beer if you go."

"You'll get me one anyway, thank you, because I helped carry this gigantic sofa up all those damn stairs. What's it made out of, solid lead?"

Vikram smiled warily. "I'm sorry to barge in on you. There's obviously a lot going on today."

"Don't worry about it," Ulysses said. He bent over to splash water on his face. "Sorry about the chaos."

Vikram laughed at that. "You're moving, of course it's chaotic."

Ulysses straightened. Unable to find a towel, he wiped his face on the hem of his shirt. "So about your ghost . . ."

Sam came in and opened the fridge, having apparently conceded the argument. "The beer isn't cold yet," he said. After a little further exploration, he stepped back, glancing at Ulysses with mounting panic in his eyes. "Actually, nothing in here is cold."

"I don't know," Ulysses said. "It was working when we did the walk-through. I think."

A moment later, Vikram said, "Did you remember to plug it in?"

Sam looked behind the fridge and swore under his breath.

"The same thing happened when my wife and I moved in," Vikram said sympathetically. "I think the property management company defrosts them during the turnover."

"He lives across the hall," Ulysses explained, and Sam's eyebrows rose. "This is Vikram. Vikram, this is Sam."

They shook hands. Vikram said, "Are you roommates? Or you're just here to help?"

"I live here," Sam said easily.

"Vikram has a problem with a ghost," Ulysses said. "We were just figuring out when I could go over and check it out. Is there anything tomorrow night that I'm forgetting about?"

"That dinner at your grandmother's," Sam said.

"Shoot." He ran his hands through his hair. "How's Saturday?"

Vikram shook his head. "She said today or she walks." He spoke lightly, but Ulysses could see the restrained fear in his eyes.

Ulysses glanced at Sam. "Do you need me for the next two hours?"

Sam leaned back against the fridge. "If you bring the last box up, I'll even go get the pizza myself."

"I can probably handle that." To Vikram, he said, "Do you have candles? Because I'm never going to find any in here."

Vikram, who had been watching their discussion with interest, nodded slowly. "Like dinner candles?"

"Sure."

Vikram's mother, Dr. Parvati Ranganathan, came when

Ulysses summoned her, and then refused to leave or speak to him. She was a tall, serious woman with her gray hair drawn back, her face a stolid version of Vikram's. She wore professional clothing, a knee-length skirt and suit coat in brown tweed and a cream-colored blouse with a bow at the neck. It was interesting the things the dead imagined themselves in. Many of them dressed like they were headed off to work, the same as they had every day of their lives. It was a habit, probably. Ulysses would have chosen something more comfortable.

"Dr. Ranganathan," Ulysses said for the fourth or fifth time. She didn't even look at him, just glared at Vikram. Ulysses sighed. "Does she speak English?"

"She was born in *London*! She speaks better English than I do." Vikram said. "Normally, she's very talkative. That's half the problem. I don't know why she's doing this." He threw up his hands. "Mum, you have to leave. Mr. Lenkov is here—"

"Dr. Lenkov."

Vikram looked over at him, one eyebrow raised, but continued: "Dr. Lenkov is here to talk to you. He's a professional."

Dr. Parvati Ranganathan crossed her arms in front of her chest and said nothing.

Ulysses wasn't used to being ignored by ghosts. Most of them had difficulty talking to the living and expressed relief when they found him. He glanced at Vikram. "Your call if you want to proceed," he said.

6

Poor Vikram looked devastated, but his spine was stiff, and when he spoke, his voice didn't quaver. "Yeah," he said. "Go for it. What do you need?"

It took more than two hours to set up and execute the banishment spell, laying out the sigil in salt on a silver-plated tea tray. He felt slightly sheepish doing so under her watchful eyes, as though he were a child in his grandmother's kitchen again, being walked through his first lessons in sigil, sacrifice, spellcraft. But it worked.

When she'd gone, Ulysses sat on the rug in Vikram's bedroom, wearily watching the other man blow out the candles. He fished a lemon drop out of his pocket and sucked on it, thinking about all the unpacking left to take care of when he got back across the hall.

"You all right?" Vikram asked, offering him a hand up.

"Just exhausted." He offered a half smile. "That took a lot out of me."

"So I see." Vikram opened the door. "Well, I just heard the missus come in, so you'd better come and meet her before you go home."

Vikram's wife, Sita, was sitting on the sofa, swarmed by two affectionate cats that must have been in hiding before. She was a beautiful woman who stood as tall as Ulysses, with dark eyes and long dark hair. "What were you doing in there?" she said mischievously, eyeing the bedroom door.

"This is Dr. Ulysses Lenkov," Vikram said. "He lives across the hall now. He's gotten rid of M—the ghost."

She blinked. "Well, in that case, welcome to the neighborhood." She got up and shook his hand. "When did you move in?"

Ulysses looked at his watch. "About three hours ago."

Sita laughed. "What did he offer to get you to come over here?"

"I just didn't want to be involved in organizing the books." He stuck his hands in his pockets. "I live with a librarian. You can imagine what it's like."

"Of course. It's a dire problem." She smiled. "Is this what you do professionally?"

"Ghost removal? Not exactly. I'm an assistant professor."

"At UW? In what?"

"Magic."

Both Sita and Vikram nodded at that. "Can we offer you dinner?" Sita asked. Her eyes flickered down at his hands. "You could invite your—wife? Girlfriend?"

"My boyfriend." It was possibly the first time he'd said the title aloud; everyone else they knew had known they were together almost from the get-go. It felt odd in his mouth, like it wasn't quite the right term. Insufficient for how important the relationship was to him, maybe. "Some other time?" he added. "We've already promised my brother-in-law pizza and beer tonight for helping with the move." He was starting to feel shaky despite the candy he'd eaten, his body reminding him that it didn't like ghosts, the muscles in his back tight like bow strings. It was time to get out of there.

If Sita noticed, she didn't comment, just said, "I'll hold you to it." He escaped out into the hallway, which was warm and stuffy. Sam was just stepping out of the stairwell carrying cardboard boxes of pizza and a six-pack.

"Hey," he said. "You look wretched. Come and eat."

Ulysses wasn't sure if he wanted to grab the pizza and devour it or wrap himself around Sam, so he contented himself with carrying the beer. "Sorry to abandon you like that." He opened the door, and Sam followed him in. Obe had apparently opened every window in the apartment to air it out and then stretched out to doze on the sofa.

Their new place was oddly shaped, because the Baskerville building was roughly triangular in its footprint. A short hallway led to the living room. On the right, a long hall led to Ulysses's office and the bedroom. The two of them toed off their shoes and turned left, making their way through the dining room to the kitchen. It was a bit stuffy, with too many boxes still on the counters, but it was a nice place. The building welcomed them; that was ultimately why they'd chosen it.

"I assume it was a success," Sam said, setting the pizza down on the table. "Hopefully they'll like us now."

"How could anyone dislike *us*?" Ulysses asked. Sam took the beer back and put it in the fridge. Ulysses shifted a box from the table to the floor, his back protesting at the weight, then realized it was labeled *Plates* and crouched down to dig through it.

"I'm going to assume that's a rhetorical question." Sam went back to the living room to fetch Obe. When he came back, he said, "I meant to ask, did you notice any spiders?"

Ulysses straightened up and set three plates on the table. "Spiders?"

"Biggish ones." Sam shrugged. "I keep thinking I'm seeing things moving out of the corner of my eye."

"You need to get a haircut," Obe said, coming in and sitting down at the kitchen table. "Your hair's flopping into your peripheral vision."

Ulysses laughed, and Sam scowled at him. "Don't come complaining when you find a spider the size of a Buick in your boot some morning."

"I'll take my chances, perforce." Ulysses sat down and flipped the pizza box open, grabbing a slice. Sam had, for some reason, gotten extra cheese with mushrooms, but Ulysses was too hungry to kick up a fuss about the impropriety of vegetables as pizza toppings. And mushrooms weren't bad.

Sam grabbed a beer and sat down next to him. "What's this dinner tomorrow for?"

"Laz is coming home."

"I thought he didn't usually come home on leave. Too far, you said."

"No." Obe twisted the top off a beer and held it out for Sam and Ulysses to clink the necks of theirs against. "He's done. Home for good."

"Really?" Sam looked like he was trying to run some mental calculations. "How long has it been, four years?"

Ulysses took a slice of pizza and sat back, propping a foot on the cross-beam of Sam's chair. "Five. Right?" He glanced at Obe. "He's twenty-seven."

Obe nodded. "He went to the academy when he was seventeen. Four years of college, one year of pilot training, and then shipped out to Vietnam for five years. I think this is the earliest he could decide he was permanently done."

Sam hissed quietly. "*Five years* over there. What the hell. Isn't that five tours?"

Ulysses shrugged. "I don't think he was in a war zone for all of it. When he visited last time, he was talking about an operation in Singapore." But the fact did take on new weight when Sam said it like that.

Obe added, "He called Celeste about a week ago and said he was back in Denver. That's all I know."

"Did something happen?" Sam asked. When they both looked at him, he shrugged. "If he was happy being a pilot, I don't think he'd choose to quit without a really compelling reason."

"He didn't tell *me* anything." Ulysses rubbed his jaw, his fingers rasping across the stubble there. "I hope he's okay."

"They'd have called us if something bad happened," Obe insisted. "Celeste is his emergency contact."

"Right," Ulysses said, unconvinced. "But I mean, they're in the middle of a war."

Sam blinked. "What does that mean?"

"That their definition of 'okay' might not be the same as mine."

When Obe had gone home, Ulysses washed the plates and tossed the empty pizza boxes while Sam wandered into the living room. Ulysses joined him a few minutes later. They'd left the windows open; the temperature had dropped as the sun set, and it was in the sixties out now, leaving the apartment comfortable.

Most of the furniture they had was from Sam's old apartment, and it wasn't quite enough to really fill the new place. They had his long, white tufted sofa, two bookshelves, and a coffee table that was currently pushed up against the wall with Ulysses's stereo atop it. There was also a striped recliner Ulysses had found a few weeks back on the curb. Most of the rest was boxes. Sam was crouched down sorting books. Ulysses rummaged around until he found a box of records.

"I thought," Sam said after a moment, "that we owned an average number of books between us. But it seems they've somehow tripled since we left the old place." He straightened up and stretched his back with a groan, still holding a fat paperback in one hand.

"I think we were misled because I didn't unpack any of the books I brought from the house to your place." He pulled out an old Ella Fitzgerald album and dropped it onto the turntable. "We can put up some shelves in the office if we need to. Built-ins, I mean."

Sam raised an eyebrow. "Can you do that?"

"Sure, piece of cake. I was a carpenter for a year between college and grad school." He flipped the switch, then grumbled when he realized he'd forgotten to plug the whole thing in and had to crawl under the table.

"You were? How did I not know that?"

When he crawled back out, Sam was watching him. Ulysses turned on the record player and speakers; this time, they worked. "It wasn't a huge turning point in my life. I was just an apprentice to my uncle."

Sam shook his head. "You have an uncle?"

Ulysses laughed. "Cass's ex-husband. He does home improvement stuff." The arm swung across and, with a hiss of static, the needle dropped onto the vinyl. Ulysses glanced over his shoulder at Sam. "Did you know that Cass has children? Twins."

"No! Where are *they*?"

"Paris." He reached out and took the book from Sam, carefully setting it on the shelf. It was *Tristram Shandy*. He didn't remember either of them owning any Laurence Sterne.

"Any other relatives you haven't mentioned?" Sam asked without rancor.

13

"About four dozen." He grabbed Sam's hand and pulled him into the clear area in the center of the room. "Don't worry about it."

It wasn't the most obvious remnant of the time he'd spent as Dionysus, but Sam liked to dance. Ulysses had discovered it was almost fiendishly easy to cajole him into it, too, which was the best part. Nearly any sort of tune could get him swaying quietly in place. When Ulysses offered him a hand, Sam allowed himself to be pulled closer, negotiating something that was nearly a fox trot while Fitzgerald sang.

"Don't tell me your great aunt Christina had children too," Sam said.

Ulysses rested his head against Sam's shoulder. "Sure. They're all Virgil's age. Live in Milwaukee and Chicago."

"But she's taken a vow of silence."

"Not when they were small." He poked Sam in the ribs. "Calm down about my family, all right?"

Sam looked down at him finally. "How's it going?" he murmured. "I forgot to say it before, but congratulations, you're on a lease."

"Yeah, yeah, I'm a real adult," he grumbled.

Sam's arms tightened around him. "You can talk to Ekaterina whenever you're ready," he pointed out. "Even if things are weird between you now, they don't have to be forever."

"They're not weird," Ulysses said. Which was kind of true. After the revelation a few months earlier that she'd known far more than previously revealed about Sam's origins, things had been exactly the same as always. They didn't talk about her secrets. They didn't talk about Sam. He came and went, spending most of his time at Sam's apartment and gradually removing his things from the house. They bickered about groceries and bits of the house that needed repair and repainting. He'd spent a weekend scraping and repainting the front door and fixing a support on the back porch. If her words were always spinning in the back of his mind, if some of their conversations had a strained undertone, well . . .

"I don't regret doing this," he murmured at last. "I would want to be here regardless. But I do wish that it didn't look like I ran away from there, rather than running to you."

Sam stopped swaying and tilted Ulysses's chin up. "Who cares what it looks like?" he asked. "You're here." Before Ulysses could come up with an answer, Sam kissed him.

Ulysses slid his fingers into the hair at the back of Sam's head. Sam smelled slightly spicy, and his jaw was stubbled under Ulysses's fingertips. Sam ran his hands over Ulysses's body and tugged at his T-shirt until he could press his palms flat against the bare skin of Ulysses's sides. Ulysses snorted and stepped back enough to strip the shirt over his head, dropping it among the boxes. Then he kissed Sam again.

When one of them broke off to breathe, Ulysses leaned forward. "What if, instead of unpacking more, we go and make sure we set up the bed correctly?"

Sam huffed a laugh in his ear. "For the record, that was not smooth and you should probably be ashamed of yourself." But he grabbed Ulysses's hand and pulled him toward the bedroom.

Chapter 2

S AM HAD BEEN AT the library for almost an hour when Dr. Edith Pearlman, the head of Rare Books, wandered in and smiled at him distractedly. "I nominated you to serve on the renovation committee."

"What did I do?" he said, trying not to sound reproachful.

"Novak came around looking for nominations yesterday and you weren't here to gainsay me," she told him, entirely guileless. Dr. Pearlman was une femme d'un certain âge, but what that age was, Sam found difficult to estimate. She wore her long white-blond hair in a neat beehive and stood five feet tall in flats. "The first meeting is at one o'clock on Monday."

He groaned and made a note of it on the blotter. When he looked up, she was still standing in the doorway, now with a more concerned expression on her face. "Sorry, was there something else?"

"There were some people here looking for you yesterday," she said. "I sent them away."

Sam sat back in his chair. "Oh?"

E. H. LUPTON

Edith shrugged. "A man and a woman, both in suits. They didn't identify themselves, but they were . . ." She looked out his office's window, then up at the witch ball Ulysses had hung above it. "I assume you weren't expecting anyone official?"

Official. Whatever that meant. "Not yesterday, and not in general."

Edith nodded. "I think—there's a chance they got your address from HR. I don't think HR had any reason not to give it to them."

"I haven't filed the paperwork to change my address yet, so they'd only have the old one." Sam sat back in his chair. His father, Howard Sterling, was the type who *could* send men in suits if he really wanted something from Sam, but he was more likely to just write or telephone Sam at the office when he discovered the old apartment's phone had been disconnected.

"There are a lot of groups that might be interested in you," Edith said. Her tone carried no information as to what she thought those groups might be. "You need to be careful."

"I—what?" Sam sat all the way up and put his palms on the desk. "What are you—"

Edith turned around and shut his office door. "Dr. Lenkov's dissertation has attracted a lot of attention. An unexpected amount, really, given how unusual your problem was. It's well deserved, in that he is a talented young man, but your identity has become something of an open secret. At least among anyone in the area with eyes to see."

"All right," Sam said, around the dryness in his throat. "I don't have power anymore. The dissertation makes that clear. I'm just a human now"—Edith snorted, and Sam frowned at her—"I mean, functionally and genetically. I know I'm not exactly what I was, but I'm nothing mystical either."

He didn't like the expression on Edith's face, serious and implacable. "You're overlooking the reason that everyone is so interested in Dr. Lenkov's work."

Sam swallowed, folding his hands in front of him. "Because he solved a problem that no one had solved before."

"Dear heart," Edith said quietly. "It's because they want to recreate *you*."

Sam's fingers were distantly tingling now. "That's—not a good idea," he managed.

"No." Edith sighed. "I hope I'm wrong, and this is nothing."

"If you're right, we're in a lot of trouble," Sam said.

The rest of the day was a bit of a loss. Sam drifted from his desk to various meetings and then back to his desk, feeling jumpy and unfocused. It didn't help that the meetings were about a plan to open the stacks to undergraduates and visitors, a plan that had generated a considerable amount of staff grumbling despite it not having been implemented yet. Because it didn't make that much of a difference to the rare books department—their items didn't circulate, so interested non-graduate students had always been forced to attend in person—he mostly sat with one eye on the door, mentally cataloging everyone who walked past.

At the end of the day, he left the building and made it as far as the broad concrete stoop outside the main entryway. When classes were in session, it was often occupied by preachers, protesters, or bands—anyone who wanted to make their voices heard. But the beginning of classes had been delayed by the bombing, and Library Mall was empty. Campus felt peculiarly hollow.

Sam slumped down on the steps. He felt like he'd spent the day proving that "men in suits" was too vague a class of people. For two weeks, there had been solemn FBI agents and plainclothes police officers everywhere, and it was only going to get worse as the students—objects of suspicion at the best of times—crept back. It hadn't bothered him until now, not really. They'd all seemed reassuring somehow.

Sam folded forward, burying his head in his hands.

When he looked up, a familiar figure was making his way across the mall toward him. Ulysses was wearing a light gray suit that had once been Sam's. With the coat slung over one shoulder and his sleeves rolled up, he looked like he should be in an ad in *Vogue*, except for his eyes, which looked tired.

He stopped in front of Sam and grinned. "You're not waiting for me, are you?"

Sam shook his head, feeling his mood lift. "Not on purpose. Just needed a minute before I head home."

"Walk with me?"

Sam let Ulysses pull him to his feet. "So what's with the fancy getup? Big department meeting today?"

Ulysses glanced down at himself, running a hand over the front of his vest. Sam licked his lips before he could stop himself. "I had lunch with some guys from a grant I'm applying to," Ulysses said, apparently oblivious.

"How did it go?"

He shrugged. "Grants, man. Who knows." Sam laughed, and Ulysses added, "I went over to the Historical Society library afterward and spent the afternoon going through Julius's papers again."

"Ah." Since they'd stolen a notebook from Alfred Barth, an associate of Sam's grandfather, back in April, they'd both spent a considerable amount of time combing through Julius's records, trying to find anything related to the demigod experiments Barth alluded to in his notes. "Any luck?"

"Nothing." He sighed. "They covered their tracks much more thoroughly than I expected."

"That's what happens when you're a suspicious bastard." They lapsed into a companionable silence. Half a block later, Sam said, "Is there a way to put up wards that would prevent someone with, well, malign intentions from finding us?"

"A human?" At Sam's nod, Ulysses frowned. "Probably not. We can ask Celeste. Why?"

Sam reported, a little sheepishly, what Edith had told him. Although he'd been turning it over in his mind all day, it sounded strangely thin when dragged out into the light. "I don't know if it's worth being concerned about, but . . . I would just as soon keep you—keep us both—safe, if we can."

He had hoped Ulysses would dismiss Edith's concerns. Instead, the other man looked a bit taken aback, as though he hadn't previously considered the points she had made. But all he said was, "We'll ask Celeste and Obe."

"Great." Sam took a deep breath and nodded.

"I'll ask Dr. Lesko if she's heard anything," Ulysses added quietly. "I doubt anyone would let something slip in front of her that they wouldn't say in front of me, but you never know."

"Thanks." Sam wanted to put an arm around his shoulders, but settled for letting their elbows jostle together. "Please don't blame yourself. Your work is brilliant—"

"Biased," Ulysses murmured, but he was smiling.

"You saved my life, of course I'm biased." Sam cleared his throat. "But still. You deserve the success you've had. If people are misusing your work, that's not your fault."

"Sure," Ulysses said, looking away.

Sam sighed inwardly and changed the subject. "Are you excited to see Lazarus?"

"Yeah. I mean . . ." He made a broad gesture. "I've only seen him for a few days here and there for the last decade."

"Were you close back then?"

"Yeah. Even after I started my undergrad, we spent all our spare time together. It wasn't the only reason I kept living at home, but . . ."

It was odd to think about Ulysses as a younger man, before Sam had met him. Sam gathered that he'd been brash, devilishly smart but not very studious, the type who spent his time running around getting into all kinds of trouble, magical and otherwise. Next to him in all the old photos was Laz: dark hair, angular face, ever-present grin. And then he'd gone away.

The family barely talked about him, which suggested that his absence was keenly felt. And now he was coming home from the war.

Evidently, Ekaterina was pleased to have her lost lamb back, because she had invited Lenkovs from all over. Sam followed Ulysses into the house and into a crowd of excited guests speaking an unparsable mishmash of languages. Obe and the eight-months-pregnant Celeste were there, of course. Virgil. No Mariah, but she was due in the next week. Ulysses pointed out a group from Milwaukee and another couple who lived in Chicago. Some of them he remembered vaguely from Samhain, but most he'd never seen. And then Laz came down from somewhere upstairs and there was practically a riot.

Sam hung back, letting the others swirl around the newcomer in a rush of overlapping voices and colors until the tide ebbed a bit. His first impression of Laz was that he was taller than Ulysses, thin almost to the point of gauntness, and stubbled, as though he'd had both head and face shaved in the recent past and then given that up. It made his eyes look very large; they were striking eyes, too, light orangey brown, almost the color of amber. But what really caught Sam's attention was the flash of recognition in them when he looked at Sam for the first time, and the hurt, quickly hidden. Then Ulysses was dragging him over and introducing them, his voice almost lost among the crowd. "This is my boyfriend, Sam. Sam, this is my brother, Laz."

Sam didn't think he'd met Laz before. He would have remembered him. They'd graduated the same year, even if they'd attended different schools. But clearly—bewilderingly—Laz knew him somehow. It felt like there was a tiny circle of silence around the three of them, just for a moment. Sam was aware that he was being assessed. There was a moment of wordless communion between the brothers, and then Laz offered his hand, and Sam shook it. Time snapped back to what it should be.

That was it. The whole group dragged in to dinner not long after. Sam wound up sitting next to Celeste, who quizzed him on Russian irregular verbs and made sure his wine glass was full and helped him figure out which pierogi were meatless. He felt oddly peaceful. His relationship with his own family of origin was rocky, to say the least; Troy still liked him, but was on the road constantly, and he and Alyson had a new, somewhat strained understanding, and those were the best of the bunch. But that was okay, because Ulysses had decided he wanted Sam around, and as part of that he got all the Lenkovs, who were boisterous and excitable, full of happy arguments and hilarious speculation and bad jokes.

They were also, as a group, dangerous, magical, and mostly Communists or at least fellow travelers, running the gamut from slightly cracked to almost nonfunctional, but honestly, he didn't mind. It was better than Francie's coldness and Howard's endless suspicious looks that seemed to imply he expected Sam to misbehave as soon as he turned around.

Sam ran into Laz again later on, out on the front porch while Ulysses was finishing something up for Ekaterina inside. Whatever else was going on between the two of them at the moment, Ulysses did the errands and odd jobs. No one would ever fault his loyalty.

Laz was sitting on the railing that edged the wide front stoop, smoking a cigarette pensively. It wasn't that shocking, really; lots of people smoked. But none of the rest of the family did, and Sam did a double-take before he realized it was *just* a cigarette. He was wearing a long-sleeved green canvas jacket with a patch that said *Lenkov* on the right side of the chest and *US Air Force* on the left, along with little insignia on the collar with bars that probably meant something, like he didn't have any civvies yet. Maybe he didn't.

The hippies were going to eat him alive.

Laz gave him a look and then raised a finger to his lips. "Don't tell them. It's a bad habit I picked up overseas."

"They won't hear it from me," Sam said. "They'll probably smell it on you, though."

Laz exhaled. "I know. You can't really fool Babushka. Not for long."

Sam laughed. "I value my life too much to try."

There was a silence that went on for a little too long, and then Laz said, "You've been hanging around a bit, huh."

Sam scratched his head. "I've been . . . that is, Ulysses . . ." He gritted his teeth and willed himself to come up with a single coherent sentence. "We got together a year ago next month."

Laz's eyes narrowed. "A year ago," he echoed, and took a long drag on the cigarette. "That sounds pretty serious."

"I mean." Sam leaned against the front of the house. "We have an apartment." Laz had to have noticed that Ulysses wasn't in residence at the house anymore. But Ulysses plainly hadn't written to tell Laz about—well, if he didn't know they were together, he probably didn't know any of it. Laz didn't seem pleased to be finding out for the first time. It was surprising—Ulysses was constantly at his typewriter, and he and Laz were close . . .

He closed his mouth and waited, one of the tricks he'd picked up from Ulysses. It went against his natural impulse, which was to Do Something, but it seemed to work, because after a minute Laz exhaled a cloud of smoke. "What do you do?"

"I'm a librarian."

Laz took a drag on the cigarette. "Sounds boring," he said eventually.

Sam started to laugh.

Ulysses came out of the house, pulling on his jacket. He moved confidently through the gathering twilight, a contrast to his brother's anxious posture.

"Everything good?" Ulysses asked Sam, glancing between him and Laz. "You ready to go?"

Laz barked something at his brother in Russian. Sam's Russian was improving, but he didn't catch a word of it, which made him suspect it was largely obscenities. It wasn't necessarily aggressive—to an English speaker's ear, Russian often sounded a lot harsher than it really was. But Ulysses stepped back with his hands raised in a pacifying gesture and said, "Hey, man, what's the problem?"

"I just want to know why I had to hear about all of this from the papers."

"All of what?"

Laz fished something out of his inside pocket and blindly shoved it at Ulysses. Sam, standing behind Ulysses, could only half see his face when he looked down, but whatever it was made him freeze in place. Sam leaned forward, peered over his shoulder.

It was a photo from the Dee award ceremony in London, published in what appeared to be an English-language magic community paper or newsletter called *Huginn Monthly*. Sam vaguely remembered the moment in the picture. He was standing next to Ulysses with an arm slung around his waist, leaning into him. Ulysses was clutching the plaque and grinning like he was about to explode. Neither of them had been especially sober at the time, or for most of the trip if he was being honest. On their left, Dr. Lesko and her wife were also smiling tipsily at the camera, Dr. Lesko clutching her own plaque. The text beneath read:

The Wisconsin Delegation: *Dr. Ulysses Lenkov (far right) was awarded the Dee prize for his dissertation at the thirtieth annual awards last night. Scion of the well-known Lenkov family, he has long been regarded as someone to watch in the field. He is pictured here with his companion Sam Sterling, his PhD advisor Dr. Nadiya Lesko, and her wife Sara Abend. Dr. Lesko received the Roger Bacon award for her ongoing research into cross-cultural rituals; she won the 1967 Dee for*

The end had been ripped off. Sam glanced at Ulysses, eyebrow raised, ready to make a quip about the way they'd identified him, but Ulysses was looking at his brother.

"I'm sorry, Laz," he said, voice rough. "By the time I realized I needed to tell you, I didn't know how to write and say any of this. It all seemed so improbable. And—"

"You could have said *something*," Laz said again, sounding equally wretched. "Just about him, even." He gestured at Sam with his cigarette.

"I didn't want the government to know about—"

"You could have mentioned there was *someone*!" He glared at Sam this time. "He doesn't look that special. Why are you so hell-bent on protecting him?"

Ulysses bristled. "A *lot* has happened since the last time you cared enough to come back," he snapped, shoving the clipping back at Laz. "I'm sorry I couldn't put my life on hold for two and a half years at a time until the next time you could be bothered to visit."

Laz physically recoiled. Sam realized the two of them would cut each other to the quick given half a chance. Without thinking, he stepped between them. "Fellas," he said, holding up his hands. And then he didn't know what else to do. In his youth, he'd resolved conflicts with Max by running away when Max tried to hit him. He and Troy had never really had any problems. Troy was easy to get along with. But Laz and Ulysses were much closer, or had been once.

Laz stared hard at Sam for an uncomfortably long moment, and then laughed. Sam exhaled. "This guy," Laz said to Ulysses, followed by another long string of Russian, still too fast for Sam to catch but less rancorous.

Ulysses stepped half a pace closer to Sam, putting a protective hand on his arm. "Nyet, nyet," he said. "It's not like that." Then switching back to Russian, he added, "Are you okay?"

Laz also raised his hands. Sam could practically see his hackles going down. "Fine," Laz said in English. "I'm fine."

"Are you?"

Laz took another drag on the cigarette and ignored the question. "Tomorrow night. Let's go out. Drinks or something." He scratched the back of his head, bringing his cigarette perilously close to his scalp. "Fun. We could do something fun."

Ulysses frowned. "Sure. Something fun."

Laz gazed at his brother and then hugged him in one sudden, fluid movement. Sam could only see the back of Ulysses's head and Laz's thin face when Laz leaned forward and said something else into his ear, too soft to be overheard.

"See you later," Ulysses said, and glanced at Sam, raising his eyebrows meaningfully.

"Ah—yeah," Sam said. "It was great to meet you. See you around." And he fled down the stairs in Ulysses's wake.

"You didn't write to him," Sam said quietly after they'd walked a block. Then he waited.

Ulysses looked over at him, as though gauging how much trouble he was in. "I didn't." When Sam didn't say anything, he added, "It's not because I was—I don't know. Ashamed."

Sam nodded. "Why, then?"

"I wasn't lying when I told Laz that I didn't know exactly what to say." Ulysses took a deep breath. "Last fall, I was . . . I didn't want to write to him that I was seeing a guy but he was probably going to die. I mean, I didn't want to put that on Celeste, even, and she wasn't working in a war zone, you know? When I write to Laz, I'm not exactly sending him my notes on *The Myth of Sisyphus* or anything."

Celeste, of course, had known about their relationship, but Sam felt like he understood something about what Ulysses was saying. It was, in some respects, a rare admission that Ulysses had even thought about Sam's mortality, since at the time he'd been very adamant that Sam was going to be fine. Sam cleared his throat. "And then when I lived?"

"I don't know." Ulysses looked genuinely stricken. "I didn't—at first I figured I was going to fuck something up and you'd leave me, and then I didn't want to say to him something I couldn't say to you at the time."

"And what would that be?"

Ulysses's eyes darted over to him, and Sam bumped him with his elbow, letting the corner of his mouth creep up.

Ulysses relaxed fractionally. "Bunch of soppy bullshit," he said, and slid an arm around Sam's waist. "And in

31

my defense, the last six months or so have been pretty intense."

"*I* wrote to *my* brother about you," Sam said, as superciliously as he could manage.

"Troy?" Ulysses said, unimpressed. "He *met* me. He had to have known—"

"He made a pass at you." Ulysses suddenly doubled over, laughing too hard to speak, and Sam enjoyed watching it. "You have a younger brother. You know what it's like. You have to—to—"

"Mark your territory?" Ulysses wheezed.

"Maybe." Sam reached out and squeezed his arm before withdrawing. Ulysses's muscles were firm beneath his fingers, the other man a constant, solid presence. "It's early," he said. "Want to stop at Rennebohm's for ice cream?"

"No," Ulysses said. "If we stop, trouble will find us, and I'm not in the mood. Let's go home."

Sam laughed. "I think the trouble will find us if it finds us, wherever we are." But he went.

Chapter 3

S AM WAS PROVEN RIGHT less than five hours later when Ulysses awoke to a ghost in their bedroom. She was an old woman who wandered gracefully through the room; it took him a few moments to understand why she looked familiar.

"I don't like what you've done with the place," she said, looking at a small painting Sam had hung on the wall to the left of the door. "You should do something about the spiders."

"We only moved in two days ago," Ulysses said, voice pitched low so as not to wake Sam. He sat up slowly. "Also, what are you doing here?"

Dr. Parvati Ranganathan turned around and raised an eyebrow at him. "You just said I had to leave my son's apartment. You didn't say I had to go anywhere else in particular."

Ulysses sighed. "Most ghosts, when they have successfully delivered their message, either to their loved ones or to me, leave."

"Yes, that's what you said." She frowned at him. "I'm still not sure where you intend me to go."

"I can't really tell you." He crossed his arms in front of his chest. "Every other ghost I've dealt with just seemed to be called to somewhere."

Beside him, Sam made a snuffling noise and rolled over, one hand blindly reaching out for Ulysses.

"You're *naked*," Dr. Ranganathan said. And then her eyes fell on Sam.

"You know, this is my *bedroom* and it's the middle of the *night*," Ulysses hissed at her. "If you want me fully clothed, you're going to have to come by during the day."

She pursed her lips.

Sam, meanwhile, had opened his eyes and was peering groggily at Ulysses. "Why are you—" he began, and then he saw Dr. Ranganathan and tensed.

"This is Dr. Ranganathan, Vikram's mother. She's dead." He tried to sound neutral, but it was past two in the morning, and his feelings weren't exactly neutral about that.

"Oh," Sam said, and yawned, as though this were an everyday occurrence. "Why?"

"I had congestive heart failure," Dr. Ranganathan supplied.

Sam nodded as though this made sense and looked at Ulysses, who shook his head. "Can you make her leave?" Sam asked.

"We were just discussing that," Ulysses said. "She's delivered her message to Vikram."

"Perhaps she has some other message to deliver?" Sam suggested. They both looked over at Vikram's dead mother.

Dr. Ranganathan's face was pinched. "I can see my company isn't wanted," she said, and turned away. "I'll just keep my secrets to myself."

Ulysses sighed. "Was there something you wanted to tell me?" he asked wearily.

"It can wait," she said over her shoulder, tone acid. "As you said, I've intruded." And she vanished through the wall.

"Sorry," Ulysses told Sam, and twisted to grab a couple of penny candies from the bedside table.

Sam accepted one, even though he didn't react to ghosts like Ulysses. He pushed himself into a sitting position, leaning back against the headboard. "Do you think we'll see her again?"

Ulysses rubbed his jaw. "I hope not."

"No?" It was hard to make out Sam's face in the dim room, but his tone was uncertain. "She said she knows something."

She had implied that. And yet. "She's been dead for six months," he said finally. "How useful could her information be at this point?" He looked down at his hands, folding the wrapper in half. "And given how forthcoming she was with her son, I don't want to spend weeks trying to coax it out of her."

Sam grabbed his elbow and pulled until Ulysses was halfway sprawled across Sam's lap. "Is there anything I can do?"

"No, but—" He paused, then reached up and straightened the small blue glass eye that Sam still wore on a silver chain around his neck. "You didn't notice anything, did you? No curse, no . . . malign influences?"

Sam shook his head. "Nothing. Nothing obvious, anyway."

Ulysses nodded. "That's what I was afraid of."

⋙ ⋘

S AM RAN INTO VIKRAM in a literal sense at seven o'clock the next morning. He was coming back from his jog, thinking about breakfast, and they collided in the Baskerville's entryway. "Excuse me," he said automatically, and then recognized him and added, "How's it going?"

'I met your mother,' he did not add. It felt like an awkward thing to announce.

"I'm all right. You?" Vikram was also dressed like he was going for a run. "Sorry," Vikram added a moment later. "You look very familiar. Did you go to MIT? Back in 1965 or something like that?"

"No, I . . ." Sam looked at Vikram more closely and felt a twinge of recognition, followed sharply by an old, aching feeling of humiliation and shame. After what felt like far too long a pause, he managed, "I was at

Harvard. We must have run into each other around town somewhere."

It was not entirely a lie, anyway, and he allowed himself a moment of self-congratulation for it. Sam was almost sure that they'd met during an incredibly embarrassing in flagrante sort of moment in a biology lab at MIT, not passed each other at the grocery store.

Vikram was nodding. "That must be it. It's good to see you again," he said. Sam glanced out the door at the street, which was already shimmering as the sun burned through the early morning clouds. He could sprint to the lake, throw himself in. It was only a few blocks. Vikram added, "I'm glad I ran into you. My wife wanted me to ask if you and Ulysses would join us for dinner on Sunday."

Sam said, "I'll ask Ulysses, but I don't think he has any plans." Then his brain caught up with his ears and he only just managed to stop himself from wincing. Maybe it would be fine. Maybe Vikram wouldn't ever remember. Maybe—

Vikram smiled. "Hey, we're neighbors, and we seem to have a hobby in common. We should go running together sometime."

"I've never really run with anyone else." Sam shifted from foot to foot.

Vikram punched his shoulder in a comradely way. "I used to have a group I jogged with back in Cambridge. A bunch of us did the marathon one year." He looked a little nostalgic. "It'll be fun. How fast do you usually go?"

Sam shrugged helplessly. "I just kind of . . . go?" He had never bothered to figure out how fast he ran or how far; he only knew it was both faster and farther than Ulysses had wanted to go on the few occasions he'd joined in.

"We'll figure it out." He nodded and left, calling "See you later!" over his shoulder.

When Sam made it back to the apartment, Ulysses was sprawled at one end of the sofa in Sam's old striped bathrobe, nursing a cup of coffee.

"I just ran into your pal Vikram downstairs," Sam said, slumping down next to him. "He invited us to dinner tomorrow."

"Mm," Ulysses said. "You're sweaty." He stretched his legs out across Sam's lap and scooted closer. "His mother came back after you left."

Sam raised an eyebrow. "What did she want?"

"To chastise me, primarily." Ulysses maneuvered until he had an arm around Sam's waist, his head on Sam's shoulder.

"For what?"

"Pick a sin. I'm surprised poor Sita held out against the onslaught for so long." He sighed. "You know, I was enjoying having a quiet life."

Sam snorted. "Since when?"

"Things have been quiet since we got back from London," Ulysses insisted.

"Minus the actual building that blew up?"

"Yes." He leaned forward and licked the side of Sam's neck, then made a face. "The bombing had nothing to do with us."

"Between that and the move, I hardly noticed the lack of ghosts, walkers, demigods, and other sundry attempts on our lives." Sam looked over at Ulysses and caught him smirking. "You're not usually this cuddly when I'm sweaty."

Ulysses set his cup on the floor next to the sofa. "Nothing makes one so vain as being called a sinner, to quote Wilde. Also, I was thinking, the shower here is significantly bigger than the one at the old place . . ."

Sam grinned and leaned closer, his nose brushing Ulysses's. "That's an interesting idea," he murmured, and kissed him.

For a moment, there were just the two of them, the rest of the world fading away from Sam's awareness. Ulysses had a hand on the back of Sam's head, and Sam had one hand knotted in the lapel of the other man's bathrobe. Ulysses tasted like coffee, and he kissed Sam hungrily. Sam thought he could just do this forever, stay in this moment and never get tired of it, the laundry detergent smell of Ulysses, the scratch of his stubble against Sam's face, the slightly ragged sound of his breathing when he pulled away. Ulysses shifted backward, tugging Sam along, until he was stretched out on his back, Sam propped above him, one knee shoved between Ulysses's muscular thigh and the back of the sofa, his other foot on the floor for stability.

Ulysses trailed a hand down his back, tugged at his hips. Sam leaned forward and bit his neck just where it connected with his shoulder, and Ulysses muttered something—Sam's name, an invitation, a request.

And then there was a knock on the door.

"Were you expecting someone?" Sam asked, pulling back.

"No." Ulysses looked down at himself. "I'm not really dressed to meet the welcoming committee."

"All right," Sam grumbled, and got up. "I'll send them away."

He had to pause for a moment in front of the door to compose himself, wishing his running clothes fit a bit more loosely. Behind him, Ulysses sat up on the sofa, clearly trying to look inconvenienced rather than partially debauched. There was another, more demanding knock.

Sam opened the door to find Laz, wild-eyed and reeking of cheap gin, a long scrape along one cheekbone and a bruise on his chin. He was wearing the same boxy jacket from the night before, now open to expose a string of dark wooden love beads with a little red tassel at the bottom hanging against his white T-shirt.

"What happened to you?" Sam asked, and then stood aside to let him in.

"Got in a fight," Laz said, shouldering past. He stopped facing Ulysses. "What are you still doing in your pajamas? We have things to do."

"Things?" Ulysses said, picking up his coffee mug. "What *things*?" He got up. "Christ, are you *drunk*? Did you even go to bed?"

"Brunch things," Laz said, ignoring his brother. "Isn't that what civilians do? They go out to brunch and they have a pretty groovy time." He flashed a peace sign, probably ironically. "Celeste is going to meet us."

"It's barely seven in the morning," Ulysses said.

The situation was spiraling out of control. Sam was still at the front door, hand on the knob, so he shut it firmly enough to get both of their attention.

"How do you take your coffee?" he asked, and Laz's expression got a little less wary. "Milk and sugar?"

Laz nodded, barely; Sam went into the kitchen and made a fresh pot. He was vaguely aware of hushed voices behind him having a conversation in rapid-fire Russian, and when he came out again Laz was sitting stiffly on the sofa. Sam offered him a mug of coffee and he took it with mumbled thanks.

"I'm going to go take a shower," Sam announced, and gave Ulysses a look. "You should get dressed, probably."

Ulysses glanced down at his bathrobe. "Yeah," he said slowly. "Laz, you okay here alone for a few?"

Laz looked up from the coffee and nodded.

"Did he say what happened to his face?" Sam asked under his breath once they'd closed the bedroom door behind them. "Do you believe he got in a fight?"

"I don't know." Ulysses dug through his drawers and grabbed a T-shirt from a Joni Mitchell concert. "It's not

41

something he would have done before, but now . . ." He sighed.

Sam thought about the bruises and nodded slowly. "I don't know. Maybe he fell and he's embarrassed." He stripped off his shirt and stood there for a moment, skin prickling. "Maybe he'll tell us when he sobers up."

Ulysses snorted. "If he remembers." He stepped into a pair of jeans; Sam's eyes followed his hands as he tugged them over his hips and buckled his belt. "I'll go keep an eye on him."

When Sam came back ten minutes later, clean and fully dressed, Laz was passed out on the sofa, his boots abandoned on the rug beside it. Ulysses was sitting on the floor next to a box labeled *Ulysses—Office*, though it plainly hadn't made it that far, flipping through a stack of letters. A full cup of coffee sat beside his leg.

"Did you call Celeste?" Sam asked, crouching down next to him.

Ulysses looked from Sam to Laz. "I'll go down and use the payphone in a minute." He hesitated, and then added, "Go look at him quick."

Sam raised an eyebrow, but he stood up and took a couple of steps toward the sofa. It was obvious when he got there what Ulysses meant—Laz had one arm thrown over his head, and his shirt had ridden up at the bottom, exposing a long scar at the front of his hip curling around toward his kidneys.

Laz woke up in the early afternoon and showered,

borrowed one of Ulysses's T-shirts, and hauled the man himself out to do something to the motorcycle—check the spark plug timing, possibly. Sam pressed his lips together and unpacked and shelved the books. When he finished, Ulysses wasn't back yet, so he started working on the kitchen.

It felt supremely ungenerous to be suspicious of Laz. The man was going through something. He was a walking raw nerve. More than that, the two of them had exchanged fewer than fifty words. Laz was clearly angry with Ulysses, or at least there were some lingering bad vibes there, but that didn't mean he and Sam couldn't find some kind of . . . friendship? Or détente, at least?

Sam was aware that he tended to be jealous of Ulysses's time. But this feeling wasn't entirely that. They'd had a quiet summer. Renting a sailboat with Celeste and Obe. A lot of not-especially-fruitful research into Julius Sterling's other experiments. Touring a seemingly endless series of apartments. Learning conversational Russian. Stripping the wallpaper in Ekaterina's second-floor bathroom. Sex. Laughter. No one had been in danger, no one had been drugged or almost sacrificed.

Did Ulysses miss the rush? Because Sam definitely did not. But he was concerned that Laz *did*.

Celeste and Obe arrived toward dinnertime with a box of witch balls, herbs, and other items to get to work on the wards. Sam let them do their thing while he went downstairs and ordered a pizza, for delivery this time. Then he went back upstairs and opened a bottle of wine.

After a while, Celeste came into the kitchen to get a glass of water. She had reached a stage of pregnancy where she looked uncomfortable all the time, and she exhaled in relief as she slid into one of the chairs. "We're about done," she said. Then she looked at him more closely. "Everything okay?"

Sam took a deep breath and fixed his face. "Just tired." She hummed and sipped her water, watching him over the rim. He tried to think of a way to explain, gave up, and eventually landed on, "I don't think I ever asked. How did you and Obe meet?"

She cocked her head to the side. She had pretty, sharp brown eyes behind large round glasses, and long dark hair that she was wearing loose around her shoulders. "Why do you ask?" she asked after a moment.

"Just curious," he said, and she sat back, crossing her legs. He poured himself a glass of wine and leaned against the refrigerator.

"It was October of our freshman year, and we were both in this comparative religion class. I think it was required. Really big lecture hall, and it was right after lunch, so I used to go early just to sit and read somewhere quiet." She looked down into her glass thoughtfully. "I'm trying to remember what I was reading."

From the next room, Obe called, "It was *Howl*."

Her mouth quirked up. "There you go. Mariah had taken me to San Francisco the previous summer and I picked up a copy. Anyway, Obe saw me reading it, and he found a copy somewhere—"

"My roommate lent it to me," Obe said, stepping through the doorway.

"And he read it so he had an excuse to come talk to me about it." She glanced over her shoulder at him. "And somehow that turned into dinner, and then lunch the next day, and we just never managed to stop."

Obe grinned at her. "Turned out she had a lot of interesting things to say about Ginsberg."

"Was anyone—I mean, it must have been tough, being a mixed-race couple." It was an awkward, parochial way of phrasing it, and he frowned at himself.

Celeste shrugged. "It was 1957."

Obe shook his head. "I'll tell you, though, Ekaterina was always very welcoming. The first time Celeste brought me over, she treated me like family."

Sam nodded. "What about Ulysses and Laz? They must have been . . . sixteen and fourteen?"

"Ulysses was reserved at first," Obe said slowly, eyes distant. "It wasn't anything personal. He's just always been protective of his family. But he warmed up after we actually met. Laz . . . he and Ulysses had this old junker they'd gotten from somewhere that they were trying to fix up. What was it?" He looked at Celeste. "Do you remember?"

She made a face. "God. Was it a Studebaker of some sort?"

Obe snapped his fingers. "Yes! It was a 1947 Studebaker Champion that had been owned by a traveling salesman who drove it into the ground." He laughed delightedly. "I used to go over in the afternoon when I didn't have class and work on it with them."

"Both of them?" Sam asked, sitting up straighter.

"Yeah. I mean, Laz wanted to know everything about engines, and Ulysses was on a quest to learn everything about everything." He looked thoughtful. "Man, he was really a piece of work back in the day."

Sam poured a glass of wine for Obe, who came all the way into the room and sat down next to his wife. "But Laz—" Sam began.

"Aw, Laz is a teddy bear," Obe said. "Don't worry about him."

Sam looked down at the tabletop. It was a chrome and teal Formica thing he'd gotten in Cambridge and been hauling from apartment to apartment for years. It was nice to be able to look at it in the new space and wonder if this was going to be a permanent home for it at last. Something about his expression made Celeste sit forward in her chair, setting her pale fingertips on his tan forearm.

"He's still trying to find his footing," she said. "The war—I mean, it's not good for anyone, but especially for Laz. It's going to take him a while to readjust."

"That's one word for it," Sam grumbled.

"And you can't have any doubts about Ulysses—"
There was a rattle of keys from the living room, and they heard Ulysses and Laz come in.

"Where's the pretty boy?" Laz said loudly in Russian, and Sam and Celeste both winced. "He's locking you out of your own apartment now?"

Ulysses's tired voice said, "Laz, don't," in English.

Celeste stood in one graceful motion. "Excuse me for a moment."

There was a pause as the door to the kitchen swung shut. Obe glanced at Sam, face wryly amused. "I see why you ask now." He put his feet up on the chair his wife had just vacated and picked up his wine glass. "Cheers."

"Cheers," Sam said. They clinked glasses and he took a sip. "How've you been? How's business?"

In the living room, Celeste was saying something in loud, angry Russian. Laz just laughed. Sam shut his eyes.

"Good," Obe said. "Business is good. We're expanding the jewelry we carry."

"Oh yeah?"

Obe nodded. "Celeste met this lady who lives on an old farm out by Paoli and makes gorgeous silver jewelry. She's agreed to let us carry her work." He hesitated as Ulysses said something, tone conciliatory but content inaudible. "It's going to be very popular, I think."

"Sounds nice," Sam said, and then the pizza guy finally arrived and put him out of his misery.

Chapter 4

S AM AND ULYSSES WOUND up going out to the Sett
  with Laz at his insistence. Sam was at least half sure
that Laz had only really wanted to invite Ulysses, but he
went along anyway. It was later than they were usually
at the bar, and the pool table in the back had been taken
over by a bunch of frat boys, but a band Ulysses liked was
setting up on a low stage in the middle of the space, so
they decided to stay. Sam looked around at the crowd,
a mix of townies and students, all talking loudly at the
small tables or standing around in groups. The room was
full of flirtations, coils of cigarette smoke drifting toward
the ceiling, the hoppy scent of beer. Ulysses steered him
and Laz toward a small table at the back.

Sam slid into the chair closest to the wall in the hope of
keeping his feet out of everyone's way, and Ulysses took
the seat to his right. Laz *subsided* into the last chair,
then twitched around, eyes skittering over the women at
the next table, the beer signs on the wall, the drummer
who was adjusting a cymbal on the stage. "Wow," he said,
turning back to them. "I haven't been here in five years

and it's exactly the same." He folded his hands on the table and looked down at his fingers for almost twenty seconds, then shoved his chair back and stretched. "I'm gonna get a drink. You want something?" He looked at Ulysses, then at Sam. "Beer good? I'll be back."

When he'd gone, Ulysses sighed and pressed his fingers to the table's worn surface. "Sorry," he said after a few seconds.

"What for?"

Ulysses shrugged. "I left you hanging on the unpacking."

"I put all the magic books in your office," Sam said, a little snippily. And then, because he was apparently congenitally incapable of remaining annoyed, he added, "I figured they'd be more useful in there, and we're out of space on the living room shelves anyway."

"All right," Ulysses said, giving Sam an odd look. "I'll measure the office for more shelves."

Sam rested his forearms on the table, frowning at the way the knobs of his bony wrists edged past the cuffs of his shirt. "What were you guys doing all afternoon?"

"We fixed a timing problem with the bike's engine. Laz has a better ear for engines than I do." He glanced toward the bar, then down at the table. When he looked up again, he caught Sam with his face unguarded and frowned at whatever he saw there. "What?"

Sam shook his head, unsure of where to begin. "I just don't think Laz likes me that much."

"He doesn't know you." Ulysses lifted a hand and ran one finger lightly along the back of Sam's right hand, a ghostly little touch. It was too much and not enough at the same time.

Sam swallowed. "I can see the way he looks at me," he said, voice quiet. "I mean, I don't care. I—"

There were raised voices from the bar and Ulysses turned his head in that direction, sat up straighter. A moment later a distinctive voice said, "Because I was busy serving my country, *asshole.*"

"Need a hand?" Sam asked.

"I got it," Ulysses said, getting to his feet. A man coming back from the bar danced backward a pace, holding his beer out of range. He was not especially notable except that he was wearing a dark suit, matching tie pulled loose, in a sea of T-shirts and bell bottoms, and his face held a startled expression that seemed to come not from the near collision but from seeing Sam and Ulysses.

The crowd swallowed both the man and Ulysses a moment later, leaving Sam frowning at nothing.

He sat back in his chair, resting his head against the wall behind him, arms crossed. "Men," said one of the women at the next table, and he laughed, despite himself.

"You're not wrong." He looked over at her and her companion. The woman who had spoken to him had pale skin, freckles, and a mass of long, frizzy blond hair draped over her shoulders. Her friend was Black and had an Afro held somewhat in check by a bright green scarf.

"Here," the friend said, offering him the joint. "Get that look off your face; it's like he kicked your puppy or something."

Sam laughed again and took it. "What's your name?" he asked, and inhaled. The smoke was acrid and swampy-smelling and stung the back of his throat on the way down. He offered the joint back to a spot somewhere in between the two of them, and the blond took it.

"I'm Galadriel," she said. "This is Buttercup. And you are?"

He raised an eyebrow and tried not to laugh, then exhaled a stream of smoke. "Usually I go by Sam, but you guys feel very formal, so call me Dionysus."

They cracked up, Buttercup clutching Galadriel's hand under the table. Sam grinned.

"So that guy," Buttercup said when she'd recovered herself. Galadriel inhaled and passed the joint to her. "What's up with him?"

Sam tried to figure out a concise way to explain Ulysses and failed. "He feels responsible for a lot of things."

"Mmhmm," Galadriel said, rolling her eyes. "Not so smart if he lets that distract him from *you*." She made a show of looking him up and down.

Sam snickered along with Buttercup, then felt a little pang of guilt. "He's an amazing person, but his life is one long series of distractions."

Buttercup claimed the joint from her friend. "Have you told him?"

"What, that he's got too much going on?" Sam rubbed his chin. "He knows."

Galadriel laughed. "No, she means—"

Oh. *Oh.* Sam's fingers were tingling a little as the drug started to light up his nerve endings. "Yeah." He ran a hand through his hair, and then did it again, enjoying the texture of it. "Yeah, he knows. We're—yeah."

Buttercup sniffed. "Good," she said, handing him back the joint.

"His brother just got back from Nam," he said, staring at the glowing orange ember at the end of the joint. "So things are . . ." He waved his free hand.

Galadriel looked a little concerned. "What do you mean?"

"His brother's going through a rough time." He took another toke and passed it back to her. The noises from the front of the bar had been dying down somewhat, but now they intensified again. He looked in that direction. There hadn't been any screaming yet, which meant that Ulysses had things under control, right? "I mean, I get it. I'm not always going to be the top of the priority list."

Galadriel, meanwhile, had both palms pressed to the table. Buttercup looked over at her when she didn't take the joint, and then leaned closer. "You okay, babe?"

"I'm—I need some air. It's really warm in here, and—" She was breathing rapidly now, sweat glittering at her hairline in the dim light. "Can we go outside?"

"Sure, sweetpea. No problem." Buttercup stubbed out the joint and then dropped the roach into a baggie she produced out of her purse. "Sorry, Dio." She got to her feet and reached out, taking her girlfriend's arm. Galadriel shoved her chair back and tried to get up, then stumbled hard to one side and went over.

"Help," she squeaked, trying to push herself back up. "I can't feel my feet."

Buttercup hauled uselessly on her elbow. Sam sighed and got up. "Here, let me," he said, and lifted her, one arm under her knees, the other around her waist. He didn't think of himself as very strong, but she was tiny and easy to hoist.

When he looked, Buttercup was staring at him. "Sorry, what?"

She shook her head. "You're just taller than I thought."

Buttercup led him through the club and out the back door. The sounds of the argument diminished as they went, and he felt himself relaxing again. Laz had been in the military, knew how to handle himself. Ulysses would be fine.

At the end of the alley he set Galadriel down on her own two feet. "My hero," she mumbled, tone dry, and then took two wobbly steps back toward the club door before her eyes grew large and she bent over to vomit next to the dumpster.

Buttercup rushed back to her, exclaiming, and Sam got out of the way. He found a spot where they could get his attention if they needed help, enjoying the breeze that was making its way along the street. The air out behind the bar smelled like a deep fryer, with a heavy pinch of yeast, but every so often something cleaner and fresher slipped through, a reminder of the coming fall. Sam turned back and surveyed the alley; Galadriel was leaning against the building, face flat against the cool bricks, making sad keening noises while Buttercup rubbed her back.

"Did she take something?" he asked. "Is she okay?"

"She'll be fine," Buttercup said, not sparing him a glance. "Sometimes this happens. Can you get her some water?"

"Sure," he said. But when he went back down the alley, he found that the door they'd come through didn't have a handle on the outside. "I'll go around."

It was surprisingly quiet for a Saturday night. Or perhaps not so surprisingly. It was lateish, he was standing on a part of East Mifflin without any bars on it, and school hadn't started yet. People were still kind of rattled from the bomb, too, and some students had gone home for a few weeks. Sam had heard stories of a few peace activists hiding out on the east side, trying to stay away from cops who might be more inclined to arrest someone for the crime than to make sure they had the right person.

He heard the sound of the sound of a payphone receiver being returned to the cradle, then footsteps coming in his direction, hard-soled shoes on cement. When he turned in that direction, the man from the bar was approaching. He was walking quickly, frowning, dark eyes darting here and there beneath knitted brows.

Sam turned away. The man called out, "Mr. Sterling?" Automatically, Sam's head whipped back, and the man raised his hand as though greeting him. He was looking at Sam as though he couldn't quite believe his luck. Sam didn't know why *he* would merit that kind of reaction. Was this some kind of drug bust? The kind of thing Howard had always tried to warn him about? Just some wild hallucination? Maybe the joint had been laced with something . . . "Mr. Sterling! Would you come with me, please?"

He could still see Buttercup at the end of the alley. She was staring at him, eyes wide. "Do you hear that?" he mouthed, and she nodded.

"Mr. Sterling," the man said. He was nearly upon Sam now, one hand reaching out to grab Sam's arm.

Sam danced backward a few steps. Get him away from there, at least. Keep Buttercup and Galadriel off his radar. "What's this about?"

"Come with me and I'll explain on the way," the man said, and reached out again to grab him.

If he hadn't had that conversation with Edith, perhaps things would have gone differently. Or if he hadn't been quite so blazed and paranoid. But Edith's concerns were still loud in his head.

"Ah," Sam said. "You know what, I don't think I'm interested." And without much more thought, he turned and sprinted away.

Behind him, he heard the man curse and give chase.

THE PROBLEM WAS THAT every time Ulysses got everyone calmed down, Laz went and opened his mouth again. The guys weren't even angry at *him*, per se—they were young and scared and on their way to the draft board pretty soon. If only Laz would stop goading them, Ulysses could buy a round of beers and everything would be fine.

"I just don't think you have the balls for it," Laz said, and the biggest and drunkest of the guys grabbed a bottle off the bar.

It was an empty bottle, so when he turned it upside down, no one got beer on their shoes, and the fact that Ulysses was clutching at that probably indicated how badly things were going. The guy was easily Sam's height and two hundred fifty pounds; he looked like he worked construction when he wasn't harassing hapless ex–Air Force captains in bars. Not, in other words, the kind of person Ulysses would have chosen to pick a fight with.

"I'm not going to stand here and be insulted by some fascist," the guy growled, and that stung. Ulysses bit back an angry reaction.

"You're free to leave," Laz drawled. The area immediately around them seemed to be holding its breath. Ulysses wished desperately for a bouncer. And then—

The bartender dropped a glass, which shattered. Laz startled badly, head whipping around, and then he bent forward with a broken noise of pain, clutching his temples. Everyone stared at him, Ulysses with concern, one hand hovering uselessly an inch above Laz's back, the rest with something between suspicion and pity. Laz straightened up an instant later, eyes wild and searching for Ulysses.

"We have to go," he said.

The huge guy took his moment and swung the bottle like a baseball bat. In a move that could only have been guided by foresight, Laz snaked a hand up and hit the inside of the man's forearm, hard. The man yelped, in pain or surprise, and two seconds later Laz was holding the bottle while the man staggered back, hand clutched to his chest. Laz raised the captured bottle like he was about to break it over the guy's head. His erstwhile attacker flinched.

"Be careful," Laz said, arresting his momentum just above the man's head. "You could hurt someone." He spun the bottle, set it gently down on the bar, and took off at a dead run.

It was a warm night and the door to the bar had been propped open. Laz didn't break stride as he exited and took off down the street. When Ulysses made it out, he looked down the line of streetlights to see Laz sprinting after a man in a dark suit, who was himself running after—

Sam.

Ulysses ran, gasping, after them. Sam was usually pretty fast, but he kept checking behind him, which tugged him off course and slowed him down. He was glancing over his shoulder as he reached the intersection with East Wash and stepped into the street without looking. Ulysses winced, hard, heart racing at the squeal as a driver slammed on their brakes. Sam danced away from the car, somehow unhurt. Even from far up the street Ulysses could hear the driver curse.

Sam took a shuffling half step farther from the hood, raising both hands in a mea culpa gesture, and then started running again. The delay had allowed the man in the suit to close the gap, and halfway down the next block he stretched out his hand to catch Sam's arm.

Ulysses tried to draw breath to shout a warning—couldn't—but then Laz was there, coiling himself to leap.

An instant later the man was on the ground, grappling with Laz. Ulysses looked at the two of them, grabbed Sam's hand, and pulled.

"We can't just leave him," Sam hissed.

"He can handle himself." But even as Ulysses got Sam moving, the stranger was throwing Laz off of him and jumping back to his feet. He looked wildly at the two of them. Ulysses stepped between him and Sam, pulling the switchblade out of his pocket, and the man retreated a pace. A large, dark car rolled up, and he dashed into the street and jumped into the passenger side. Seconds later it took off in a squeal of rubber.

Laz, halfway through getting up, winced at the sudden noise. Ulysses walked over to offer him a hand. "What the hell was that?" he asked. When Laz just stared at him, he added, "How much of that did you see, back in the bar?"

"I don't know," Laz said. He ran his hands over his scalp, as though he had enough hair to get disarrayed. "Bits." He scowled. "Aren't you forgetting to say something? Perhaps *thank you, Laz, for saving my boyfriend*?"

"Thank you for saving him," Ulysses said automatically. "But since when does your foresight work like that?"

Laz shrugged. His chest was still heaving from the run, but the openness had left his face again. "It comes and goes." He bent to tie the laces on one of his boots, then got up again, a little stiffly. "Speaking of, I'm going to go find a drink. Somewhere that's not infested with motherfuckers like those guys back at the Sett." He spat. "You coming? Or—" he cut his eyes over to Sam, who was still standing where Ulysses had left him, face pale in the lamplight. "Guess you got other problems."

Something tense and unhappy settled into the pit of Ulysses's stomach. Sam didn't say anything, just looked at the two of them, lips pressed together. When Ulysses looked back at his brother, Laz was already walking down the street.

"Laz!"

"See you around," Laz shouted over his shoulder, waving one hand lazily. He didn't turn back.

Ulysses took a ragged breath. He was still clutching the knife in one hand, forgotten, so he shut it and returned it to his pocket. "What happened?" he asked Sam, because *someone* was going to give him a coherent explanation, damn it.

"When you got up, I talked to the girls at the next table. One of them felt sick, so I helped her outside. While I was out there, that guy in the suit came up, and I decided I didn't like the look of him." He shrugged.

Ulysses sighed. "You just started talking to them?" He stepped closer. "Man, you reek of pot." Which actually helped explain how this delightful new friendship must have sprung up. He shut his eyes. "Do you ever just . . . not take what someone is handing you?"

When he opened his eyes, Sam had taken a step back, crossed his arms in front of his chest. "Are you—are you blaming me for someone trying to kidnap me?"

"No! No, of course not." Ulysses rubbed his forehead. Sam's face was shuttered, and Ulysses stepped forward and hugged him on a sudden impulse. "I'm glad you're okay."

Sam was shaking. It took a worryingly long time for him to untense enough to hug back, finally resting his forehead against Ulysses's neck. "I don't understand what happened," he muttered. "I didn't *do* anything, Ulysses."

"I know you didn't." He took a deep breath. It wasn't a bad smell, honestly. Earthy, green. It was Sam. "Come on, let's go home."

Chapter 5

S AM WAS QUIET ON the walk back. But Ulysses hadn't gotten a doctorate to not hear himself talk, so he took care of filling the silence for both of them.

"Laz's premonitions used to be short things," he said. "He'd see enough to get out of the way of a ball that was thrown at him. Split-second glimpses." He shook his head. "And I never saw him act like they caused him distress. What's changed?"

They were climbing the steps of the Baskerville when Sam said, "The war. I mean . . ." He waved a hand in a way that was clearly meant to indicate most of Southeast Asia.

"But he . . ." And then Ulysses paused, because he actually wasn't sure on that point. What *had* Laz been doing for the last five years?

They went into the apartment. Sam vanished almost immediately into the bedroom, and a minute later Ulysses heard him get into the shower. He stared at the closed door, feeling oddly helpless.

Sam was resilient. They'd been attacked more than a few times and he'd always been fine. Now, though, he looked fragile, and Ulysses wasn't sure what to do.

He'd gotten something wrong. More likely, he'd gotten almost everything wrong, and he didn't know how to get back in the right again.

He paced around the living room a few times, checking the wards restlessly, and then subsided into the recliner.

What *was* up with Laz? He thought of his brother as a high school student. He'd been studious and focused, whip smart but easy to overlook because he was quiet. They'd done almost everything together—car repair, jujitsu lessons, Ulysses's early forays into trying to help the ghosts that appeared to him. Ulysses had barely seen him sneak a beer.

The Air Force Academy had stressed Laz out, but it was meant to, right? Something about learning to perform under pressure. Each time Ulysses had seen him, he'd seemed tired but in good spirits. He excelled in his studies. He loved engineering, he loved planes and learning to fly. And then, something that had been pretty unthinkable when he'd enrolled in 1960 happened: he graduated and was sent to Vietnam.

Ulysses had seen him only sporadically since he'd been overseas, though they'd written. He wasn't sure what Lazarus had been assigned to do. He'd mentioned a willingness to fly anything he could get his hands on, including transports, helicopters, and reconnaissance jets. Bombing raids? It was certainly possible, although it hurt to think of his little brother doing that. The rest of the time, he'd worked on engines, as far as Ulysses knew. And now he was home, and he was jumpy, uncomfortable, explosive, stumbling drunk at seven in the morning.

What a disaster.

He needed—Ulysses chewed on his lower lip. Laz needed something, that much was clear. But Sam also needed—

Before he could finish either thought, Sam wandered out of the bedroom in a white T-shirt and a pair of soft pajama pants, hair curling damply on his forehead. His expression, while not exactly hangdog, was also devoid of his customary ebullience. His eyes were red-rimmed.

"How's it going?" Ulysses asked. "You look a bit . . ." He waved a hand, as though that were explanatory.

Sam looked at him, the corners of his mouth bending slightly down. He was halfway across the living room now and seemed frozen in place. "I'm fine."

"Are you still stoned?" He tried not to sound accusatory, but Sam stiffened.

"No. And I'd appreciate it if you'd stop acting like I brought this on myself somehow. The whole thing was . . ."

"Awful?" Ulysses suggested.

Sam looked a little surprised to hear him say it, but nodded and drifted closer. "I didn't expect whatever the hell that was."

"It's deeply weird," Ulysses agreed. "I haven't heard of anything like that happening here."

Sam took a deep breath, shifted his weight slightly. "Any idea who was behind it?"

Ulysses rubbed his forehead. "I assume it's related to the men Dr. Pearlman warned you about. But who exactly they are . . . no idea. There's the cult that went after Hugh, of course, but he was a full-fledged god and you're not." He hesitated before adding, "And there's certainly no shortage of besuited weirdos roaming around campus since the bombing."

"I suppose," Sam said. He was in range now. Ulysses held out a hand, and Sam let himself be drawn into the recliner. He sat sideways across Ulysses's lap, head on his shoulder, long legs sticking out absurdly over the arm of the chair. "Is there anything we can do?"

Ulysses wrapped his arms around Sam's waist. "There's a warding spell I've heard of that would prevent anyone from physically finding our apartment. With a few caveats."

Sam pulled back and looked at him. "Caveats," he said warily. "All right. What are they?"

"It doesn't work if they've already been here since we moved in, so if it were Vikram or Laz trying to kidnap you, they wouldn't be confused by it. If you or I tell someone where we live, I think they'll be able to find it, so we'd have to be careful. And it wouldn't prevent them from waiting outside and grabbing you, like they did today." He took a deep breath and steeled himself, because he guessed that Sam was not going to like the next part. Ulysses certainly didn't. "Also, it's blood magic."

As he'd expected, Sam started to pull away. "Ulysses—"

"Not—I mean, it's not the human sacrifice-y type of blood magic. More like we put some of our blood in a bowl, use that to paint the sigil on the door, and then do the spellcraft and sacrifice."

Sam's lips made a displeased line. "What's the sacrifice?"

Ulysses shrugged. "Probably a rooster or something. They're associated with warnings."

"Wow, that sounds a lot like the bad type of blood magic," Sam said dryly. "That's . . . a lot like the spell Julius did on his mausoleum, actually." His voice sounded a little thin, like remembering what Julius had done disturbed him. It disturbed Ulysses, and he didn't know all the details.

"Well, it worked," he said obstinately.

"It didn't keep us out!"

"It wasn't supposed to!"

Sam's face did something emotionally complicated, and then he leaned closer and rested his forehead against Ulysses's. "It seems like—you'll have to forgive me if I've got this wrong, but what I've gathered is that any form of blood magic is dangerous, and letting you get accustomed to doing that kind of thing is probably dangerous to you. I think you've said as much. So let's not."

Ulysses shut his eyes, disappointed and relieved. "No?"

"I don't think they're going to try to break in here and grab me while I'm sleeping, Ulysses. They know where I work. Also, if they learned anything from today, it's that you're terrifying, so . . ."

He laughed, taken aback, despite the seriousness of the moment. "Am I?"

"You didn't see yourself and Laz coming down like a wolf on the fold," Sam said. "It was amazing."

Ulysses took a deep breath. "I didn't know what Laz was planning. I just knew I had to get you away from there."

Sam kissed him with a sudden desperation. Ulysses couldn't breathe, found himself clutching Sam's hip as Sam bent to kiss his neck, one hand running across Ulysses's chest and down his arm, gripping his bicep. Post-shower, Sam smelled like petrichor and shampoo, and Ulysses tried to pull him closer, his heart rate picking up.

Wordlessly, Sam slid off his lap and stood, offering a hand. Ulysses allowed himself to be pulled to his feet, and then they stood chest to chest, Ulysses looking up at Sam's face. "What—" He broke off, his voice threatening to betray a lot of messiness, and paused before trying again. "Sam. What do you want?"

Sam exhaled noisily. "Just . . . remind me that I'm human."

Ulysses said, "Sam," in a voice that was still a little too raw.

"You don't have to sweep me off my feet or anything. I just want—I need—something. A distraction." He looked frustrated with his own inarticulateness.

The entirety of the evening unraveled in Ulysses's stomach and he closed his eyes. He'd saved Sam, but from what, and how could he stop it from happening again? He couldn't. All his knowledge and he couldn't protect Sam. He couldn't do *anything*, not really.

But perhaps he could offer some comfort for now.

"You *are* human," he said finally, aware that the pause had been a long one. "The ways in which you aren't are academically interesting but ultimately unimportant. And even if you weren't, I swear I would be here anyway."

Sam took a breath but didn't say anything, and Ulysses wondered if he'd said something wrong. Eventually Sam opened his mouth, but then he just shook his head. "Forget it."

Oh. Ulysses grabbed his wrist before he could turn away. "No, don't go. I'm sorry. I was thinking."

Sam raised an eyebrow. "What about?" He didn't sound totally won over, but he wasn't leaving anymore.

"How to sweep you off your feet." He looked Sam up and down, slowly, trying to put some heat into it. "You're tall, if you hadn't noticed. Makes it a little tricky."

Sam turned back toward him. "Makes what tricky?"

"This." He raised the wrist he was holding and dropped a shoulder, catching Sam right at his center of gravity, just above his navel. Then he straightened back up, Sam neatly draped over his shoulders. Sam yelped, and

Ulysses staggered on the first step before he adjusted to the unevenly distributed load.

"Ulysses!"

"Hush. This is what you wanted." He started for the bedroom.

Sam made a strangled noise, half laugh, half outrage. "This is not dignified!"

"I'm sorry," Ulysses said. "Was sex supposed to be?" He used Sam's feet to nudge open the door. It was a good five steps to the bed, and Sam's squirming made him lurch to one side. "Careful there."

"You be careful."

Ulysses tried to reverse the procedure to throw Sam onto the bed, overbalanced, and nearly pitched over directly on top of him.

Sam was laughing and trying to catch his breath. He reached down and tugged at Ulysses's T-shirt until he moved up the bed. "Hi," he said, suddenly quiet.

"You okay?" Ulysses murmured.

Sam bit his lip. "Kind of. Not really. No." He took a breath and fixed Ulysses with those odd, pale green eyes. "I'll get over it, but—"

Ulysses leaned forward and kissed the apologies out of his mouth, then kept going, threw a leg over his hips and kissed the side of his neck. The feelings that Sam was going through, he had no idea what to do with, but sex he thought he could handle.

Pulling back slightly, he ran his hands down Sam's chest and hiked up his shirt. Sam sat up enough to pull it over his head, then settled back on his elbows, face still troubled. Ulysses traced a finger over his collarbone and tried to remind himself to slow down, take his time, try to make this good.

Sam tended to see himself as a little too tall, too thin. But he was wrong; he was like a Greek statue, elegant, grand, and beautiful to the point that Ulysses didn't always even know how to look at him. All the running hadn't made him bulkily muscular, but it had helped fill him out a little, made him look healthy again. His tan skin was smooth, unmarred by their experiences. Ulysses bent to bite his shoulder, kissed the mark, then worked his way down his chest.

By the time he reached Sam's hips, the other man was watching him with something approaching reverence, breathing unsteadily. Ulysses could feel how fast Sam's heart was going as he pulled the thin cotton pants down and dropped them off the bed. Sam was naked underneath, hot to the touch, and the sound he made when Ulysses closed a hand around his hard-on was obscene and amazing.

Unexpectedly, Sam bent one leg and rolled them over, straddling Ulysses's hips. "You're still fully dressed," he muttered reproachfully, tugging at Ulysses's shirt.

Ulysses didn't argue, just helped Sam yank his clothes off, then waited while Sam surveyed him, running a finger over a scar here and there before leaning down to kiss it. He felt like a scrapbook of misadventure, covered with marks that lingered long past the end of the associated traumas. Sam ran his fingers over a group of odd, not-quite-circular fingerprints on his shoulder, the remnants of a curse-infected injury earlier in the spring. Sam was looking at them like they were breaking his heart, and Ulysses was not about to let him get feelings all over a perfectly good seduction, so he rolled them back over and pinned Sam's shoulders.

"It's fine," he growled. Sam's eyes were half-lidded and dark, and he kissed Ulysses more intensely this time, arching up to grind his erection into Ulysses's, until Ulysses had to pull back to catch his breath. "What do you—"

"I want you," Sam muttered, "inside me. Now. Ulysses. Please. Now. Ulysses." The last syllable turned into a hiss when Ulysses reached down and stroked him again. Sam wound his legs around Ulysses's waist, barely giving him enough space to reach out and fumble the jar of lubricant out of the bedside table. His hands trembled a little as he slicked himself.

It was as he entered Sam that it happened. One moment he was there, holding himself still while Sam breathed through his body adjusting, and then he was inside Sam's senses as well. It was overwhelming, like getting caught by an unexpected wave and dragged under. He could physically feel the bed against his back, the reverberations of his own movements, Sam's arousal, Sam feeling things from Ulysses's side as well and knowing what he was feeling in some kind of weird feedback loop, and below all the physical stuff Sam's emotions, love and lust and fear and anger and all the other darker things he was trying to ignore.

It was too much. He felt like he had just fallen headlong off a bridge or over a waterfall with no sense of where the bottom was. The anxious roil in his chest did battle with exhilaration. He probably should have stopped, shut his eyes and tried to sort out what was happening, but Sam made an urgent noise, rolling his hips, and Ulysses started to move. Sam was digging his fingers into Ulysses's back and murmuring something like encouragement or love in his ear; Sam's emotions were a ragged mess, and Ulysses wasn't much different. He was caught between two mirrors, feeling each movement into infinity. There was something different about the bond between them, hot and tight and sparking, that he couldn't quite get enough brain cells together to understand. He had just enough time to think that this wasn't going to last and maybe it shouldn't, and then Sam was coming, biting his shoulder hard as he did, and the pain dragged Ulysses into his own orgasm.

He collapsed on top of Sam, sweaty, sticky, shaking. Sam wrapped his arms around Ulysses, gave him a moment to regroup and piece his mind back together.

"Hi," Sam muttered, when Ulysses managed to lift his head and make eye contact.

"Sam," Ulysses said, and then stopped, unsure where to go from there.

Sam laughed quietly, nervously. "Was that because of the bond?"

71

"I . . . almost certainly." Ulysses managed to roll to the side, landing on his back on the crumpled sheets. "And the answer to your next question is I don't know, and I can't think of anyone I could ask without dying of shame."

Sam curled up on his side, draping an arm over Ulysses's chest and pressing his face into his neck. "It seems fine."

"Does it?" Ulysses looked up at the shadows on the ceiling, tried to remember what time it was, what day and month. "That was terrifying."

"We didn't die."

Ulysses found himself grinning. "No, we didn't. And we—I mean, are you all right?"

"Do you have to ask?"

"I guess not." He took a deep breath and then yawned, surprising himself. "The department keeps a a small collection of books in the staff lounge so the undergrads don't find them. It's the, uh. The stuff that's a little risqué. I'll see if there's anything relevant."

"And if there isn't?"

Ulysses shrugged. "We could write something."

Sam managed, "That would really cement your reputation," before he started laughing too hard for words.

"I mean, it doesn't have to be *illustrated* or anything," Ulysses said, and he was laughing too. But when he stopped and took a breath, he didn't like the direction his thoughts headed in.

"What?" Sam asked, lifting his head to look at him. He must have tensed slightly or made an unhappy noise. Possibly Sam was just much more keyed into Ulysses's feelings than he'd assumed.

Ulysses avoided his eyes. "That wasn't intentional on either of our parts." He paused, but Sam didn't answer right away. "Am I mistaken?"

He heard Sam take a deep breath, felt the cold seep between them as he drew back. "I didn't do anything deliberately."

"That means that the bond is changing." He cracked his thumb and the first knuckle on his left hand, because the other arm was still wrapped around Sam. "And . . . I have to assume this kind of change is a problem. Moving to a less stable, less intentional pattern is—not good."

"Is it?" Sam sat up, pulling all the way away from him.

"Isn't it?" Ulysses sat up too, feeling like a gulf was opening between them. "What if it starts happening all the time, uncontrollably? Do you really want to know what I'm doing all the time? Feel what I'm feeling? Be one person with two bodies? It's hard enough to deal with when I expect it. I don't want to live in that all the time. I'd go mad."

Sam's face shuttered and he rubbed his forehead. "It wasn't that bad, was it?"

Ulysses said, "Sam," and didn't like how raw his voice sounded. "You don't have any training, and you don't understand what could happen here. You could end up like Virgil, or worse." He ran his hands through his hair.

"You don't know why he's like that!" Sam stood up and bent to snatch his pants from the floor where they'd landed. "It's not because of some . . . some quasi-mystical bond between him and your mother!"

"What is this?" Ulysses snapped, watching him dress with tight, efficient movements. "You always take me to task for not protecting myself. But now I want to protect both of us and you're angry."

"No!" Sam said, too loudly, and then squeezed his eyes shut. "All right, yes. Because we don't have any evidence that is going to get worse or—or *damage* one of us."

Ulysses crossed his arms. "I think you are inappropriately blasé about that possibility."

"And I think you're being a control freak," Sam said. Then he stopped, looking shocked with himself.

Ulysses felt frozen, pin pricks in his palms and the soles of his feet. "I'm . . . I'm just trying to keep you safe," he managed at last.

Sam nodded slowly, mouth pressed shut like he didn't trust himself to speak. Then he turned away.

"Where are you going?"

"I'm going to read for a while," Sam said without looking back. He crossed the room and stopped, one hand on the doorknob. "You should get some sleep. It's late."

"Sam," Ulysses said, and the door shut between them.

Chapter 6

ULYSSES TOSSED AND TURNED for an interminable time, half convinced that at some point he'd roll over and find Sam asleep next to him. But he never did. Instead, he eventually dropped into a dream where he was watching Sam and Livia talk to each other from across a crowded room.

That had never happened. At the best of times, Livia would have cheerfully murdered Sam, and he suspected the feeling was mutual. He'd never seen them exchange more than a few terse words at a time. But in the dream, Sam said something and Livia threw back her head and laughed. Uncomfortably, he suspected they were talking about him, and that if he could hear what they were saying, he wouldn't like it. But no matter how he tried to get over there, the room somehow kept him apart from Sam. Even shouting did no good, because Sam couldn't hear him above the hum of the party.

He woke up sweaty and alone. It was mid-morning and the apartment was silent. When he put on his robe and made his way out to the living room, Sam was gone.

Ulysses's stomach turned over. He had to sit down for a few minutes until the room stopped spinning.

Once he no longer felt like he was going to die or pass out, he realized that the whole place smelled like freshly baked bread. He'd been dumped more than a few times, but no one had ever bothered to bake for him before they left. He went into the kitchen and found a large loaf of bread on the counter under a towel, along with a note:

Had to leave to pick up Ellen at O'Hare. Didn't want to wake you. Enjoy the bread. Remember we're supposed to dine with Vikram and his wife this evening at 7. –S

"You made a real hash of that." It was Dr. Ranganathan, standing in the corner next to the refrigerator. "He was upset when he left."

"How upset?" Ulysses asked, then realized he didn't really want to hear it from her.

"Up all night baking bread." She shrugged. "I have to admit, that's an emotion I have difficulty parsing. But there was some real violence in his kneading."

Ulysses checked the percolator, which Sam had left on the stove. It made about six cups of coffee, and Sam had left him—enough for one cup. Well, that was something.

"Were you just watching him all night?" he asked over one shoulder.

When he looked around, she shrugged. "Being dead gives one an enormous amount of free time and a different perspective on how to spend it."

"I bet." He took down a mug and filled it with lukewarm coffee. "What time did he leave?"

"Seven." Dr. Ranganathan looked across the kitchen, like she was looking through the wall into the living room. "He was pacing back and forth before he left. As though he wanted to go in and talk to you, but he didn't dare." She rolled her eyes.

The coffee tasted like battery acid. He added sugar, which made it taste like sweet battery acid, possibly an improvement. "He didn't say anything?"

"Not to me. I don't think he knew I was here." She tilted her head to one side. "You can see me. And Vikram and Sita can see me. Why is that?"

"Almost everyone can see some ghosts under certain circumstances," Ulysses said, waving a hand. "If it was someone they knew and loved, or if they're in a place with a lot of background magic, it's more likely. But I can always see them."

"What a blessing," Dr. Ranganathan said dryly. "Are you saying your lover can't see me because he doesn't want to?"

"No, because *you* don't want him to." He sipped his coffee again, considering. "Although both are probably true."

Ulysses got on his motorcycle. He wasn't quite sure where he was heading; it had been a long time since he'd ridden out of town to clear his head, racing aimlessly along the country roads. Why waste the gas, when he could go find Sam and talk about whatever problem he'd come up against until he came across a solution. Or—not talk.

He and Sam didn't fight. That was the thing. They had disagreements sometimes, but Sam was congenitally opposed to the kind of shouting matches that characterized romantic relationships on television and in films. He was easygoing, almost to a fault. For him to react like he had to something Ulysses had said . . . well, Ulysses was aware he'd fucked something important up. He just didn't see quite what.

He wound up at the Red Gym. That was mildly worrying in itself: was he really getting so dull that he was going to lift weights instead of . . . He realized he didn't quite know what.

And he *was* going to lift weights.

After his workout, he stood in front of the odd, castle-shaped building for a moment, one leg thrown over the bike. The magic building was on the west side of campus; to get there he'd turn right, ride along Langdon, and then go up the steep hill on Observatory Drive and follow that for a while.

Without thinking too hard about what he was doing, he turned left. At the end of Langdon he jogged over one block onto Gilman, heading toward Pinckney Street and the house.

The house.

He didn't live there anymore. It wasn't *his* house at all. But it was still a grand old place, worthy of some kind of name.

Still chewing on that, Ulysses let himself in the back door. The kitchen was quiet; he walked through into the living room and found his father, face buried behind a newspaper, seated on the sofa.

"Hey, Virgil," he said, dropping onto the couch next to him. "How's the economy?"

There was a long silence, and then Virgil said, "Bad."

"Is it?"

There was a rustle as Virgil folded the paper up. "Inflation's up," he said. "Few years, very bad. Nixon."

"Well, I mean, Nixon," Ulysses said, and Virgil smiled. It was a bit surprising to have Virgil focused and responding. The older man was fifty-four but hardly looked it; perhaps because his face was so constantly at rest, it had never had the chance to settle into lines. Instead, his skin was smooth, if weathered-looking. His bright blue eyes were the same as Ulysses's, but he had sandy brown hair, a small scar on his chin, and a trim mustache. He wore a tweed suit as though he were still going to the office every day, but no tie. Following an impulse Ulysses couldn't quite explain, he asked, "Do you ever know where Mariah is?"

Virgil tilted his head. "Paris."

Ulysses smiled weakly. "I mean more specifically."

Virgil nodded and glanced at the clock. "Orly."

Ulysses heard footsteps on the back stairs. A moment later, Laz clattered in from the kitchen and dropped into the armchair. "Don't go around harassing Virgil about whatever twisted shit you're into."

Laz didn't look hungover, although he had dark rings under his eyes and a livid scrape on his cheek. "What have you been up to?" Ulysses asked.

Laz grinned. "This and that."

An alarm went off in the kitchen. Laz twitched, but it was Virgil who got calmly to his feet. Ulysses followed him into the next room and watched as he turned the timer off and opened the oven. Ulysses tossed a pair of oven mitts at him. Virgil didn't look over, but he did put them on before he pulled the baking dish out and set it on top of the stove.

"You can turn off the oven," Ulysses suggested.

"He knows," Laz said from the doorway. "Give him a second."

Virgil glanced over at them, one eyebrow raised, then reached out and turned off the oven.

"What did you make?" Laz asked.

Virgil shrugged. "Didn't."

"Looks like a quiche," Ulysses said.

Laz nodded. "Do you think Babushka has that earmarked for something, or can it be breakfast?"

Ulysses looked at Virgil, who made a complicated head motion as though he were weighing the idea and said, "Yes."

They were all silent for a moment. "Yes, she has plans?" Ulysses said eventually. "Or yes, we can eat it?"

"Yes," Virgil said, and both Ulysses and Laz stared at him for a long moment.

"Useless," came a voice from behind them. Ulysses turned to see his grandmother, a tiny woman with long white hair and bright blue eyes, scowling. "Americans always claim education is the way to get ahead. But look at you all. So much learning. So little use." If they'd been outside, she would doubtless have spat to accentuate her point. Instead, she set her parcel on the counter and walked around to the stove, shooing the three of them out of the way. "You are hungry? Yes?" She looked from face to face. "All right, go and sit."

Virgil took his slice out to the dining room table, leaving the two stools in the kitchen for Laz and Ulysses. Ulysses got himself a cup of coffee and one for Laz as well, because the guy did look a little rough beneath the swagger, and sat down to watch Babushka as she bustled around making herself tea.

"Well?" she finally grumped at him. "You have a question?"

"Do I need to—"

Babushka shook her head sharply. "You stink of questions."

Ulysses took a bite of the quiche and tried to decide which question she wanted him to ask. Or perhaps expected was a better word. He had so many at the moment, and they all felt equally urgent.

When he finally opened his mouth, what he asked was, "Did Julius Sterling have followers?"

Babushka didn't do anything as amateurish as drop her teaspoon or freeze in place, but Ulysses thought there

81

was a rigidity to her posture that hadn't been there a moment before. On his left, Laz was definitely looking askance at him, but probably because he had no idea what Ulysses was talking about.

"Followers, no," Babushka said. "He had Dr. Barth. And some assistants." She paused. "Barth had students as well. Residents."

"Did any of them know what Sterling was doing?"

"Barth," she said immediately. "Although. Did he know the full extent of Sterling's plans?" She shot him a look, a reminder that *he* probably didn't even totally understand them. "You know what they say about two people keeping a secret."

Ulysses shut his eyes. "We've heard rumors about a group that's trying to capitalize on the—the subjects of his research."

"The god children, you mean," Babushka said, leaning on the counter. "Interesting." Then she was quiet for a while. Laz looked over at Ulysses again, obviously hoping to divine what exactly was being discussed. Ulysses took another bite of quiche and didn't meet his eyes. Eventually, Babushka shook her head. "It's a bad business. I could have predicted that if any of the godlings survived, someone would try to exploit them. Do you know where they are?"

"Other than Sam and Hugh?" He tried not to let his eyes dart sideways at Laz. "No, I do not." He sighed, trying not to look too closely at his impulse to secrecy. "They were all local twenty-five years ago, but it's been so long. I have some birth dates, some initials that might be encoded. Not really enough to trace anyone."

She pressed her lips together. "Very few groups here," she said finally. "Very few people who are powerful enough to command the kind of loyalty and respect one would need to take on a godling. It might make Mr. Trouble look like a viable alternative." Babushka smiled crookedly at him, then turned away, digging through a drawer until she produced a pencil stub and a small notepad. Muttering, she scribbled down a few words, paused for a long moment, added one more. She tore out the paper and folded it, pushing it across the table to him. "There. That's where I would begin."

There were three names: Garcia, Landover, Ranganathan. He raised an eyebrow. "The assistants?"

"Residents." Babushka made a face. "I cannot prove they are culpable. But they were around at the time."

"Thanks," he said, sliding the paper into his pocket. "That's exactly what I needed."

Laz followed him out onto the front porch. Ulysses paused on the steps, looking back at him. "Is Sam okay?"

Ulysses shrugged. "He's . . . he was a little shaken up, but he's fine."

Laz dug out a pack of cigarettes and lit one, studying him during the silence. They were two years apart in age, but Laz seemed both unaccountably young and much older at the same time. He looked calmer than he had the day before—sleep must have knitted the raveled sleeve of care or something. Meanwhile Ulysses just felt tired.

"What do you call this place?" he asked Laz. "I mean, you haven't lived here for so long. Do you still think of it as *home*, or . . ." He realized belatedly that Laz probably didn't appreciate the reminder of his absence.

"I used to call it Gooseberry House when I was talking to my teacher, back in Thailand." Laz smiled a little and took a drag on his cigarette.

Ulysses frowned. "Gooseberry? After those bushes Cass took out back, what, a decade ago?"

"No, after that line in *Eugene Onegin*." Laz rolled his eyes. "It was just a joke. Don't worry about it."

"Oh." But it had a certain ring to it, he had to admit.

"Walk with me?" Laz said finally, gesturing to the sidewalk. "I'd like to hear about how you and Sam met. If you don't have anything better to do."

Ulysses took a deep breath and pushed away the ever-present awareness of an overwhelming list of things to research and too few hours in which to do them. "Sure."

Laz flashed him a grin as he came rattling down the steps, half excited, half mischievous, and for a moment it felt just like old times.

SAM KNEW ELLEN WAS exhausted because she let him take her luggage and haul it back to the car while she trundled along behind. She was wearing a yellow dress, badly wrinkled from travel, that came down to her knees, with a matching yellow cardigan that she removed as soon as they stepped out into the Chicago heat. She had braided her long red hair for the trip and it was leaking out of its queue, giving her a rumpled look very much at odds with how she usually presented herself.

"Davao City—which is the durian capital of the Philippines, if you didn't know—to Hong Kong, Hong Kong to Japan, Japan to San Francisco, and then SF to here," she said when she got in the car. "I've been in an airplane for a day and a half." She frowned. "Maybe longer. I crossed the international date line a couple of times, I think." She yawned and rubbed her face. "How's Ulysses? Did you find an apartment?"

"He's fine," Sam said, tapping his fingers on the steering wheel. It was hot from the sun, and the mild sting was a good distraction from the drift of his thoughts. "We did finally find an apartment. Actually, we just moved in on Thursday."

He turned the key in the ignition. Ellen stopped frowning at the side of his face long enough to buckle her safety belt. "Is everything all right?"

"Fine," he said blandly, and rubbed his jaw. Stubble caught at his fingers; he hadn't shaved before he left. "It's been great. The neighbors are very friendly. And—and Ulysses's little brother just came back into town, too." He carefully reversed out of the parking space and made his way to the cashier, and then out of the ceaseless field of asphalt onto the access road that returned to I-90.

He could hear Ellen fidgeting. "Moving in together can be stressful," she said at last. "You might find you argue more than usual. Harry and I certainly did. You're establishing new patterns, and that can be difficult even for long-time couples."

"Well, but we've technically been living together since April." And it wasn't like they'd been fighting about whose job it was to do the dishes.

He still took solace when she shook her head and said, "It's not the same. He was staying with you. Now you're—you're equals. You've got both of your things at the place, I assume, instead of just your furniture and a duffle bag of Ulysses's clothing. This is a big step. Of course it puts stress on your relationship." She shifted in her seat. "I think it took us a good six months before we really figured out how everything was going to work, and we'd been together for a few years at that point."

"I'm a little surprised you came back while Harry is still over there," Sam said.

"Yes, well. Things are very political in the UW math department at the moment." She sighed loudly. When he risked a glance, she was leaning back in the seat, eyes shut. "The Army Math research think tank was headquartered in Sterling Hall. Now that's all shut down and there's rumors they're going to close it forever, so there's a lot of math researchers looking for new jobs. I needed to claim a spot before the department gave them all away, because it will look better when Harry is done and we're looking for full-time teaching positions elsewhere."

Sam nodded. "How's his research going?"

"Slowly, but he's having fun." She opened her eyes. They were just pulling onto the highway heading north, rolling past fields of tall corn and wildly green soybeans. "He thinks he'll be done by Christmas."

"And if he's not?"

She rubbed the fingers of her left hand together in a way that meant "money."

"Ah." There were plenty of intricacies about the PhD student life that Sam, who had stopped after his master's, knew about only peripherally. Research grants were one of these.

"What was it like?" Ellen said suddenly, and he knew somehow that she'd been itching to ask the question since she'd gotten into the car.

"The bombing?"

She waited.

"I don't know. Disconcerting."

Ellen punched his shoulder. "Come on, man."

"I don't know!" Sam watched the dotted line between the lanes flicker past for a moment. "We were in bed. It woke us up, and it was obvious something had exploded, but we didn't know what. The next day, I think Celeste called and said it was Sterling Hall, and we walked down to look at it." He cleared his throat. "There was—all the glass was gone. It probably broke every window for

87

blocks around. Big hole in the side of the building. And it blew all the leaves off the trees."

"Whoa."

"Yeah." Sam shook his head. "It didn't feel real. It still doesn't. It's possible that we should have seen it coming, with all the protests and the police and the tear gas . . ." But there had been a couple of firebombings, and a few that had failed to go off. "A physics researcher died. So when I say I don't know what to say about it . . . that's what I mean." They sat in silence until Sam asked, "Can you explain to me what they were doing at Army Math? I've read the articles, but . . . were they doing any magic research?"

Her eyes narrowed. "What do you mean? What happened?"

He took a deep breath and told her about the men in suits.

"You think they're related to the bombing?" Ellen sounded skeptical, and he didn't blame her.

"I don't have proof one way or another." He hunched forward a little, gripping the steering wheel. "It's just weird."

Ellen rolled her eyes. "Well, I'm happy to be the one to tell you that your paranoia is dialed up too high. They didn't have anything to do with magic there. Just math."

"What does math have to do with the army?"

She scoffed. "Lots of things. If you want to fire a missile from point A and hit point B, you need math. If you want to drop a bomb from 30,000 feet up and hit *anything*, you need math. If you want to improve your weapons, you need math. If you want to model the conflict on a computer, you need math." She gave him a sidelong look. "Not magic, so tell Ulysses to calm down."

"I'd love to," Sam said honestly. "Why not magic?"

"It's not very efficient." Ellen yawned suddenly. "I'm sure you could create a spell to get one bomb to its destination very precisely, but do you know how many bombs they drop per day?" She shook her head. "Plus magical types tend to be 4F, or anti-war, or both. Ulysses's brother is unusual in that regard. But they'd need a thousand of him to be able to do anything."

Sam relaxed his grip on the steering wheel and leaned back. "I see what you mean."

Ellen spent a few minutes staring out the window for another few minutes before she added, "I'm not saying it's totally impossible. Just unlikely."

Sam exhaled. He could hear Ellen drumming her fingers on the door handle. "I'll keep an ear out around the department, all right? I don't know if anyone would be dumb enough to talk, but if they do—"

"Thanks." Sam tried to smile. "I appreciate it."

"It'll give me something to do." She sighed and curled up against the door. "Sam. On Mindanao I went to the beach every day and did math in the sand. It was gorgeous. White sand, blue water, fresh coconuts, the ripest pineapple I'd ever experienced. . . . Now I get to go through another Wisconsin winter. Without Harry." She groaned.

Sam nodded sympathetically. "Are you doing a fall show? Could take your mind off things."

"I don't know." She sighed again, but uncurled slightly. "We didn't write all that much this summer. A bunch of scenes from *The Tempest*, but not a full show's worth. And I have a long choral number from a *Hamlet* musical we didn't wind up finishing."

"You could do all the *Tempest* scenes as the first act, and then do that after intermission." He thought for a while, the miles unspooling under the tires. "Call it a staged reading."

Ellen considered this. "I'd need someone to help direct," she said after a while. "I always have my hands full with the music."

"You could—"

She said, "Sam."

He took a deep breath. "Have I been volunteered?" he asked. "I don't know anything about directing."

"You'll be great." Ellen patted his hand. "Don't worry about it."

Chapter 7

S AM LET HIMSELF IN quietly and leaned back against the door when it closed, taking a deep breath. It was mid-afternoon, warm and humid, and Ulysses had the windows open. The air smelled faintly of the herbs that Celeste and Obe had hung over the door, and more strongly of the bread he'd baked that morning. He could hear Springsteen playing on the stereo in the office. Ulysses had moved things in his absence; the coffee table was now where it belonged, in front of the sofa.

Sam felt tired and lonely, despite having spent most of the day with Ellen. Coming home made the cold spot behind his sternum worse, because he was going to have to talk this out now. For the first time since the early days of their relationship, he wondered what Ulysses would do, whether the bond *was* too overwhelming for him and if he'd leave over it. It was everything he'd avoided thinking about all day, and the weight was suddenly crushing.

He envied Harry and Ellen in some ways. Of course, their path as two academics was not going to be easy, but there was something straightforward about it that Sam didn't get to have. No magic, no gods. Just two people who loved each other and wanted to build a life together.

He toed off his shoes and hesitated. The door to the bedroom was open; he could go relax, let the tension of the road melt out of him. He'd barely slept the night before. It would be good for him. Or he could be brave and go into the office. They could have it out. He knew what was probably the right thing to do, and he knew what he wanted to do, and he let the two pin him to the spot for a moment, staring at the doors.

And then he screwed his courage to the sticking place as best he could and went into the office. It was a biggish room with east-facing windows, bright but without direct sunlight at this hour, warm but not stifling. There was an avocado-colored tufted chaise longue he hadn't seen before along the far wall, with a few boxes of books piled between it and the door. The previous occupants had abandoned a desk beneath the windows, and that was where Ulysses sat now, reading glasses perched on his nose as he peered at a book. Sam stood behind him for a moment, breath sticking in his chest, unsure if he should interrupt, and then Ulysses looked over his shoulder.

Sam said, "Where'd that come from?"

"Mmm?" Ulysses turned, then took off his glasses and stretched. It was a bit of a shame, because he was one of those annoying people who looked extremely sexy in glasses, but Sam enjoyed watching the play of muscles under his T-shirt as he moved, the skin visible where it rode up. "Laz and I found it on the curb. How was the drive?"

"It was O'Hare," Sam said. "Hot, construction, tolls."

Ulysses raised an eyebrow. "Do you want to lie down before dinner? You've got time."

Sam shrugged. "I thought we should probably talk." He looked down at his stocking feet. "Want to grab a beer?"

"I think we're out," Ulysses said, pushing his chair back. "I gave the last one to Laz after he helped me carry the chaise up the stairs. Or did you mean go somewhere?"

"No, yeah. A bar or something."

Ulysses got to his feet. "Sure."

They walked in near silence toward the Square. Fret Not Bar, on the corner at the top of the hill, had a sizable patio that was largely empty at five in the afternoon, so they took their drinks outside. The cast-iron chairs were not exactly comfortable, but they kept him grounded, the discomfort preventing his mind from flying away on the sensations of the breeze and rising warmth, the dark bitter beer and the lingering smell of cedar aftershave that trailed behind Ulysses. They sat facing each other, Sam's knees taking up too much room under the table.

Ulysses seemed to run out of steam and just stared at him, one hand loosely curled around his pint glass. "You're Utnapishtim's wife," he said after a while.

It took Sam a moment to place the reference, and then he gave a short bark of laughter. "Utnapishtim's wife, the one who left Gilgamesh loaves of bread when he failed at his quest for immortality and slept for seven days? Does that make you Gilgamesh?"

Ulysses grinned. "Of course I'm Gilgamesh. Strong, beautiful, powerful, wise?"

"Oh my god." Sam covered his face, trying to keep his laughter in check. "Not humble, of course."

"No, sorry. It's a hero thing." Ulysses tipped his head back. "I suppose you'd make a good Enkidu as well. Made by the gods, civilized by sex, best friend and lover of the king."

"Since he's the one who always gets to ask Gilgamesh if he's sure about whatever damn fool thing he's doing, I'll take it," Sam said, smiling down at his beer. Then he took a deep breath. "I'm sorry I walked out last night."

Ulysses looked at him carefully. "I'm—well, I'm sorry you spent the night on the sofa, for one."

Sam nodded, taking a drink of his beer to cover over how lost he felt. And, if he was being honest, his annoyance. Wasn't Ulysses supposed to say something about how he was sorry for being a control freak or something? Wasn't that how these things worked? But Ulysses was still just staring at him, like he was some kind of puzzle that would come into focus if only he could get the right perspective. Sam was half surprised he didn't put his glasses back on to look more closely. "I didn't really sleep, to be honest."

Ulysses's mouth turned down at the corners, but he didn't press. Sam watched as he sipped his beer and set the glass down, tracing a finger through the condensation. "What happened?" he asked eventually. Sam snorted, and he shook his head. "I mean—I upset you. But I don't understand how, exactly."

"No?" Sam shut his eyes. "Really no?"

When he looked again, Ulysses shrugged. It was somehow a very Gallic gesture; he must have picked it up from Mariah at some point. "You seemed to take what I said about the bond very personally."

"'Maybe," Sam said. "Probably because it's my fault, and I'm—how do you get rid of it without getting rid of me, Ulysses?" He took a deep breath. "And I'm not convinced it's a bad thing."

"You mean us, our relationship?" Ulysses sat forward and caught his hand. Sam had an odd, twisty moment in which he wasn't sure whose feelings he was feeling, or maybe that was wishful thinking, or maybe they were just feeling the same thing. "You don't really mean that. We only just moved in. We can't—"

Sam shook his head. "I mean the bond. I think I like it. I don't know that I want it to go away." They stared at each other. Ulysses's face was frozen in a strange expression, halfway between fear and something softer. Sam wondered how they could know each other so well and yet be stuck in this moment where everything felt so foreign. "Do you not like it?"

There was a long silence during which Ulysses was no doubt reassessing Sam's sanity. "Why don't you tell me what you like about it," he said eventually.

Sam shifted in his seat. "I can't tell you exactly. I haven't always had the best experiences with magic, but it's part of who you are, and I want to be part of that. And the bond has been useful a few times, you have to admit."

"Mmm." Ulysses leaned back again. For a long moment, he just watched Sam, a slight frown on his face. Sam surprised himself by staring back, although he felt scrutinized and his heart had been racing since they sat down. "You're right about the utility of the thing, although I can't wholeheartedly agree it's a net positive. But I promise to keep an open mind during my research. All right?"

Sam supposed it was the best he was going to get. It was a compromise, of a sort. "Thank you."

"So is that—are we good?" Ulysses still looked slightly stricken, and Sam fought the urge to either put his forehead on the table or launch himself across it at the other man.

"Ulysses. We're good." He forced himself to take a deep breath, lowered his voice. "Just remember what I am, all right?"

He looked confused. "I know what you are."

Sam drank the rest of his beer in one long rush, slightly embarrassed by how vulnerable he felt. "We'd better get to the liquor store. We're supposed to have dinner at seven, and it's already almost quarter past six."

"Is it really?" Ulysses drank the last of his and stood up. "Think that place on State Street is open?"

"Probably." Sam looked down at his hands for a moment. Then, surprising both of them, he hugged Ulysses. If they hadn't been in public, he'd probably have done a lot more. As it was, he contented himself with patting the other man on the back, hand sliding over his thin cotton shirt before pulling away.

"WHAT DO YOU MEAN, Ekaterina gave you the name Ranganathan?" Sam asked as they stepped out of the liquor store. It was a ten-minute walk back to the Baskerville building, and they were just going to make it by seven. Ulysses wasn't exactly sure how time had gotten away from them.

"No first name." He sighed. "I asked her about possible students or assistants who might have known about the experiments."

Sam slowed down for a few paces, then shook his head. "Julius died in 1953, and Vikram was in Boston in '65 doing his PhD. Unless he's significantly older than he looks . . ."

Ulysses looked at him curiously. "How do you know that?"

Sam cleared his throat. "I was also in Boston at that time."

"He went to Harvard?"

"No, he went to MIT. We just . . . crossed paths." Sam looked away. "He remembered me. Or—he thought he recognized my face when I saw him yesterday. I don't think he knew where from, and I decided not to remind him."

"Wait," Ulysses said. "When you say crossed paths—"

Sam was blushing. That was interesting. "I mean we met once, that's all."

"Did you—" He lowered his voice. "Sam, did you sleep with him?"

"*No!*" Sam said, loudly. A few passersby turned to look at him.

Ulysses stopped walking and put a hand on Sam's arm. "Maybe you'd better tell me the whole story."

Sam looked around but, apparently finding no convenient holes to throw himself into, sighed. "Private space is, as you might guess, at a premium in the undergraduate dormitories, both at Harvard and at MIT."

Ulysses nodded as though he'd ever lived in a dorm. "A common issue for students, I hear."

"I was seeing this guy from MIT. Or, I don't know, seeing him is a bit generous."

"You were making time," Ulysses suggested, and Sam laughed.

"Yeah, that's . . . yeah." He looked down for a moment, clearly steeling himself. "We were out one night, and he got it into his head that we should go by this lab in the biology building on MIT's campus that he had a key to, and—"

"One thing led to another?" Ulysses wiggled his eyebrows.

Sam groaned. "Vikram walked in because David couldn't be quiet." When Ulysses glanced over at him, he was flushed and wouldn't meet his eye.

Ulysses had to bite the inside of his cheek to stop himself from laughing. "I didn't realize," he said. "I, ah. I thought that time at Picnic Point was an aberration—"

"It was!" Sam said, too loud, too exercised. "Because of this!"

Ulysses gave him a sidelong glance. "Was Vikram shitty about it?"

"No. No, no. It was just embarrassing. A lot of people in that position would have called my father and told him what happened." He looked down at his feet. "I was not quite twenty-one at the time. I think you can imagine how *that* conversation would have gone."

Howard was a lot of things, but *understanding* was not an adjective Ulysses would have chosen. "Fair enough. Self-preservation is a reasonable goal." He handed the bottle to Sam while he pulled his keys out of his pocket and opened the door to the building.

They were halfway up the stairs when Sam said, "You're not . . ."

"What, jealous?" Ulysses pursed his lips. "I think I can provide a better night out than necking in the biology building."

"Angry."

"Annoyed on your behalf, maybe." Ulysses stopped on the fourth-floor landing. "Why would I be angry? I'm almost thirty, and I haven't exactly been a saint. You've met Livia. And she's hardly my only ex."

Sam looked at him, the edges of his mouth turning down. That was the problem with gods. They were beautiful and exciting and just a little territorial. And even if Sam wasn't a god . . .

He remembered, abruptly, Dionysus calling him Ariadne that night up north, and frowned. She was the wife of Dionysus, at least in mythology, and Dionysus was very loyal to her. After her death, he'd retrieved her soul from the underworld and brought her to Olympus to make her a goddess.

Facing Sam, the story seemed suddenly less sweet.

Guilt flitted over Sam's face. "What?"

Ulysses backed him up into the corner behind the door and kissed him. "Nothing. Don't worry about it." He pulled away and took the wine back from Sam. "This is not the moment for revelations. We're going to be late." It was a few minutes after seven by the time they were knocking on Vikram and Sita's door. Ulysses had assumed they'd be annoyed by their guests' tardiness, but instead Vikram looked a little harried. "Please, come in," he said, stepping back to let them by, then yelping as one of the cats made a beeline for the exit. There was a clatter of pots and dishes from the kitchen, just audible over the radio that was blaring in there.

It was a relief, if Ulysses was honest. Even with Sam's assertion that Vikram couldn't have been the Ranganathan Babushka named, he'd been worried. But everything felt very normal. He looked over to see one cat winding its way around Sam's ankle, the other watching him from the back of the sofa. They were just cats. The apartment was a bright, pleasant space full of spindly legged furniture and normal mementos of their life together. Nothing odd to be seen.

He remembered the wine he was carrying and offered it to Vikram.

"Sorry," Vikram said, slightly sheepish. "We forgot how prompt Midwesterners are."

"It's all Sam," Ulysses admitted. "My Russian grandmother barely admits that time exists."

"Didn't she use to teach?" Sam asked.

"The UW was better about allowing professors their eccentricities in those days, I suspect." He started to crack his knuckles, then checked himself. "Or everyone was too frightened of her to say anything."

"Your grandmother was a professor?" Vikram asked, passing him a glass of wine.

"In the Department of Magic Studies, yeah."

"Isn't that where you are as well?" Vikram poured a second glass for Sam and a third for himself. "How did that happen?"

So he told the story of how she'd been recruited, making it funnier than he usually did. Most of it was hearsay at best anyway. He'd been about two, Mariah pregnant with Laz, when they'd suddenly moved from Cambridge to Wisconsin, and he knew the stories he'd been told rather than remembering them himself. The difficulties he'd learned about only later of getting the correct visas for a defected Bolshevik.

By the time he'd finished, they were sitting in the living room, and the cats, Jagger and George Harrison, had taken up residence on Sam.

"Just push them off if you don't like them," Sita advised, drying her hands on a towel as she came out of the kitchen. Sam looked over at her, eyebrows knitting together. For a moment Ulysses thought Sam had seen something surprising, but then his face cleared to a smile and he introduced himself, all charm.

If Sita noticed this slip, she didn't give any sign. She was as delightful as she'd been when he'd first met her. Calm, with a quick, dry wit. Vikram got her a glass of wine, and Ulysses watched the way she smiled when he handed it to her, the way their fingers brushed. He wondered idly how much she'd meant it when she'd said she would leave if Vikram didn't deal with the ghost. It was hard to judge, even now that he'd spent more time with the late Dr. Ranganathan. Sita didn't give him the sense of someone who made idle threats. But she also clearly loved Vikram and didn't seem like she would walk away from him. Not easily.

He thought for a while about that choice, and about Sam and the bond. Then Sam looked over, one eyebrow raised fractionally, and drew him back into the conversation.

THEY WERE STILL THERE two or three hours later, sitting around the table. Sam leaned back, half drunk and relaxed. The cats buzzed around under the table somewhere as Vikram told a funny story about trying to recalibrate some kind of machine in his lab.

Sam found that he liked Vikram and Sita. He liked them immensely, despite the fact that they were suspects. Although in what, for what. . . .

Perhaps that was the wrong way of looking at it. Sam himself had an evil grandfather, so he couldn't claim too much of a moral high ground. Neither of their hosts could have been directly involved.

"How did you meet?" he asked during the next lull in the conversation.

They gave each other one of those shared couple looks, waiting to see which of them would tell the story.

"I finished my PhD in '66 and got a job at the UW," Vikram said. "And she had just finished her residency and moved back here."

"You grew up here?" Sam asked, looking over at Sita.

She nodded. "Middleton, really. My father was retiring and my stepmother's health hasn't been great for quite a while, so I wanted to be near them, and I got a job at Wisconsin General."

"Did you just run into each other around campus?" Sam looked from Sita's face to Vikram's. "The hospital is right around the corner from the bio building, isn't it?"

"Actually, her father introduced us," Vikram said. "At his retirement party."

"I think he invited me just because he wanted me to meet Vikram," Sita said. "Of course, Vik didn't know about the scheme and didn't ask me out for six months—"

"Much to her father's annoyance," Vikram said, laughing. "He came back for a department luncheon and asked me what was wrong with me."

Sita looked over at him, surprised. "He never did!"

Vikram nodded. "That was when I finally went round to your office and asked if you wanted to get dinner."

"You never told me that."

Vikram looked sheepish. "I didn't want you to think I was just there because your father twisted my arm."

Sam glanced over at Ulysses, who was swirling the dregs of his wine this way and that. "How long have you been married?" he asked.

"Nine months," Vikram said. "Since right around New Year's."

Ulysses looked up, apparently doing math in his head. "It's nice that your mother got to attend," he said blandly.

"Oh, no," Sita said, "we eloped to Hawaii. His mum hated me."

"She didn't hate—"

"No, she just didn't want you to marry me."

"Why not?" Sam asked.

Sita threw up her hands. "Superstitions."

"No. No." Vikram made a gesture and nearly knocked over his wine glass. "She lived in the West her entire life. And she was a scientist herself. It never made any sense that she would be superstitious. It was some kind of excuse she made up."

"She said my zodiac was wrong or something. No, what was the word she used—"

"Inauspicious," Vikram said.

"Yes. You see?" Sita shook her head.

Before Sam could stop himself, he leaned toward Ulysses and murmured, "She sounds like your grandmother."

Ulysses snorted. "And then she came back to haunt you for six months," he said to Sita. "That must have been awful."

Sita nodded. "It was very fortunate we found you when we did. You saved our marriage." She raised her wine glass to him.

Ulysses flushed happily and looked down at the tablecloth, and Sam grinned. "What did she do?" he asked. "Professionally, I mean."

"She was a pediatrician," Sita said, gesturing broadly. "She worked at Wisconsin General Hospital back in the '40s! You'd think she would have been excited to have an OB for a daughter-in-law."

Vikram took her hand and kissed her fingertips, murmuring something Sam didn't catch, and she melted, her face turning pink and pleased. A moment later, she looked up and grabbed the wine bottle, pouring herself another glass before holding it up to everyone else. Sam accepted, Ulysses shook his head.

"How did you two meet?" she asked.

Sam took a sip of his wine. "I was part of one of Ulysses's investigations." He watched her as he spoke, because he had suddenly realized what she reminded him of. It was like an image suddenly coming into focus, and he almost shook his head and looked away because he didn't want to consider it.

"What does he investigate?" she asked. Vikram gestured toward the back of their apartment and she nodded, eyes widening. "Oh! Ghosts and things, really?"

"Yeah," Sam said. "Something like that."

Sita leaned forward, squinting at him. "But he fixed the problem?" she asked.

Sam glanced at Ulysses, too drunk to do anything about what was probably an inappropriate level of fondness on his face. "That's what he does. He fixes problems."

Ulysses leaned back in his seat, draping one arm across the back of Sam's chair. It was a casual move, and before he could second-guess himself, Sam leaned back into it. Ulysses was saying, "Sam makes everything sound much more exciting than it actually is, most of the time."

Sam laughed, because it was a joke meant for him alone. "I don't think that's true."

Sita smiled at the two of them. "When was this?"

"Last fall," Ulysses said.

"The end of October," Sam added, frowning to himself. "Our first date was the twenty-fifth."

"That wasn't our first date," Ulysses said. "I bought you dinner a week before that."

"That wasn't a date. That was an apology for the"—he made a hand gesture, realizing belatedly that it was vaguely obscene when he heard Sita giggle—"for that ritual."

"You kissed me!"

Vikram was laughing now too. "When are you getting married?"

Sam said, "No," and felt Ulysses turn to look at him quizzically. "My parents' marriage is kind of a mess, and I just—you know, it's just letting the government decide whose relationships are important."

Ulysses clicked his tongue in a way that felt reminiscent of the way Ekaterina expressed disapproval. "I'm disappointed you don't see fit to make an honest man of me," he said dryly.

Everyone was laughing now, and Sam looked down at his hands on the edge of the tablecloth. "Sorry to shock you by bringing our sinful lifestyle into the building," he said.

Across the table, Vikram was wiping a tear from his eye. "So Sam, are we going to go running tomorrow or what?"

Sam shifted, suddenly feeling awkward. "I don't want to slow you down," he said uncertainly. Ulysses made a scoffing noise, as though his response was wholly phatic.

"It'll be fine. We can go at whatever pace you're comfortable with." Vikram grinned. "Tomorrow, five thirty?"

Sam raised his glass and indicated Vikram's empty one. "Are you going to be up that early?"

"Sure, sure." He made a beseeching face. "Come on, I haven't had anyone to run with since my last running partner moved to Milwaukee."

Sam glanced at the table. The problem was that he liked Vikram now. He was genuinely very nice and funny, and he seemed to want to be friends with them. And as concerned as Sam was about what Vikram was going to say when he finally remembered where he'd met Sam before, this right now was lovely. "Sure," he said, and Vikram whooped. "Five thirty. I'll be waiting."

Chapter 8

D RUNK SAM WAS VERY affectionate. He cooed over the cats when they rubbed against him. He kissed Sita on the cheek and shook Vikram's hand. And once they were out in the hallway, he cornered Ulysses up against the door of their apartment, sliding an arm around his waist from behind and bending down to mouth at Ulysses's neck while he tried desperately to work the lock. It made Ulysses dizzy. Or maybe that was the wine.

They stumbled in and Sam vanished into the darkness while Ulysses did the prosaic things like locking the door and toeing off his boots. When he turned around, Sam had gotten their one floor lamp turned on before sprawling out on the sofa. It was long enough that he could stretch his legs out, and he looked like a Grecian king when he did it, something oddly regal in his bearing.

Dr. Ranganathan didn't appear to be around. Thank goodness.

Ulysses unlaced Sam's shoes and pulled them off, because Sam didn't appear interested in doing it himself, feeling the weight of Sam's eyes on him all the while.

He was abruptly conscious of the way everything felt like a ritual when your boyfriend was a drunken demigod. Maybe the barrier between the sacred and the profane was more permeable in those moments, or maybe the idea that things could be divided at all was an illusion born of the Enlightenment.

What was a ritual, anyway? It was something separate from your normal life. It was something you entered into intentionally, usually via some sort of spoken phrase or action. Except traditionally, Dionysus subverted those things, didn't he? The god from outside, the rituals of the forest instead of the temple . . .

He opened his mouth to ask Sam and then abruptly changed his mind, because with the mood Sam was in, that would be all he talked about for the rest of the night, and they had other things to address. "Did you have any observations?" Ulysses asked instead.

"Mm." He shifted his legs, making room, and then stared at Ulysses in silence until he sat down. Sam reached down and pulled at his shoulder until he let himself be turned, settling his whole back against Sam's chest. He could feel the gentle rise and fall of Sam's breathing. Sam wrapped an arm around his waist.

Ulysses relaxed and waited, expecting more perseverating about Sam's first encounter with Vikram. But what he eventually came up with was: "Sita's like me."

When Ulysses managed to pull back and turn, Sam was looking away, so Ulysses got his profile: the strong nose, high forehead, half-closed eyes. It was not explanatory. "She what?"

"A failed god," Sam said. "Didn't you sense it?"

Ulysses shook his head slowly. "She doesn't look like you and Hugh."

"Hugh and I both had power and lost it," Sam said thoughtfully. "I don't think that happened for Sita. She never quite got there in the first place."

"Why not?"

"Don't ask me why things are the way they are," Sam told him. "That's your job to figure out."

Ulysses didn't know what else to do, so he reached out and took one of Sam's hands. Sam looked down as though surprised by the point of connection. "She's older than you are," Ulysses said.

Sam nodded, biting his lip. "There was an experiment before me, wasn't there? Your grandmother told you about it."

"She said the child died as well as the mother," Ulysses pointed out.

Sam was quiet for a moment. "Maybe she's wrong," he said, and then added, "or death isn't the barrier we think it is."

Ulysses shivered, thinking about what he'd done to—for—Hugh. "Maybe." It was a line he'd lived on for a long time but had always turned away from trying to understand. "Even in the '40s, sometimes medicine managed some things, right?"

"I suppose," Sam said. He trailed a finger along Ulysses's collarbone, and Ulysses waited to see what he was going to do next. The lamplight spilled over both of them, staining Sam's skin golden, painting shadows under his cheekbones and lower lip. "What are you thinking?" he asked abruptly. "When you look at me like that I always wonder."

"Like what?" Ulysses tried to figure out what his own face was doing. "I was just noticing how pretty you are." Sam made a face, and Ulysses laughed. "You can't have missed how people look at you. Everywhere we go, I see them checking you out."

"I'm tall," Sam said dismissively. "People look."

"Is that what you think?" Ulysses reached up and cupped his cheek with one hand. "Sam, you're amazing." Slowly, he drew his thumb across Sam's lower lip, watched his eyes darken.

Sam leaned forward, and then stopped inches from Ulysses's face. "Can I kiss you?"

Ulysses took a breath and said, "Yeah."

Sam kissed him, gently at first, as though something might break if he came on too strong. With the truce between them still new and slightly fragile, maybe he was right. Ulysses slid his hands up Sam's chest and returned the kiss, pressing deeper. Sam tasted like wine, and he felt warm and vital. Sam looked disappointed when Ulysses pulled away, then made a breathless little laughing noise when he only moved enough to straddle Sam's lap, leaning forward to kiss him again, pressing him into the arm of the sofa. Sam shoved a hand into the back pocket of his jeans, a possessive gesture that made Ulysses smile against his mouth. He moved far enough to find the buttons on Sam's shirt. Always so many tiny buttons with him.

Sam kissed his ear, the side of his neck. "I hate to be the one, but is this a great idea?" he murmured.

"Probably questionable at best," Ulysses said, pushing the shirt open and off Sam's shoulders. "But I intend to worry about that later."

"What's the line?" Sam shrugged the shirt the rest of the way off, then sat forward enough to strip off his undershirt. His eyes were half-lidded, mouth red from being kissed, and it only made him more attractive.

"No penetration." Ulysses pressed a kiss to the top of Sam's sternum. "That seems to be where the problems arise."

"All right," Sam said. He plucked at the hem of Ulysses's T-shirt with one hand, then slid his fingers up underneath it. Ulysses swayed forward into his touch, Sam's fingers sliding over his stomach. It was there—he could feel the bond suddenly, humming between them, not quite loud enough to drown out other sensations, but the strange symmetry of touching and being touched was there at the back of his head. He pulled away slightly, just enough to pull his shirt over his head, then reached for Sam's belt.

Sam made a noise as Ulysses's fingers grazed his cock, already half hard. "This . . . Ulysses, we should . . ." His

113

hips pressed forward into Ulysses's touch. "I mean we shouldn't."

He was probably right, damn him. Ulysses was drunk, but not enough to throw all caution to the wind. Not when it came to magic. Not yet. Or at least, not this time. Ulysses sighed. "Yeah," he said at last. Sam reached out and pulled him into a hug, burying his face in the side of Ulysses's neck. Ulysses shut his eyes and tried to breathe. "So much for the delights of living in sin, huh?"

Sam laughed. It didn't make everything better, but it helped.

SAM LAY IN THE dark, listening. It was sometime between four and five, because it always was when he woke up. The room held the soft sound of Ulysses breathing, his steady quiet heartbeat, every now and then a creak of floorboards or a soft rustle as an intermittent breeze flowed through the open window. Outside there were birds just beginning to flutter around, the distant occasional rumble of tires on asphalt. At four in the morning, the world was laid open.

Eventually he slid out of bed. He found his running clothes in the dark and dressed quietly. He hardly needed to; Ulysses tended to sleep—well, like the dead felt like an inappropriate simile, given how much time he spent actually speaking with the dead, but he was a sound sleeper when they weren't being accosted by spirits.

He locked the apartment door behind him at 5:20 and bent down to loop the key onto his shoelaces. It was stuffy in the hall between the apartments; he went to the window at the far end of the space and carefully slid it up. The Baskerville was roughly wedge-shaped, and originally had six or seven apartments on each floor. Over time, the apartments had eaten each other, until on the fourth floor they were down to two, with a hallway that neatly bisected the floor.

At 5:32, Vikram came out of the other apartment in a T-shirt that said *MIT Athletics*. He looked exhausted, hair sticking up in every direction, and when he saw Sam he offered a tight smile. "Good morning."

"Hangover?" Sam murmured.

Vikram eyed him. "So young," he muttered. "You'll find out someday."

Sam wondered if he would. If there was one single, solitary benefit to having been Dionysus, it had to be hangover-related. If there was any justice in the world.

They went down to the street, and Vikram took a few steps, rolling his neck. "Why don't you set the pace?" he told Sam.

They headed up the hill toward the capitol, Sam trying to guess how fast Vikram might find comfortable. For his part, Vikram seemed to be feeling chatty, and with a few questions Sam knew that his parents had been born and raised in London, then moved to New York for medical school. Vikram had been born in Evanston, then they'd moved to Madison when he was two, and to Vancouver a few years later.

"And then Boston for grad school?" Sam asked, and then winced inwardly. But had he really thought that if he didn't mention the city, Vikram would somehow not bring up the circumstances of their first meeting?

But Vikram just nodded. Perhaps he really didn't remember. He said, "I did my undergraduate work at Princeton."

"New Jersey, then Boston, and then back to Madison." Sam shook his head. "Man, you've lived everywhere."

"What about you?" Vikram asked.

"I was born in Madison and grew up here. Then I went to Cambridge for school, grad school in Manhattan. I lived there for a while. And then I moved back here last summer." It had been just over a year, he realized with a little shock. In June he'd come back, and hit it off with Harry and Ellen in time to go to their wedding in July.

"Do you like it?"

"What, Madison?" Sam blinked at the question. "I don't know." Was that still true, though? It had been a while since he'd thought about it. Before the—before, he'd hated it. His driving ambition for most of his youth had been to get out of Wisconsin and put as much space between himself and his family as possible. But now there was Ulysses. And he was . . . reconciled to the place? Attached, even? The city had grown on him, at least. "It's where I live," he said at last.

"I hear you, man," Vikram said. They were passing the Tenney Locks and turned to follow the footpath through the park. "Sita's like that too. I don't think she would have come back except for her father, you know?"

"What about her mother?"

"She died when Sita was born," Vikram said. "Her father raised her. She has a stepmother, but her father only married her about ten years ago."

"That must have been tough," Sam said, because he felt he ought to say something. "My mother also died in childbirth."

Vikram snorted. "Wisconsin General did not have a good reputation there for a few years, as I understand it." They went through a short under-road tunnel lit with one orange sodium light. The horizon in front of them was beginning to glow as sunrise approached, but that was still a while off. "It's quite terrifying, the things that can go wrong. Although I'm sure I have a skewed view, being married to an obstetrician." He sighed. "Do you want to have children?"

Sam cleared his throat. "Not really, no." Then he forced himself to actually think about that. "I mean, I don't know. Kids are great. I just assume that I probably won't, for obvious reasons. Why, are you guys thinking of—"

"Yes," Vikram said. "It was one of the things we were fighting with my mother about, actually."

"Did she want grandchildren?"

Vikram shook his head. "Just the opposite. It was very strange behavior, honestly. No Indian woman has ever been upset to hear she might have grandchildren! I worried that she was becoming a bit demented toward the end of her life, but the behavior continued after she died." They went another block before he added, "*Do* ghosts usually keep the mental state they had when they died?"

"I haven't met that many," Sam hedged. "You should ask Ulysses. He's the specialist."

Vikram nodded. "He doesn't take you around to his hauntings?"

"Sometimes." Sam scuffed a foot on a rough patch of sidewalk and took a couple quick steps. "How long have we been out here?"

Vikram checked his watch under the next streetlight. "About thirty-five minutes." He looked around. "I'm pretty sure we said we were stopping at half an hour. We must have missed a turn somewhere."

"Is that a problem?" Sam asked. "I usually run this way. I guess I wasn't thinking."

"This is fine. I think it's probably a mile and a half back to the apartment from here." Vikram grinned. "From the way you talked, I assumed you weren't much of a runner. I didn't realize you were running five miles a day."

"No, I just—I never quantified it." Sam thought about his meandering routes across the city. "I just go as far as I feel like in the time I have."

Vikram laughed. "That's wild."

"Is it?"

He snorted, or maybe he was just out of breath. "If you're not measuring anything, how do you know what you're doing?"

"Ah ha," Sam said. "There's your mistake right there."

ULYSSES OPENED HIS EYES in the gray-dark bedroom to see a spider walking across the ceiling. It was, improbably, about the size of his fist, and he found himself rooted to the spot, heart racing, trying to decide if this was a dream.

As he watched, the creature reached a spot directly above where he was lying and stopped. He stared at it. It, presumably, stared back, although that seemed like a funny thing to think about a spider. Then it jumped.

It vanished halfway down with a little pop that startled him awake in the sun-warm bedroom. He could hear the shower running. His nerves were being gently sandpapered. It was morning. He had a hangover.

Ulysses had made it as far as the kitchen by the time Sam was out of the shower and dressed. The percolator was still doing its thing, and he had slumped down, half against the wall, on the leeward side of the small kitchen table. Sam came waltzing out in a brown suit, looking like he got paid to look that good, and Ulysses was caught by the urge to rub his face all over Sam's vest so everyone would know who he belonged to. But since that required him to get up, he didn't.

Sam glanced at him, one eyebrow raised. "Rough morning?"

Ulysses shut his eyes. "Remind me to be more temperate in the future where alcohol is concerned."

"Will it help?" He filled a glass of water, then set it and the bottle of aspirin in front of Ulysses with an unnecessarily loud click. "Vikram was in rough shape this morning too."

"Poor guy." Ulysses shook two aspirin into his palm and swallowed them. "I didn't use to get hangovers."

Sam shrugged. "Want something for breakfast?" he asked, and opened the fridge.

"Coffee." The percolator began to boil, and he wrenched himself to his feet.

Sam handed him the milk and shut the fridge. "I'll see if I can stop by the store later. We're out of everything." He sat down at the table; Ulysses could feel Sam's eyes on him as he moved around the space, pouring two mugs of coffee, adding milk and sugar, handing one to Sam.

"How was your run?" Ulysses asked when his brain had kicked in enough to remind him that had happened.

Sam looked unusually grave. "Vikram is a lovely guy, and Sita is the daughter of the first woman. The baby Ekaterina thought died."

"You're sure?"

"He all but told me." He sighed and drank his coffee. "I'm worried this is going to make living here awkward. Too many secrets."

Ulysses hummed and didn't point out that some of the secrets were Sam's own. "We should just tell them. There's not a good reason not to."

"There's lots of reasons not to," Sam contended. "They'll hate us. They'll—"

"Why will they hate us?" Ulysses broke in. "It's the truth. *We* didn't do anything; Julius Sterling did."

"Because we're going to make their lives more difficult," Sam said. "And because people aren't always extremely logical when it comes to what they hate or why." He rubbed his face.

Ulysses tried to imagine, just for a moment, Sam growing up without the combined influences of his father Howard and stepmother Francie. A Sam who hadn't been under a geas that tried to constrain his behavior from the ages of four to twenty-four, who felt much less conflicted about everything that he was. But then again, that would be Dionysus, wouldn't it? And he'd met Dionysus—he was amazing, but he wasn't Sam. Except that he was.

Ulysses was going in circles, and his head still hurt. "Don't worry," he said instead. "After all, you and I got through learning about Dionysus without you hating me." He hesitated, then added, "I even killed you and you didn't mind."

Sam looked up at the ceiling. "I think that suggests there's something wrong with me for being so forgiving."

But when he looked back, he was grinning. "Maybe it's your innate charm."

"That's probably it," Ulysses agreed, and drank his coffee.

Chapter 9

O N TUESDAY, ULYSSES GOT to work later than he
wanted to and had to sit through a couple of
meetings before he was allowed to go back to his office
and hide. He was teaching three classes in the upcoming
semester, plus one section of the big Magic 101 lecture,
and he needed time to prepare syllabi, ensure that the
book lists had been sent to the bookstores, outline a few
lectures, make notes for his TAs, and complete other
sundry academic tasks that hadn't been on his radar
when he'd decided there was something glamorous about
being a professor.

He'd been at it for a little over an hour when he heard
Dr. Lesko making noise in her office next door. Steeling
himself, he got up and knocked on her door.

"Ah, Ulysses," she said when he walked in. "If this is
about the honors section of Magic 101, I decline. Clever
undergraduates are a disaster waiting to happen without
putting all of them together in one place." His former
advisor was tallish, fiftyish, gray haired, with a passion
for men's suits and strange orange eyes she kept hidden

behind blue-tinted glasses in public. Now, though, her face was bare, and he felt like she could see all the way through him.

"It's not that." He sat down. "I need to ask you a few questions."

She looked at him square in the face, and when he couldn't hold her gaze, she shook her head and turned her attention to the papers on her desk. "Your predecessor in that office, Dr. Martin Sullivan, used to come in here and sit silently for hours at a time. Then he'd thank me and leave." She gave him a sharp glance, then looked down again. "If you are inheriting his idiosyncrasies, I shall be very dismayed."

Dr. Lesko's office was physically a mirror image of his: a smallish space with windows along one wall, webbed with tape the facilities people had used over the cracks; bookshelves where there weren't any windows; and a desk in the middle. There was a photo of her and her wife Sara on the desk and one of Sara and three large dogs on the windowsill, alongside a few rose quartz crystals and a gyroscope. He took a deep breath, reminding himself that of his options, she was probably the least embarrassing and most likely to be helpful.

"It's about Sam," he managed.

She nodded, turning a page over. "I presume nothing terrible has happened, since you're sitting there calmly."

"That's not fair."

"Isn't it?" She picked up a pen, scribbled something in a margin, and set it down again. "You do tend to wear your heart on your sleeve." No one actually thought that about him, he was fairly sure. He heard her sigh. "He hasn't broken up with you, has he? It seemed like things were going well. You certainly seemed obnoxiously infatuated with each other when last I saw you together. Rumor has it that you've rented an apartment."

"No," he said. "Rumor" was probably Babushka, and he was going to ignore the fact that they'd apparently been gossiping about him. "We're fine. We haven't—" He decided abruptly that this was a conversational dead end. "I'm interested in any information or resources you might have about magical bonds."

She raised an eyebrow. "I wondered when we'd have this conversation."

Ulysses cracked the first two knuckles on his right hand, thumb and index finger, then stopped, looking at his hand. He rubbed the calluses on his palm. "Sometimes I can feel his emotional states," he told her. "He can find me, in a geographic sense." He licked his lips, suddenly a catalog of nervous tells.

"And?" She folded her hands and looked at him. "You wish to know?"

"Is that what you were trying to tell me about, back in April?"

She leaned back in her chair. "That's right," she said dryly. "What did I say? Is this wise? And you told me—what was it again?"

"That it was a fait accompli."

125

Dr. Lesko nodded, lips pressed together. "In other words, you were given a warning, which you chose to ignore, presumably because you were horny."

Ulysses briefly wondered if he could just die where he sat in order to escape from this. "That's not—I wouldn't typify what happened like that."

"Wouldn't you?"

They stared at each other.

Finally, Ulysses took a deep breath. "I've seen some of the literature on romantic bonds. The research is not great, but it always seems to come to something like: after many years together, magical talents can rub off on people who are very close to each other. The effect seems to be minor. A fortune teller's partner might develop a facility with reading cards or tea leaves, but probably won't ever have prophetic dreams." He looked down at his hands again, cracked the rest of his knuckles in order. "It's difficult to prove, because so much of it seems to be the sort of thing that people might just learn from years of proximity."

"And that isn't what's happening to you," Lesko filled in when his silence went on too long. "You're able to feel Sam's emotional states, you said."

"Emotions and physical sensations in some situations. And he can feel mine."

She nodded. "You find this distressing." She eyed him. "Why is that?"

Because it was overwhelming? Because he liked the boundaries of his own body? Because he didn't want to lose himself? "What if it doesn't subside?"

"*What if* indeed." Dr. Lesko steepled her fingers. "There are two components to consider, I think. First, Sam is a god—"

"He's not," Ulysses said. "He doesn't have access to—"

She shook her head. "I'm aware that he's not Dionysus anymore. However, you yourself referred to him as *hypostatically Dionysus* in your dissertation, did you not?"

"In a sense, that's true. But in practical terms—"

She ignored him. "I suppose there is a question we could ask about whether a god without their powers is still a god. However, the problem you are facing is not a philosophical one."

"As I said. In practical terms, he hasn't got any power *or* knowledge of magic."

She shrugged. "Obviously there's something about him. Maybe the universe still sees him as god-shaped. Maybe Dionysus set something in motion." She pinched the bridge of her nose. "Gods are difficult to study. We know almost nothing about them, and—well. You're possibly the leading expert, as frightening as that statement is to make." Dr. Lesko picked up a pen and tapped it on her blotter. "You're not willing to leave Sam? Or stop—"

Ulysses looked out the window. They were on the twelfth floor. Unfortunately, it didn't open, so flinging himself out would be tricky. "No," he said at last.

"Then you're going to have to learn about mental shielding." She got up and rummaged through one of the shelves until she located a small book with a green cover. "Take a look at this. It's a good starting place."

Ulysses took it, bemused. "What about the rest of it, Sam being—" He broke off, not sure how to say it. "I mean, he was Dionysus, but he's still *Sam*," he finished in a horribly soft tone.

"Mm. He's lovely. But I'm afraid that being the cherished of the gods rarely ends well for anyone." She shrugged, putting a hand on his shoulder and guiding him to the door. "However, you seem opposed to the alternatives. So either you'll find your way through . . . or you won't." Lesko smiled in a way that felt both sympathetic and detached, and pushed him gently back into the hallway.

Laz was comfortably ensconced in Ulysses's chair when he got back, thumbing over that string of wooden love beads like a rosary. He was dressed in jeans and a plain T-shirt and that damn military jacket again. Ulysses raised an eyebrow; Laz was clearly trying to look relaxed and nonchalant, but his shoulders were tense.

"Hey!" Laz leaned back in the chair, pressing his palms together. "There you are. Nice office. What's with the tape?" He gestured at the windows.

"The bombing," Ulysses said.

Laz reached out toward the broken window, then stopped himself at the last moment. "What, *here?*"

"It broke windows all over this end of campus. Think we got off pretty lightly by comparison. Probably someone's old spell."

"Oh." Laz looked at the taped-over cracks again, then around the office like he was seeing it for the first time.

"Not that I don't appreciate the visit," Ulysses began, "but could I—" He tried to edge around the desk.

"What's this?" Laz asked, sitting up suddenly and grabbing for the photo of Ulysses and Sam that sat on the desk. "When were you at Stonehenge?"

"June," Ulysses said. "It was the weekend I got the Dee. Dr. Lesko dragged us out to see it." Her wife had taken the photo when they weren't paying attention. Ulysses had been supremely hungover and Sam exhausted, draped over Ulysses's shoulder; they'd bickered over the map while Stonehenge sat in the middle of a field behind them. Ulysses couldn't look at the picture without remembering how awful he'd felt, and how happy.

"You look happy." Laz let Ulysses take the frame from his hand. "I went out to Truax this morning."

"What?"

"The Air National Guard base? At the airport?" Laz's eyes searched his face. "The 115th?"

"Sure." Ulysses shifted. "Why?"

"They're still finishing my separation paperwork." He scratched his face. "If you want to know why we haven't won the war yet, it's because someone didn't finish their paperwork on time." He chuckled to himself. "Anyway, I went and talked to some guys I know out there about what happened on Saturday."

Ulysses leaned against the edge of the desk. "Oh?"

"No one had any idea what was going on." He moved restlessly, turning in the chair to look out the window. "I'm pretty sure it wasn't the Air Force orchestrating that. Which means whatever happened, it's not because of me."

Ulysses sighed. "No one thought it was because of you, Laz," he said gently.

Laz didn't say anything, just looked at him. Finally, he seemed to accept this, and sat back again. "Can you give me a ride out to East Wash?"

"Sure. What's out there?"

"A car dealership." He crossed his legs, tapping one of his boots against the wall behind the desk. "I heard they had some used GTOs. I wanna test drive one."

"What are you looking for?"

"A '68 or a '69, maybe." He went on, talking about horsepower and compression and torque, all of which felt like a language that Ulysses had once spoken but was no longer fluent in. But it was nice to see Laz engaged and enthusiastic, even if it looked like it'd been a week and a half since he'd last bothered to shave and he had dark rings under his eyes.

There was a polite tap on the door, which swung open before he could respond. Dr. Lesko was there, holding another book.

"Ah, Lazarus," she said, and he stood up like a general had just walked in. "I heard from your grandmother that you were due back, but at the time she wasn't sure when."

"The Air Force does like to keep people guessing, ma'am," Laz said.

"Think how awful things would be if the military was at all efficient," she said, smiling. "Thank you for coming back in one piece, by the way."

Laz shrugged, looking down at his feet. "I got lucky," he said. Ulysses rather doubted that.

"Be that as it may," Lesko said. She shot Ulysses a covert glance that he did not miss, then returning to Laz, she added, "Are you busy right now?"

Laz looked back up. "Not especially. I was just waiting for U to finish his work."

Lesko nodded. "Could you take a look at the toaster oven in the break room? It's not heating correctly."

Laz rubbed the back of his neck. "I'm happy to, but I don't have any tools on me."

"I'm sure we can find some," Dr. Lesko said cheerfully. "Why don't you go take a look and see what you think you need."

Laz glanced over at Ulysses.

"I'm going to be an hour or two," Ulysses told him. "You might as well go."

"Cool," Laz said. "Race ya."

When he'd shuffled out, Lesko handed the book to Ulysses. "Thought you might find this interesting as well." It was a slim volume entitled *How to Improve Your Mental Shielding*.

"Not much to it, is there?" he said, flipping through. It was typewritten and mimeographed; he could feel himself getting a headache from reading it already.

Dr. Lesko shrugged. "If it solves your problem, then . . ."

"Did you get this at a free festival somewhere?" he demanded. "Was the author selling it himself out of a battered suitcase?"

"Don't knock it until you've tried it is all I'm saying." She turned away and shut the door behind her.

T HE LIBRARY WAS TRYING to get Sam's attention.

It was an odd sensation. He was paging through a bible from about 1615, preparing to catalog it, when something tugged at his awareness. It reminded him of the feeling of suddenly looking up from a book to realize that his neighbor was practicing the drums. Once he was conscious of it, he didn't know how he'd ever missed it.

"All right," he said aloud. "What is it you want?"

He felt a pressure drawing him toward the door of his office. Stepping out into the hallway, he looked across the reading room to the large glass windows and, through them, the fourth-floor hallway. A few grad students were walking toward the elevators, and someone from whatever they were calling the technology department pushed a cart with slide projectors stacked up on it. He could hear the wheel squeaking, shrill but distant.

The elevator doors slid open and two people in dark suits stepped out.

Sam had a few seconds to review his options. Panic, run, stay and find out whether they meant to arrest him on some charge or just drag him out without a word.

Edith's office was behind him, next door to his own, and the entrance to the stacks was at the end of the hall. To his right was a third office used primarily for interns and filing cabinets. So he went left, straight through the door into the stacks.

Something plucked at his sleeve and he followed it deeper into the shelves. Nothing back here had ever been designed for student access, so the shelves were scavenged and mismatched, the filing system idiosyncratic at best, with some things filed by Library of Congress number, some with an older Cutter number system, others kept with the materials they were donated with. As he wove his way through, the sense that he was being led grew stronger, almost dizzyingly so. And then there in front of him was a heavy steel door.

Had it been there before? Stupid question, of course it had. He vaguely remembered the red glow of the exit sign. Stairwells did not simply appear. But how had he never bothered to see where it went?

He heard a distant sound, probably at the door to the stacks. He was going to have to ask Edith about all of this, but some other time.

The staircase did not, thankfully, have an alarm on it. It wound around and let him out on the State Street side of the building, into a beautiful early fall day. The sun was shining, students were wandering along with their friends, librarians were coming back from lunch somewhere nearby. As he stood there, catching his breath, a couple walked past hand in hand; he abruptly wished Ulysses were there to help him.

Sam wasn't sure it was a great habit to reach out through the bond to see if he could find him. Not that it would have done him much good to know Ulysses's exact location. He wasn't around. Sam was going to have to be his own protector for the time being.

He spotted a black Plymouth parked near the curb on Lake Street. Trying to look nonchalant, he wandered over and scribbled the license plate number on a scrap of paper. Then he went around the building to the north side and found a spot from which he could peer around the corner.

He leaned against the side of the library and tried to pretend he was having a cigarette. He remembered, somewhat, a time when the building itself would have whispered to him, reassurances and information. It didn't have a lot of cither in human terms; it didn't understand the world in the way humans did, so what it offered was rarely useful. It found pigeons and seagulls fascinating. There was a leak in a bathroom on the third floor. A chipmunk in the ventilation. A pneumatic tube blockage. Grad students necking in the cages on the fifth floor. But he recalled finding comfort in its chatter, during the time when he had been, increasingly, Dionysus, and able to hear it all so much more clearly.

It was odd, now that he thought of it. What had spurred the bond to change? Ulysses hadn't seemed concerned by the timing, just by the fact that it was happening. But wasn't the timing a little bit suspect? It wasn't as though they'd hit some special length of time as a couple. Ulysses had been staying at Sam's place since April, so signing a lease together didn't seem like the same sort of milestone. Moreover, if the bond was becoming more erratic because of Sam somehow, where was the power coming from? Sam didn't have any power. Ulysses had proven that himself.

Hard-soled shoes crunched on cement; he peeked around the corner to see the besuited figures approaching the car. They appeared to be having an argument as they got in; he heard a certain tone without being able to make out the words. Neither of them spotted Sam watching as they drove away.

He went back around to the front door and up to his office. Edith was on her way out for a meeting and looked only dimly surprised to see him.

"You missed some visitors," she said, in a tone that indicated exactly what she thought of them.

"Lucky me."

"Perhaps." She fished a business card out of her pocket and passed it to him. "Timely little disappearing act you pulled."

He shrugged, looking at the card. Division of Criminal Investigation. He looked up at her. "Do you believe they're for real? I've never heard of this bureau."

"No idea." She glanced at her watch. "I've got to run, sorry."

He found the phone book in her office and carried it into his. It took a few false attempts and unsympathetic secretaries before he found who he was looking for.

"Wisconsin State Motor Vehicle Pool, this is Sharon."

"Sharon, hi," he said. "I just have a quick question for you. There's a car out here on Langdon, parked in a loading zone, thought it might be a government vehicle based on the license plates, in which case I don't want to have it towed, you know?"

"Of course. What's the license plate?"

He read it back to her. "It's a big black Plymouth Satellite."

"Oh, yeah," she said sympathetically. "Those are all Division of Criminal Investigation cars. Better leave it alone."

"I'll tell the boss," Sam said. "Thanks."

When they'd hung up, he sat in his office for a while in silence. So there was a legitimate government agency behind all of this, even if he didn't know why they'd been chasing him so late at night. Very little from that night made sense. He sighed.

The positive side was that he now had a fact. He didn't know exactly what he was going to do with it, but he had it. And that was something.

Chapter 10

I T WAS LATE AFTERNOON by the time they got to the dealership. Ulysses trailed along behind Laz as he went from car to car, peering through windows, occasionally pointing out a fact about this or that one's engine.

Finally Laz stopped and turned around to face him. "What's going on? You seem . . ."

Ulysses frowned. "What?"

Laz shrugged. "Kinda checked out, I guess." There was a long pause. "You used to love this stuff."

"I just have a lot on my mind." He watched Laz open the driver's side door of a late model red Pontiac GTO convertible. Ulysses obediently lifted the hood and propped it open when he pulled the hood release. "Sorry, tell me about the cylinders again," he said when Laz got out again.

"Is something going on?" Laz hesitated. "Beyond the—you know."

"A few things." He smiled, but he could tell it wasn't reaching his eyes. "Are you going to test drive this one?"

Laz nodded. "If the salesman ever gets up the guts to come over here."

"You could've shaved first."

Laz rolled his eyes. "Have you ever thought about trading the bike in for a car?"

"Not really. I like motorcycles." He bent forward to look at the coolant tank. "Does that look like a leak that was cleaned up?"

Laz also bent over to examine it. "What are you going to do if one of you breaks a leg or something?"

"What was I *ever* going to do, with or without Sam?" He straightened up, pulled off his sunglasses to rub the bridge of his nose. "Call an ambulance, call Celeste and Obe. . . . Back in April, Sam's friends Ellen and Harry drove me to the hospital."

Laz scowled. "What the hell happened in April? You didn't tell me about that."

"It's a whole story." Ulysses smiled, but he could feel his fatigue permeating the expression. "Don't worry about it."

A salesman carrying a clipboard appeared. He was in his mid-forties, hair parted decisively and shellacked to his head so there was no chance of it moving, wearing a neat but not especially attractive suit. "Gentlemen, welcome. Can I help you?"

Laz smiled. "I hope so." Ulysses watched as he and the salesman started with a brief discussion of the V8 engine, what Laz was looking for in general, this car specifically, test driving it, and on and on. Laz was a bit awkward, but he clearly knew what he was talking about, and his enthusiasm was infectious.

Suddenly, there was a loud noise from the far side of the lot—a car backfiring or something, Ulysses never found out exactly what—and Laz jumped. It was a small, fluid gesture that ended with him crouched wild-eyed against the door panel of the car, one hand pressed against his chest.

The salesman sputtered something about coming back with the keys and fled. Ulysses crouched down next to him.

"This is new."

Laz squeezed his eyes shut and nodded.

Ulysses wasn't sure what to do, but he went with his instinct to reach out and offer Laz a hand. Unexpectedly, Laz took it. His palms were clammy and calloused and he gripped Ulysses tightly, the sinewy muscles in his forearm bunching and relaxing visibly. Ulysses wasn't sure why he was surprised. Maybe they hadn't held hands since they were children and Ulysses was reacting badly to seeing a ghost. Laz was a grown man now. Older than Sam.

After a while, Laz opened his eyes and looked over at Ulysses ruefully.

"Is this how it is?" Ulysses asked.

Laz took a shaky breath. "Sometimes." He let Ulysses pull him to his feet. "Sometimes it's worse." He patted his pockets and found a pack of cigarettes, shoved one in his mouth and lit it with trembling fingers.

Ulysses put his hands in the pockets of his jeans, feeling awkward. "Have you seen anyone about this?"

"No one helpful." Laz exhaled a stream of smoke and leaned back against the car, tense but clearly aiming for insouciance.

"What did they say?"

"Time heals all wounds. Some bullshit like that. It's all in my head." Laz shrugged. "It's not that bad, compared to some I've—"

The salesman returned with the keys then, and Laz stopped talking. The salesman stared at Laz for a moment, shifting from foot to foot. "You just get back?" he asked at last.

Laz opened his mouth to respond, then closed it again and wound up inclining his head slightly.

"Thought so." He looked down at the shiny toes of his shoes. He was an odd age, about fifteen years older than Ulysses—too old for the draft, too young to have served in World War II. Possibly Korea? But he didn't have the bearing of someone who had been in the military. It being Madison, he was as likely as not to be a pacifist, and Ulysses found himself bracing, just a little, for what he was about to say. What he eventually came out with was, "My son's going to be drafted." It wasn't quite a plea for help, or a confession. Ulysses didn't know what it was.

A spasm passed across Laz's face, and then he said, "I'm sorry. Best of luck to him."

The salesman smiled unhappily and Laz smiled unhappily back. "Thank you," the man said, passing the keys over to Laz.

Ulysses dragged himself up the stairs to the apartment sometime after eight o'clock. When he opened the door, he saw Sam sitting on the sofa in the living room cradling his guitar, and Ellen sitting on the floor bent over a large and ill-organized stack of papers on the coffee table. Behind them, the eastern sky was mostly dark. He could see their reflections in the windows they had yet to find curtains for.

"You should give the altos the fourth of the chord," Sam was saying. "Then you can resolve upward on the next phrase."

"The fourth," Ellen scoffed, not looking up from whatever she was scribbling. "Where did you learn music theory?"

"Okay, give them the seventh, then."

Ellen frowned. "Play the chord with the B flat. Let's hear it."

Sam played a chord, and she sighed. "Fine, we'll do the seventh." Then she glanced up at Ulysses. "You looked unduly perplexed."

Where *had* Sam learned music theory? Ulysses was only vaguely aware that Sam played guitar, because although back at the old place he could occasionally be heard noodling around out on the fire escape or in the next room, he rarely played in front of Ulysses. But here he was, arguing about chord progression?

"Do I?" He gripped the strap of his satchel with one hand. "What are you guys up to?"

"A musical setting for three scenes in *The Tempest*," Ellen said. "We have to arrange it for choir before we can hold auditions."

It was all the reading that was the problem. Sam mostly read fiction, but occasionally he read nonfiction, and it gave him *ideas*. He'd started learning Russian from a book, as though Russian were something you picked up rather than had foisted on you.

Meanwhile, Ulysses was still plugging away, doing the one thing he did well. It wasn't quite fair, somehow.

He finally met Sam's eyes and saw the corner of his mouth quirk up ruefully. "Hey," Sam said. "There's food in the kitchen. I went grocery shopping after work. Also, Ellen brought takeout from the new Chinese place."

"Thank you," he said. Ellen shrugged, looking back at her paper, where black notes were dancing across staff lines in an ever-more-complex pattern.

Sam said, "You're welcome to stay and listen if you want. It's not likely to sound like much right now, though."

Ulysses hesitated a moment, because that would have been delightful. He'd become quite fond of Ellen and Harry's productions, and it was tempting to find out how the sausage got made. But he had work to do, so eventually he made some excuse and went into the office.

W HEN ELLEN HAD GONE, Sam put his guitar back in its case and went into the office to put it away. Ulysses was asleep on the chaise, a book open across his chest, reading glasses still resting on his nose. Sam paused, watching him doze. The rings under his eyes that had vanished in the wake of his dissertation defense were starting to reappear, and Sam pressed his lips together unhappily.

Sam grabbed a scrap of paper off the desk to act as a bookmark and rescued the book, setting it on the desk at about the same moment Ulysses made a noise and opened his eyes.

"Sam?"

Ulysses reached out and caught his hand, tugging him down, although the chaise wasn't a large piece of furniture. But Ulysses sat up slightly to make room, and Sam perched on the edge of the seat, facing him.

"Didn't mean to fall asleep," Ulysses managed. "What time is it?"

"Tenish." Sam reached out and gently lifted Ulysses's glasses off his face. "You can't have been asleep for that long."

There was something about the way Ulysses's face looked once his glasses were gone, vulnerable and open for just a moment. Sam rubbed a finger against the stubble on Ulysses's jaw, watching his eyes drift shut at the sensation, and then leaned forward and kissed him.

It was a normal kiss, gentle, lovely, slow, but Sam realized halfway through that he was feeling the bond again, a quiet companion there with them. Had he always felt it and just not put a name to it? He tensed; when he pulled back, Ulysses leaned forward and pressed his face into Sam's neck, one arm around his waist, breathing in a shuddery, unhappy way. Sam fought the impulse to slide into Ulysses's emotions and focused on the comforting feeling of his body, solid and undemanding, pressed against his own.

"Are you hungry?" Sam asked finally, speaking more or less into the back of Ulysses's head. "You didn't eat yet, did you?"

"No." He pulled back and yawned. "Had a beer with Laz. That's all."

"What was the occasion?"

"He bought a car." Ulysses stretched his back and then followed Sam into the kitchen. "There's something going on with him."

Sam thought that much was obvious just from looking at the guy, but he didn't say so. Instead he raised his eyebrows in what he hoped was an expression of mild surprise. "What is it?"

"I don't know." Ulysses slid into one of the kitchen chairs and went through the leftovers on the table, finally coming up with a container of slightly congealed chow mein and a fork. "He started to talk and then changed his mind. Couldn't get it out of him after that." He sniffed the noodles and took a bite.

Sam wrinkled his nose. "I could make eggs or something if you want."

"That would be nice." Ulysses gave the chow mein a long look and put it down. "Tell me about your day. You're working on a new show."

Sam told him about it while he beat eggs in a bowl and melted butter in a frying pan. Then he told Ulysses about the DCI officers.

Ulysses was quiet for a while after that, until Sam turned a slightly wonky omelette au fromage out onto a plate and set it in front of him.

"What do you think?" Sam asked, feeling like his voice was a little too quiet. But Ulysses was looking down at the plate, flexing his right hand like he'd been cracking his knuckles when Sam wasn't paying attention.

Finally he sat back. "Honestly?"

Sam crossed his arms, leaning against the sink. "When have I ever not wanted honesty?"

Ulysses shrugged. "I think you should call them. Set up a meeting."

"Really?"

The other man glanced at the empty chair across from him, then cocked his head and stared silently at Sam until he took the hint and sat. "They seem very set on meeting with you one way or another. If you make the call, you get to control that meeting." He took a bite of the omelet. After a moment, he added, "I could come with, if you'd like."

"I'd like to keep you as far away from them as possible," Sam said darkly. "Anyway, I need you available to post bail if they arrest me."

Ulysses rubbed his chin. "Why would they arrest you?"

Sam blinked. "Do they need a reason?"

"Typically, yes."

Sam ran his hands through his hair. "In my experience, if cops want to hassle you, they will. It doesn't matter why; they can always make things up. Or find a reason."

Ulysses gave him a long look, like he was trying to formulate a question he wasn't sure he wanted to ask. Sam decided to put him out of his misery. "I used to be the bail guy among my group of friends back in Manhattan. Because I wear suits and I look respectable." He shrugged. "Lot of protests in 1968, you know?"

Ulysses ran his eyes over Sam, as if silently appraising how respectable he looked in his shirtsleeves and vest, and took another bite of the omelet. "This is delicious, thank you."

"You're welcome." Sam folded his hands together and took a deep breath. "Ulysses—"

Ulysses looked up and evidently saw something in Sam's face that made him set down his fork. "Hmm?"

There was a loud knock on the door.

Chapter 11

THEY BOTH STOOD AT the same time, and Sam made an impatient motion. "Finish your dinner. I'll deal with it." He pushed his chair back in. "It's probably Vikram asking about running tomorrow."

But when he opened the door, he discovered Laz.

The man looked rough. Or maybe that was just his default state. Whatever it was, the yellow lighting in the hallway made the shadows under his eyes stand out starkly purple against his pale skin. His stubble gave the lower part of his face an unhealthy gray cast.

"What's up?" Sam asked when he realized he'd been standing in surprised silence for too long.

"I'm here to help," Laz announced in Russian.

The boxes were pretty much unpacked, and—he looked at Laz again. "Help with what?"

"Just wait." It took Sam a moment to realize he'd switched to English, and then he switched back. "Where is my brother?" He shouldered his way past Sam as he said it and flung open the door to the hall closet.

"He's in the kitchen," Sam said, although it took him a moment to come up with the word *kuchne*. Laz, head still inside the closet as he searched for something, didn't appear to notice the effort, or care.

Ulysses came through into the living room. He was still wearing the slightly befuddled expression that had been on his face since he'd awakened, as though not entirely convinced this wasn't a dream. Sam gave him an imploring look.

Laz straightened up and shut the closet door. "Ulysses!" he shouted, like a warrior greeting a brother-at-arms, and tossed him an object.

Ulysses caught it automatically. It took both of them a moment to register that it was a sheathed short sword.

Sam stared at it, mystified. When he glanced back at Laz, he was hefting a hand ax he'd found in there. "What on—"

There was a loud, high-pitched scream from across the hall.

Ulysses said, "Was that—"

Laz had already sprung out into the hall. Ulysses followed, barefoot, with Sam right behind. There was another scream, and then Laz kicked in the door with startling efficiency.

Laz and Ulysses were through the door as soon as it swung open. Sita and Vikram were cowering at one edge of the living room, trying to get away from a handful of tentacles, big ugly things with suckers, that were emerging from a round hole in the center of the shag

149

rug in the living room. Something was making a low, rumbling noise that made Sam feel rushed and panicky.

Laz put himself between Vikram and Sita and the tentacles, while Ulysses turned toward the threat. But Sam hesitated, looking at the scene. The tentacles were really artful, long tapering things with big suckers, pale on the underbelly and dark purplish-red on top. Like props in a movie.

The air had that strange, electric feel of a lot of magic, but it wasn't divine. Dionysus's magic, and Hugh's—Arawn's—too, had a deep, earthy smell to it, like soil. This was more sulfurous, like a just-extinguished match, and it made Sam's fingertips tingle. He opened his mouth to tell Ulysses, but—

Ulysses must have moved wrong, too close or too fast, because suddenly one of the tentacles lashed out whip fast and wrapped itself around his wrist, yanking hard on his arm. He half shouted. Laz leaped forward, brought up short when one of the tentacles took a swipe at him.

Sam wrapped his free arm around Ulysses's chest and yanked him backward, but the tentacle stretched and held. Ulysses made a pained noise.

Across the room, Laz shouted, "The sword!" Sam grabbed it out of Ulysses's off hand, and brought it around in an arc, swishing through the tentacle. He and Ulysses sprawled backward in an ungainly tangle as Ulysses came free. Somehow, luckily, he landed partly on top of Sam rather than on the sword blade.

Ulysses rolled to the side and sat up, looking down at the piece of tentacle still clinging to his arm with a dazed expression. Sam reached out with shaking hands to pry it away. He'd expected it to be rubbery, somehow; instead, it was almost too smooth, slightly cool to the touch, firm like a muscle. Beneath it were quarter-sized welts, red and angry, one with blood welling up in the center. But that was wrong, wasn't it? Octopi didn't have stingers. So what—

"Ulysses," Sam said.

"I'm okay," he replied, not taking his eyes off his arm.

"That's great." Something moved out of the corner of Sam's eye, and he looked up. In a calm voice he didn't quite recognize as his own, he said, "We have another problem."

Ulysses looked at Sam's face, and then turned in time to see the first of the spiders crawl out of the portal.

They were very large, for spiders—bodies about the size of chicken eggs, so that Sam could clearly see their milky white eyes even from a distance. They moved slowly, erratically, and their backs were an iridescent black. There was something intriguing about them, even as the more rational part of his brain shouted in revulsion and shock. It was as though he'd had a nightmare and it came to life.

Some of the spiders were moving toward Laz, drawing shouts from Vikram and Sita. Others seemed drawn to Sam and Ulysses. Most of them, actually. Sam scrambled to his feet and hauled hard on Ulysses's arm.

Not that Ulysses was paying attention. "Do you think they're drawn to magic?" he asked, staring at the creatures.

"What does that mean?"

"More of them are coming toward us. And look at how they're—" Ulysses licked his lips. "It's hard to explain how it feels, but I think they're looking for magic users."

Sam tried to understand that. "They're—*what*?" His nerves were already so frazzled that if the spiders were adding to the general chaos, he couldn't tell. But Ulysses seemed very firm on that point as he struggled to his feet. Sam gripped his shoulders, steadying him.

Ulysses locked eyes with Laz. "Get them out of here," he said, gesturing at Vikram and Sita. Laz complied, swinging his ax at any spiders that came near as the three of them made their way to the door.

"How do we get rid of them?" Sam asked.

"We need to close the portal." He patted his pockets. "Do you have a pencil?"

Sam did. Ulysses turned his back on the entire scene, focusing on the sigil he was drawing on the wall, so Sam put himself between Ulysses and the advancing spiders. He could feel *something* as got close, although was that what Ulysses was talking about? One outrunner leaped—Jesus Christ, they could *jump*—and Sam smacked it away with the sword in a move that was more tennis backhand than sword stroke. The rest paused for a moment, like they were thinking. "Any time now," Sam shouted over one shoulder.

The noise was almost a roar now, rushing wind, an approaching train, the angry surf, and it was getting hard to hear over it, harder to think. "Can you make it to the kitchen?" Ulysses shouted back. "Get a container of salt."

Sam ran. A few long strides took him to the kitchen, and then he was panicking, casting about almost blindly until he lit on a familiar navy blue cylindrical container.

The run back felt like sprinting into a headwind. The spiders had reached Ulysses's legs and were trying to creep up. He kicked one away, smacked another hard with his hand and sent it flying, and then Sam was there.

Ulysses grabbed the container. Keeping hold of Sam with one hand, he wrenched the spout open and flung it end over end into the portal like a grenade.

A TERRIBLE, NOISELESS EXPLOSION knocked the two of them to the floor. Ulysses tried to fling himself in front of Sam to protect him, but they wound up more or less huddled together against the coffee table.

The silence was almost as deafening as the noise had been. Ulysses felt like he'd been spat up on a beach, the ocean still thundering through his veins, even as the world remained perfectly motionless. He sat up, ears ringing, and saw that the room was exactly as it had been when they were over for dinner, except for his scribbling on the wall. The tentacles were gone. The spiders were gone.

Beside him, Sam groaned and sat up. "What was that?"

Ulysses shook his head. "No idea."

"Another type of demon?"

"Not coming through *that* portal." He rubbed his face with both hands, making sure nothing else was bleeding. "It almost felt like something someone invented as part of a test."

"For us? They couldn't have known we would be nearby."

"Really?" He raised an eyebrow. "At ten o'clock at night? Across the hall from us?"

Sam gathered his legs to his chest. "We go out."

"Not on a Tuesday night," Ulysses said with some asperity.

Sam fell silent for a moment. "And the thing with the salt?" he asked eventually.

"Salt has been important throughout human history," Ulysses said, vaguely aware that it sounded like a lecture and not caring. "All those expressions. Someone being worth his salt, Roman soldiers being paid in salt—"

"That was a myth," Sam wailed. He grabbed Ulysses by the shoulders, and that slight pressure sent him sliding to the ground again. He had all the inner strength of a cooked noodle left. "They didn't get paid, they were volunteers. Pliny— Stop laughing."

He couldn't. "Anyway, the idea of using salt to repel evil is also very old, and *not* a myth. And almost everyone has salt."

Sam, braced above him, looked at him like he was crazy. Maybe he was. His arm still hurt—he'd almost lost track of that—and he couldn't stop laughing. Finally Sam leaned forward and pressed his lips to the corner of Ulysses's mouth, just the barest hint of a kiss before he was up and tugging Ulysses back to his feet. Ulysses staggered into him, knocking him sideways into the wall with the sigils on it. Laz was just coming back through the front door of the apartment, Vikram right behind him.

"All clear?" Laz asked, but he was already lowering the ax.

"Yeah," Sam told him, steadying Ulysses. "It's fine."

Ulysses was a familiar combination of exhausted and relieved and elated. He wanted to fall over, to grab Sam and drag him off somewhere more private, and also to make sure nothing like that ever happened again. He looked over at Vikram, who had Sita's hand clutched in both of his, feeling fiercely protective of them.

"Is Ulysses okay?" Sita asked, shaking free and striding into the room. "He doesn't look so good."

"He'll be fine," Sam said. "He just needs a little time. And to eat something."

"He's bleeding!"

Ulysses looked at her, then down at his arm. The circular welts were swollen, bright red against his pale

155

skin, and now each had a spot of blood in the center. Some were worse. "Oh." He snagged Sam's handkerchief out of his pocket and blotted at them ineffectually, hissing as they started to sting.

Sita sighed. "Vik, darling, go grab a roti from the kitchen. Sam, help me get him on the sofa before he falls over so I can bandage his arm."

It was a while before he could really collect his thoughts. It couldn't have been that long, because when he came back into the moment, Sita was still bandaging his arm, and she seemed pretty efficient.

"Your color looks better," she said, glancing up at him. "Feel like talking now?"

"Yeah." He flexed his hands. "Tell me, why were they here?"

Sita looked up at him, stilling. "I don't know. I was hoping you'd have the answer to that, since you seem to be the expert."

He sat up. "It was almost like the intent was to frighten you."

"Well, mission accomplished." She fastened the gauze with a little metal clip. "You should be able to take that off tomorrow. If you have continuing problems, you should go see a doctor."

Ulysses took his arm back and looked around. Sam and Laz were standing next to each other, Sam trying to explain something to Vikram, Laz scowling. Everything else was in order, as far as he could sense.

"Thanks," he said. He got to his feet slowly; he was doing better at standing up now. Sam followed his motion with worried eyes.

"How do we keep them from coming back?" Sita asked. "Can we?"

Ulysses looked at the sigils he'd drawn already. "They shouldn't be able to reopen the portal tonight." He fished the pencil out of his pocket and added one more, a little apotropaic marking for protection of a home. "Tomorrow, I'll get Celeste and Obe to help set up some proper wards for you."

Vikram reached out to shake his hand, then clapped him on the shoulder. "Thank you. I don't know what we would have done without you."

Ulysses shifted uncomfortably. "We'll talk again soon."

The three of them went back across the hall. Laz set his ax down absently next to his boots and sank down on the sofa. "I can't believe you," he muttered, curling forward, head in his hands, elbows on his knees.

"What did I do?"

Laz groaned. "You trust *him* to watch your six instead of me?"

"I trust *you* to get the civilians to safety," Ulysses snapped, not trusting himself to glance over at his boyfriend. "If you can't play nice, get out of here. I don't have the energy for petty bickering tonight."

"Fine," Laz said. For a moment, Ulysses wondered if he was going to walk out, but all he did was sigh and flop sideways, the fight abruptly going out of him. "Can I crash on your sofa tonight?"

Ulysses finally looked at Sam, who met his gaze, one eyebrow twitching. Without a word, he turned and went into the kitchen. A moment later Ulysses heard the water go on in the sink.

"Stay if you want." He took a deep breath and let it out, trying to throw off the leftover shakiness of the fight. "It's not very comfortable."

"I've slept in worse places."

Ulysses fetched a pillow and a blanket from the closet in the office. "Laz," he said when he got back, "how did you know to come here?"

"Mmm?" Laz rolled over, looking blearily up at him. "What do you mean?"

"You showed up before Sita began screaming."

Laz shook his head. "Tomorrow, all right?"

"Fine."

He spread the blanket over Laz and went down the hall to the bedroom, gently shutting the door behind him.

Everything was as he had left it. The bed was neatly made, the bedside lamp steady and yellow when he turned it on. The room was quiet, a cool breeze through the open window bringing with it the smell of impending autumn. There were no spiders.

He pulled his T-shirt over his head and went into the bathroom, brushed his teeth. The mundanity was pleasant; the mintiness of the toothpaste and the familiar exercise of moving the bristles around somehow soothed him. He washed his face gingerly, trying not to get the gauze on his arm wet. When he straightened and looked at himself in the mirror, he saw his same old face, tired eyes, hair that could use a trim. He dried off and went back into the bedroom, shucked off his jeans, and collapsed onto the bed.

Sam came in not long after. Ulysses watched quietly, eyes half open, as he wandered the room, taking off his vest and unbuttoning his shirt. Then he must have dozed off a bit, because when he woke up Sam was pulling the covers back and crawling into bed next to him in the darkened room. He was wearing a pair of old pajama bottoms, no shirt. Ulysses rolled over and draped himself over Sam's torso, because Sam was warm and perfect.

He felt Sam shift a little, wrangling him into a more comfortable position. Then a deep breath. "So," he said after a while, "Laz is staying tonight."

It wasn't exactly a question, and Ulysses shut his eyes, pressing his face into Sam's neck. "Is that a problem?"

"No." Ulysses wasn't sure that was the truth, but he didn't chase it. A long moment passed. Sam said, "You're worried about him."

"A bit."

Sam snorted, but he didn't pursue the matter. Instead, he wrapped an arm around Ulysses's ribs. "What was that?" he asked quietly. "Demons?"

"No." Ulysses yawned. "It was a trap. I don't know exactly what it was trying to do. It almost looked like it was meant to push Sita hard enough that she'd show her powers." Like when your father stabbed you, he didn't add.

He heard Sam's hair rustle on the pillow as he shook his head. "She doesn't have any powers."

"How sure are you?"

"A better question is why aren't you sure?" Sam exhaled softly. "I thought you had a way of judging these things."

Ulysses made a noncommittal noise. "I'm just trying to come up with a reason."

"Does there have to be one?" Sam kissed the top of his head.

"It makes a lot more sense that there would be some rationale than that someone would expend the effort to stochastically send that kind of thing after a biochemist and an obstetrician."

Sam hummed. "Or after a librarian and a university professor?" he said quietly.

"But it— I— They," Ulysses sputtered, and then subsided, scowling. Finally he moved enough to look at the side of Sam's face in the dim light from the clock. "Fine."

Sam turned his head slightly. "What if this is somehow related to that guy in a suit who chased me?"

Ulysses hugged him, as though he could somehow chase away the thought with the strength of his arms. But even he couldn't deny there was a logic there. And he really didn't like it.

Chapter 12

S AM GOT BACK FROM his run a bit after six thirty and climbed the stairs back to the apartment, thinking of the color of the sunrise and the strawberries they'd had in England in June. It was a little unfair for the sky to be so beautiful when everything felt like it was spinning out of his hands.

The apartment's windows offered a clear view of the pink and orange sky. No Laz on the sofa: the spare quilt had been folded precisely and set on top of the pillow. Ulysses would be displeased to have lost the opportunity to question him, probably. Sam shook his head.

Ulysses was still asleep as Sam crept through to the bathroom, but when Sam got out of the shower, he was up, leaning one shoulder against the wall and brushing his teeth in a slow, meditative way. He glanced appreciatively at Sam as he pushed back the curtain and reached for a towel. Then Ulysses looked away. Sam wasn't sure what to do with that. "You're up early," he said finally.

Ulysses bent forward and spat in the sink. "It's a lifting day," he said when he straightened.

"You don't want to take a day off because of what happened?" Sam's eyes strayed to Ulysses's arm, no longer bandaged. The welts were still livid against his skin, but they weren't bleeding, and he moved with his usual fluidity.

Ulysses raised an eyebrow. "What time did you leave on your run this morning?"

"Five thirtyish."

"You fought the same as I did."

That wasn't entirely fair and Ulysses knew it, but Sam could recognize a losing battle when he came across one. He knotted the towel around his waist and stepped out of the shower onto the small bath mat. Ulysses had pulled on a pair of jeans but was still shirtless, and as Sam's eyes trailed along his chest and down his stomach he suddenly felt like there was no air in the room.

What would he have done normally? Shove the man up against the closed door and make them both late. Instead, he edged past, trying not to breathe or make eye contact until he was safely in the bedroom and dressed. When he looked up, Ulysses was leaning against the doorway, watching him, and the look on his face broke Sam's heart a little. His fingers stuttered in the process of tying his necktie. Was this how things were going to be?

He didn't realize he'd spoken aloud until Ulysses said, "Is *what* how things are going to be?"

"Some strange version of shacking up where we're both just miserable all the time?" Sam pulled savagely at his tie and felt the knot go crooked. With a strangled noise, he fumbled at the ends, trying to loosen it.

Ulysses stepped forward and chased his hands away. "I'm not miserable," he said.

"You can't see the expression on your face when you're looking at me."

Ulysses sighed. Sam stood as still as possible as he worked the knot loose and lined up the ends of the tie. "I mean, it's true that I'm unhappy about the bond acting up and the feeling that I can't touch you the way I want to." He carefully knotted the tie, hands running through the motions Sam had done himself a million times. "But it isn't like my feelings for you are going to change just because we can't make love for a couple of days or something." He tightened the knot very gently and tucked the tail of the tie into Sam's vest, smoothing his palm across the buttons.

"That's not really—" Sam caught his hands before he could step back. "If the bond is intrinsically bad, or if it's . . . rotten or something, the easiest way for you to fix the problem is to get rid of me. Isn't it?"

"Sam . . ." Ulysses's voice sounded raw. "That's not an acceptable solution."

"It would fix the problem, though. Wouldn't it? Don't lie to me."

"Yeah, well, you can fix a broken wrist by cutting off the arm at the elbow. Doesn't mean it's a good way to do

163

it." He kissed Sam's knuckles. "I'm here for keeps. You know that, right?"

Sam's breath hitched. "I . . . yeah."

Ulysses looked at him for a quiet moment. Then he reached up and laid one hand on Sam's cheek. His fingers were cool compared to the overheated mess Sam was, and tense when Sam covered them with his own. Ulysses was as nervous about this as Sam was, and the knowledge was inexplicably soothing. Before he could second-guess the impulse, he bent and kissed the other man, carefully and deliberately.

Ulysses pulled back first and gently ran the pad of his thumb over Sam's lower lip. "Better?" he murmured.

"Yeah."

Ulysses stepped back and stared at him as though trying to decide whether to take Sam's word for it. Then he nodded abruptly. "Good."

Sam looked down at his clothes, trying to remember where he'd been in his routine and what he was missing. Beside him, Ulysses was pulling on a T-shirt for a band—or perhaps a guy—named Rodriguez. "Here," he said, handing Sam his watch. "I'll go put the percolator on."

"HEY, ULYSSES!"

Ulysses jerked back to the present. He was resting on the end of a bench between sets, and suddenly

Vikram was crossing the gym toward him. He shut his eyes for a moment. He'd always enjoyed feeling a little invisible in the weight room, and instead here was Vikram, coming across the space in a T-shirt with the sleeves cut off, waving at him. He raised a hand in greeting.

"Nice to see you," Vikram said, coming to a halt in front of the bench. He obviously hadn't slept well; he had dark rings under his eyes, and he looked tense, ready to jump if something went off.

It was a look Laz had been carrying around lately. Ulysses frowned. "Is there a problem back at the apartment? You didn't come here looking for me, did you?"

"No. I play basketball with some of the guys from the meat science lab on Tuesdays." Vikram folded his arms a little uncomfortably. "Did you get a chance to talk to your sister yet? I'm sorry, I know it's still very early, but—"

"No, yeah," Ulysses said. He'd called her from the lobby payphone only to find that Laz had already been over to see to her and Obe. "They can come this afternoon. Is there a time that works for you?"

"Oh," Vikram said, sounding surprised. "Five o'clock?"

"I'll let her know." He waited, trying to discern if something else was required of him. "How's Sita doing?"

Vikram shrugged. "I don't think either of us got much sleep last night."

"She's quite something," Ulysses said, watching the other man's face. "Do you know if there's any magical talent in her family?"

Vikram shook his head. "Not that she's ever mentioned."

"And you've never seen her doing any magic?"

"Are you asking if she does stuff like you?" He shook his head. "No way. She's very practical."

As though practical were the opposite of magic. Babushka would love that. "She *is* named for a goddess," Ulysses said, trying to sound like he was joking.

"That's as far as it goes." Vikram gave Ulysses an odd look. "Why?"

"I'm just trying to figure out why that happened," Ulysses said. "As attacks go, it was unusual, to say the least."

There was something odd in Vikram's face that Ulysses couldn't identify. "We're lucky to have you as neighbors," he said slowly. "Nothing like that has ever happened to either of us before."

Ulysses pressed his lips together. "Yeah," he said, "I was very surprised as well." They stared at each other unhappily.

Finally Vikram sighed. "I'm sorry. It's unkind of me to insinuate that you had anything to do with this. You and Sam and your brother saved us, and you're bringing Celeste to help protect our apartment . . ." He shook his head. "You must think I'm very ungrateful."

"I think you're under a lot of stress," Ulysses said, and Vikram nodded.

"I don't think I told you, my lab was damaged in the explosion. To say nothing of what Sita's been dealing with at the hospital. So all day for the last few weeks I've been sweeping up broken bits of my research and trying to catalog what needs replacing and what data has been lost." He spread his arms, then let them drop to his sides despondently. "And on top of that my mother's ghost, and now this."

"I'm sorry about all that," Ulysses murmured. Then he really had to finish his set and unrack his weights, so he lay back, centering himself beneath the bar. Somewhat to his surprise, Vikram stepped around the bench to stand next to his head.

"If I'm spotting you, I stand here, right?"

"Sure." He took a deep breath and lifted the bar. For a moment he held it above his chest, arms outstretched. Then he slowly lowered it, just until the bar touched his pecs.

"What is this?" Vikram asked, watching the bar make its return journey. "Two hundred pounds?"

Ulysses paused fractionally at the top of the arc. "Two hundred five," he managed.

"Is that a lot?"

He did another four reps and re-racked the weight. "Relative to what?" he asked. After a moment, he added, "I hurt myself last April and had to stop for a while. I'm still getting back to where I was."

Vikram laughed and leaned on the bar, watching as Ulysses got to his feet and began to unload the bar. "Why do you do this?"

Ulysses scratched the back of his head. "It's fun," he said eventually. It wasn't quite the right word. The actual feeling sat somewhere between meditation and satisfaction. He wasn't sure there was a word for it.

"Really?" Vikram looked surprised, and Ulysses shrugged. Vikram seemed to consider this for a while. Then he asked, "Do you ever play basketball?"

S AM STEPPED OUT OF the library at one o'clock and found a spot near the door from which he could keep an eye on Library Mall. He tried not to look around like a suspicious character in some detective film, but it was tough. A variety of students milled around downtown, making their way to the bookstore, meeting friends, a few radicals trying to discern if it was safe to come out of hiding yet. Sam wasn't wildly conspicuous in his suit, but the undergrads were still giving him sidelong glances as they passed. He folded himself onto the wide railing that ran around the forecourt and tried to fade into the background.

In all those old Raymond Chandler movies, the cops Philip Marlowe had to meet with were either inept or lazy—or both. Sometimes corrupt, too. Even the smart ones were easily outmaneuvered. Sam didn't need to worry about this; they couldn't possibly have anything on him, and if they did, he and Ulysses would figure something out.

Two figures in dark suits detached themselves from the crowd of passersby and made their way toward him. One was short and austere, with light brown skin and auburn hair cut in a severe bob. The other was tall and Black, with dark eyes and a face that seemed to exude good nature. If they played good cop, bad cop, he had no problem guessing who was who.

"Mr. Sterling," the woman said, coming to a stop in front of him. "You've been a hard man to get a hold of."

He shrugged. "I was a little turned off when one of your goons chased me across the Square after dark."

The woman's face grew, if anything, more severe. She looked at the man. "Did you hear anything about that?"

The man looked genuinely baffled. "I can't imagine a scenario in which that kind of behavior would be necessary," he said. "No one is trying to arrest him."

The woman's face tightened into an unhappy scowl. "Make a note, would you?" she asked, and the man pulled out a notebook and scrawled something. The woman looked back at Sam. "That wasn't us, to be clear. Or if it was, we'll have a word with whomever did it." From her tone of voice Sam was concerned that when she said *a word*, she meant she was going to stab them.

"I appreciate that," Sam said.

"Right." She straightened her jacket with a sharp tug. "I'm Special Agent Penelope Greenspoon, and this is my partner, Special Agent Melvin Robinson."

"A pleasure," he said, and shook her hand, then Robinson's. She didn't look like a Penelope, but he supposed her parents had named her before she'd become terrifying. "Could I see your badges?"

They both handed them over, which was a relief. Sam wouldn't have been able to tell if they were counterfeit, but he also didn't think imposters would bother to have made fake badges. He returned them.

"Mr. Sterling, we'd like to invite you to come with us to our field office," Robinson said, tucking her badge back into her coat pocket.

"Why?" His mood sobered quickly. "Am I being investigated?" The only lawyers Sam had contact information for lived in Brooklyn. It was possible his sister Alyson could recommend someone, or Sterling Enterprises no doubt had a corporate counsel. . . .

"You're not currently the subject of an investigation," Robinson said, phrasing it specifically enough to give Sam a little pause. Also, they weren't exactly required to tell him the truth, were they? But he did get the feeling they meant no immediate harm, whatever that was worth: it was an unusual intuition for him, and he wasn't entirely sure where it was coming from. "We have some papers discovered in the Sterling Hall wreckage that we would like you to advise us on."

"Me? Why me?"

Greenspoon cleared her throat. "The documents have become important to our investigation into the bombing, but we're not able to read them. A professor who looked at them thought some of the alphabet looked like shorthand. Our secretary concurred but was unfamiliar with that particular style."

Sam frowned. "Someone told you I know about shorthand?"

"Several individuals in the history department mentioned you as an expert." She looked at him severely, as though she didn't quite believe what she'd been told. "We're not asking you to provide a translation if you're unable, but if you could assess the documents, that would be a great assistance."

Sam had helped teach a few history graduate students how to read original documents, including shorthand, back when he was working at the Historical Society. The whole thing sounded like grasping at straws to him, though. He scratched the back of his head to hide his perplexity. "All right, I can take a look."

Chapter 13

IT WAS THE MIDDLE of the afternoon, and Ulysses was bent over a stack of paperwork while Milo and Ingrid—a pair of eight-year-olds who'd decided his office was an interesting place to hang out after trailing after him from the faculty lounge one day over the summer—opened his mail and talked about a movie they'd seen recently that seemed to be called *Beyond the Planet of the Apes*, or possibly *Beneath* or *Above* it. Ulysses had missed something at the beginning of their conversation and now felt hopelessly out of step every time he tuned back in. Fortunately, things seemed to be proceeding without much input from him. Behind his desk, his little transistor radio burbled quietly, just loud enough that he could hear some melody underneath the chatter but not easily make out the notes.

"How many of these movies have there been?" he asked eventually.

The kids looked at each other. "Two," said Milo, a short kid who had sandy blond hair and thick glasses.

"I think they're making another one, though." Ingrid was slightly taller than Milo and didn't wear glasses, but her haircut was nearly identical to his. "I think I saw it in a magazine."

"Which one did you like better of the two you've seen?"

This spurred some debate. Ingrid had liked the spaceships in both of the films, but the first one was slightly superior. Milo, meanwhile, thought the second was better because they had telepathy. Ulysses was unclear if 'they' meant the apes or some other group of antagonists.

Ulysses had vague memories of seeing the first one. "What about the end of the first one?" he tried. "The final shot with the Statue of Liberty?"

Both kids shrugged.

"I thought it was the Earth as soon as they landed," Ingrid said airily. "It wasn't that much of a surprise."

"No, you didn't," Milo said. "How could you know?"

"Because they had horses! Were we just supposed to believe that horses evolved on a planet hundreds of light years away?"

Milo appeared to be gearing up to argue when the door, which had been only half closed to begin with, swung all the way open to reveal Sam standing in the doorway.

Both kids looked at him with some interest.

"Ulysses," Sam began.

"Who are you?" Ingrid asked him.

"He's the guy in the picture," Milo said in what he clearly thought was a whisper. Ingrid leaned forward from where she was sitting and looked from the photo to Sam, frowning.

"Meet my assistants," Ulysses said finally, fighting the urge to rest his forehead on the desk. "Milo and Ingrid."

"Someone trusted you with their children?" Sam hissed.

"Not as such." Ulysses glanced at the kids, who looked as furtive as he felt. "They were bored and I needed someone to sort my mail."

Sam nodded, still looking concerned. "Where are your parents?"

"My dad teaches Norwegian and my mom is a botanist," Ingrid announced proudly. "And Milo's dad is a geology professor."

"Do they know where you are?"

Milo shrugged. "They know we're on campus."

Ulysses found a handful of change in his pocket. "On that note, I think it's probably time you guys clocked out," he said, handing the coins to Ingrid. "Thank you for your help."

The kids glanced between him and Sam and then left in a hurry. Ulysses could hear them whispering about whether and to what extent Dr. Lenkov was in trouble as they walked down the hallway.

When Ulysses turned around from shutting the door, Sam had slumped down into one of the chairs the kids had vacated. "They sort your mail," he said, voice flat.

"I couldn't find any undergrads one day." He sat down in the other chair, knees almost touching Sam's. "Then they kept showing up."

Sam shook his head. "Because you probably pay them in Coke."

Ulysses nodded. "And peanut M&M's, sometimes."

"God knows what their parents think," Sam said, and then laughed suddenly. "Do they even know? Are the kids supposed to be somewhere safe?"

"This is safe! Mildly educational, even."

"Mm." Sam smiled as he shook his head. Then, suddenly, his face fell. "Ulysses . . ."

Ulysses sat forward. "What's up?"

"I met with the DCI agents." He took a deep breath. "They have—they found some documents in the basement of Sterling."

"All right." Without thinking, he reached out and caught Sam's hand. "Start from the beginning."

Sam took a shuddery breath. "One of the things that the FBI, the DCI, and I don't know who all else have done with the bomb site is go through all the wreckage for leads. In the basement, they found a significant cache of papers."

Ulysses rubbed his jaw with his free hand. "What does this have to do with you?"

"It's in a shorthand no one could figure out. I've given a few workshops on reading handwritten documents, and someone heard about that and wanted me to take a look."

"What was it?"

"A combination of an old shorthand system from the '20s and some Aklo." Sam chewed on his lip. "The Aklo was being used as a one-to-one substitution for English to disguise certain words."

Ulysses's chest tightened as the penny dropped. "Words," he repeated.

"Names." Sam looked upset again. "Specifically, Howard's name."

They sat in silence for a moment. Two. "Did you tell them that you recognized the name?"

Sam scoffed. "I'm not a complete amateur. I told them I needed to confer with some colleagues about the contents but I'd produce a transcription." He took a deep breath. "It's a long document—possibly some kind of dossier. I haven't had a chance to take a close look at most of it yet, but there's a good chance Howard's not the only one mentioned."

"Yet?"

"They gave me a copy." Sam groaned and rubbed his forehead. "I'm going to have to tell them I have a conflict of interest, aren't I?"

"Probably." Ulysses hesitated, thinking. "Do they have any idea who the papers belonged to?"

"If they do, they haven't let on," Sam said. "Someone with an office in Sterling Hall. It probably isn't a huge leap to suggest they may be in the cult that went after Hugh last spring." He looked down at his shoes, body tense, distress reverberating through him and into the bond.

Ulysses didn't need to guess why. He got to his feet and leaned past the desk, turning up the volume on the radio. Sam looked at him quizzically when he tugged at the other man's hand. "Come on. Are you going to tell Howard?" He pulled again, and Sam got to his feet. Ulysses stepped slightly closer, slid one arm around his waist, and started to dance.

"I should." Sam was stiff in his arms as he said it. "Shouldn't I?"

Ulysses nodded slowly. As far as he was aware, Sam had seen his father once since that night up on Madeline Island, and it had been at Ulysses's instigation. "Do you want me to tag along?"

"No." Sam began to sway weakly in time with the tune. "I can handle him. I'm not afraid." After a moment, he laughed weakly. "After all, he's unlikely to stab me again."

"True enough." Ulysses raised his arm and spun Sam. "That doesn't mean you have to go see him in person. You could write him a letter. Or you can leave it, and he won't be any worse off than he was before."

Sam leaned his forehead against Ulysses's, eyes closed. "I want to be the kind of person who would tell him."

"Then do it." Ulysses tightened his arm. "But wait until you have a better idea of what's going on, so you only have to do it once."

Sam made a small noise of agreement. "What is this?" he asked after a moment, opening one eye.

"I don't know. Just a song." The sweet-voiced singer was crooning about plane crashes. Ulysses frowned. "Don't take it as a portent or something."

Sam pulled back far enough to look at his face. "Really, though?"

Ulysses licked his lips, but before he could answer, there was a knock on the door. Sam sighed and stepped backward, just out of Ulysses's reach. Ulysses opened the door.

It was Vikram. "It took me forever to find your office," he announced, stepping in. "I thought you might like a ride back to the Baskerville." His eyes roamed the taped-up windows, evaluating how hard they'd been hit by the blast. Then he looked over at Sam and grinned. "Running tomorrow?"

Sam scratched his head. "Sure." He glanced at Ulysses. "I'd better get back to the library."

Ulysses nodded and watched him go.

They drove back downtown. Celeste and Obe were waiting in the hall; Celeste, very pregnant, looked understandably tired, and Obe's normally cheerful face was set in a worried expression. Nothing got better when they actually walked into Vikram's place.

"What the hell happened in here?" She looked around, as though there would be something still visible from the previous night's adventures beyond the scribbles on the wall and the splintered door lock.

"Didn't Laz tell you?" Ulysses crouched down where the portal had been, holding one hand an inch above the floor.

"Not really." She turned to look at the sigil on the wall, frown deepening. Obe put the box he was carrying down and came to peer over her shoulder.

"Bad plan to use blood like that," he said after a moment.

"Blood?" Vikram asked sharply.

"It's a good warding spell," Ulysses said defensively. "Also, I was in a rush."

"That doesn't make it a good idea," Celeste snapped. "You need to be more careful. Think what would have happened if they'd broken it."

Ulysses opened his mouth to respond, but Vikram cut him off. "What would have happened?"

"Snap back," Obe said, bending over to dig through the box. He straightened up with a hammer and nail. "If he'd lost control of the spell, he could have been hurt or killed. The use of blood in the spell ties it to him in a way that it ordinarily wouldn't be."

Vikram nodded, brows knitted. "Why did you do it?" he asked, looking at Ulysses.

"It's a stronger version of the spell." He glared at Obe. "Now if you can all be quiet, I want to ask the building what it thinks happened."

Celeste sniffed, but no one else spoke, so Ulysses folded his legs into a half lotus and shut his eyes.

He had thought it would be difficult to quiet his mind, but the residual magic tugged at him almost right away. It wasn't like talking to a library, with its quietly whispering books. The Baskerville had been built in 1914 and led a relatively unremarkable existence since then. He stretched out and found the cold boilers in the basement waiting for the fall, electrical and gas lines, stairways and fire escapes and garbage chutes, the infrastructure that infiltrated and circulated, the building's breath. There were moments happy and tragic in its past, all buffed into a smooth golden thread by time's passage. A few deaths here and there, a few births to balance them out. Nothing to distinguish it from any apartment building of a certain age.

And then there was the night in question.

It had felt for the building how Ulysses imagined a car crash might feel for a car, and wasn't that a terrifying statement. Not painful, but fast and sudden and jarring. The building had been, in some way, bilocated. One foot on sea and one on shore, as Sam would probably say. Did the building have any idea where the other location was? When he asked, all he got in response was confusion.

He drew away slowly, and the apartment let him go. It had generally positive feelings toward its inhabitants, but it was frightened, if that was the right word. Ulysses felt unpleasantly responsible for the intrusion.

When he opened his eyes, Celeste was sitting on the sofa, watching him, face unreadable. "Sorry," he said, trying to shake himself all the way awake. "How long was I out of it?" He could hear Obe moving around somewhere deeper in the apartment, and who knew where Vikram had gotten to.

Celeste shook her head. "Twenty minutes." She squared her shoulders, looking at him. "You doing okay, U?"

"I'm fine." He uncoiled and stretched. When he looked up, she still had the same expression of concern, and he wasn't sure he liked it. He knew it meant he'd done something she thought was dangerous or foolish, usually both. He wondered, for a moment, if she could see the marks that lingered on his arm through his jacket sleeve. "Am I missing something?"

She shook her head. "You and Sam should get out of here."

"What?" He looked around, but he was still sitting in the middle of the rug in a nice, large apartment, one that was occupied by two normal professional-type people. "Why?"

"I have a bad feeling about those spider things." Her mouth turned down at the edges. "I've never heard of anything like them." Laz must have told her about that.

He shrugged lightly, getting to his feet. "We handled it, though."

"Sure, once. What if they come back?"

"I don't know." They stared at each other until he joined her on the sofa. "This is how life works, Celeste."

"Not everyone's life." She sighed and stretched her back, looking uncomfortable. "You know, we hoped that you'd settle down a bit."

Obe and Vikram's voices were drawing nearer. "Who's we?"

She ignored him. "You've got a job and responsibilities now. You could stop risking your neck like you're still twenty-two."

Ulysses shut his eyes. "It's just something that needs doing."

Celeste shook her head. "Why does it have to be done by you, though?"

He didn't have an answer to that. Instead, he looked away and watched Vikram come in, carrying a chair, Obe behind him.

"What's up with Laz?" Celeste asked after a long silence.

"What do you mean?"

"He showed up all twitchy at practically the break of dawn, looking like he hadn't slept in a week." She paused, and then added, "Every time I see him, I get the feeling there's something he's keeping from us."

Ulysses sighed. "He's not required to tell us things, you know. I understand that among normal, non-intuitive people, secrets are actually quite common."

"Well, he's not living with those people, is he?" she snapped. They stared at each other, and finally she said, "I thought maybe he would talk to you."

"I hoped he would too," Ulysses said bleakly. A noise across the room caught his attention—Vikram offering a hand to Obe, who was stepping backward off the chair. "I've been trying."

"Keep trying," Celeste advised, and patted his leg. "Now go eat something before you pass out."

Chapter 14

A FTER WORK ON THURSDAY night, Ulysses went back to the apartment and stared into a cabinet. It was dinnertime, but he couldn't bring himself to choose anything to eat, or indeed to care. He was tired. Classes hadn't even started yet and everything was exhausting. Meetings, paperwork, what total bullshit. What he really wanted to do was sleep for an hour, then wander down to campus and take Sam out to dinner somewhere nice, talk through their problems, make everything right again. Failing that, he wanted to go to the gym and lift heavy objects until he was too tired to deal with all the *feelings* currently kicking around inside of him.

But there were diminishing returns on lifting twice in one day, and Sam had diner plans with Ellen.

"That's the third time you've sighed into that cabinet," said a familiar voice. "I don't know if you're aware, but disapproving of its contents is not going to change them."

He turned to see Dr. Parvati Ranganathan watching him from the kitchen table. She was sitting elegantly, legs crossed at the knee, formal but relaxed. "To what do I owe the honor?" he asked dryly.

"Nothing *you* did," she said, voice dripping with acidic sweetness. "I just enjoy having company in my old age."

Ulysses raised an eyebrow. She smiled back. He watched her expression grow icier as he joined her at the table. "Is it more fun if I pretend to ignore you?"

"It's not fun at all." She recrossed her legs in the other direction; something in her remembered restlessness, even if she no longer had a body to feel it in. "What did you say your surname was?"

"Lenkov."

Dr. Ranganathan frowned. "That professor was a Lenkov."

Ulysses said, "*I'm* Professor Lenkov."

She snorted. "Not the one I'm recalling, unless you've grown several inches and changed genders."

"You spoke with my grandmother?" The words tumbled out unintended. Of course they'd spoken; Babushka had implied as much. But somehow this little bit of vulnerability pleased the ghost.

"Once or twice, yes." She smiled a thin smile.

"What did you talk about?"

There was a long pause as she examined him. "Perhaps you should ask her."

He thought of Babushka's list of names, her silences and lacunae. "I'm asking you," he said, but she was gone.

He tried to stop himself from sighing again. Failed. Then he pulled himself together and walked over to Gooseberry House.

He left his boots in the front hall and followed the voices through to the kitchen to find Aunt Cass and Mariah in the process of opening a bottle of wine. Quite possibly not their first, either, although it was barely six thirty. Babushka was clearly elsewhere; the two of them wouldn't have been drinking in the kitchen if she were around.

"Nephew!" Aunt Cass greeted him, shoving the bottle in his direction. "Be a dear and open this, will you?"

It was a white from Côte du Rhone, suggesting it had arrived with Mariah. He picked up the corkscrew. "Is Laz in?"

"No," Mariah said. She was beautiful as always, fully as tall as him, with long red hair and dark blue eyes. Most days, Ulysses felt a good ten years older than she looked. "He's gone on a job interview."

"Don't know why," Aunt Cass said. She had dragged the other stool around to the far side of the kitchen peninsula and now perched on it in front of the stove. Ulysses could hear a timer clicking, the quiet whoosh of the oven as something cooked.

"All that lounging around on the porch, smoking and drinking, coming home at all hours, it was driving me to distraction," Mariah said. "A job will straighten him out."

"How dreadfully capitalist of you," Cass said. Mariah laughed.

Ulysses finally pried the cork out with a little pop and set the bottle down again. "Where's the job?"

"For the record, I don't care a whit if he decides not to take payment or to get paid in ration coupons or god knows what," Mariah said, as though that was somehow a less capitalist option. "He just needs to get out of the house and keep more regular hours, and a job will give him a reason to do that."

"I suppose," Cass said doubtfully. She got up and poured wine into her glass and her sister-in-law's. "Nephew, grab a glass and join us."

Ulysses could only find an old coffee mug, but it held the wine as well as a fancy glass would've. Cass filled it and he leaned against the counter. "Did you arrange the interview?" he asked Mariah.

"I did," she said. "An old friend of mine runs an art gallery on State Street."

Cass raised an eyebrow. "Carla?"

"Do you know her?" Mariah asked.

"Oh yes. She dated Paul right after the divorce." Ulysses cleared his throat, and she made a dismissive gesture. "Don't worry, it was a long time ago. And she jumped ship pretty quickly, proving my estimations of her intelligence were correct." She cackled, and Mariah raised her glass.

"Do you think he'll be back soon?" Ulysses asked.

"Who can say, darling?" Mariah turned more fully toward him, crossing her ankles. "In the meantime, I'm happy to see you. Your father tells me you're . . ." She

187

hesitated and glanced at Cass. "Comment est-ce qu'on dit qu'il emménage avec le petit . . ."

Cass wrinkled her nose. "We'd say 'shacking up,' I think."

Mariah nodded. "Your father tells me you are shacking up with that young man now."

"Sam," Ulysses said, sipping his wine to hide his surprise at the fact that Virgil had been the informant. "That's true."

"The godling," Cass said, into her wine glass.

Mariah glanced at her and sniffed. "Oh, yes. I'd forgotten that part." She looked back at Ulysses. "How is it?"

"Fine."

Mariah made a tsking noise.

"What do you expect me to say?" Ulysses asked.

Cass slid off her stool and went around to the fridge, carefully not making eye contact with either of them.

"You could say that your relationship is a state of bliss! That you entertain ideas of marrying this boy someday. That—"

Cass set a plate on the counter in front of her and dropped a wedge of brie onto it. "Be a dear and open this, won't you?"

Mariah picked up the package, which necessitated putting down her glass. Cass took a moment to refill it. "Mariah, let the boy have his privacy. You can see he's happy. That's enough."

Ulysses mouthed a silent "thank you" at his aunt. She winked.

"Actually, Aunt Cass, I'm glad to see you here," he said. "I ran into an interesting creature the other day."

"Oh yes?" She resumed her seat and looked at him expectantly.

"Large spiders that seemed to be able to sense magic." It felt almost too simple to lay before her, but he needed a topic change.

To his surprise, she raised both eyebrows. "They *sensed* it?" She leaned forward. "What did they look like?"

"About the size of chicken eggs plus legs. Cloudy eyes, like they had cataracts. Otherwise pretty much how you'd expect a spider that size to look, I guess." He sipped his wine. Mariah had found a package of crackers and a knife and was arranging the cheese plate. Her attention appeared to be only on her task, but he knew she was listening.

Cass shook her head. "I don't recall hearing about anything like that. Have you?" She glanced at Mariah.

Ulysses's mother was frowning. "No, not at all." Slowly, she picked up a cracker, mind clearly elsewhere. "I've seen a few spiders of semi-magical origin in my time. They were all quite large. "

"How large?"

She shrugged, puffing out her cheeks in a way that felt very French. "Bigger than a Labrador. They don't do very well. Increasing a creature's size that radically is hard on its joints."

He whistled. "Is it possible someone cooked these up themselves?"

"Sure," Cass said. "I've seen movies . . ." She trailed off for a moment, thinking. "It's not unknown for animals to be able to sense magic above specific levels. There are a few species of birds that can do it. And some types of fungi grow differently in more magical areas. But none of them *feed* on it. I don't think they could."

"How so?"

She sipped her wine, then reached out and cut a slice of cheese. "There's not enough ambient magic in most places. There's . . . to be honest, even magicians with ambient magic in sufficient quantities are pretty thin on the ground. You know there's only a few people like you running around. I can't think someone like Celeste, say, would have enough ambient magic to be worth attacking." She wrinkled her nose. "Don't get me wrong; Celeste is an excellent practitioner, one of the best in the Midwest, if not the country. But her talents are quite different from yours."

Mariah eyed her sister-in-law, but nodded.

Ulysses closed his eyes for a moment. "I'm not—"

"Oh, my darling," Mariah said, a bit sadly. "Of course you are." He opened his eyes to find both women watching him.

Not for the first time, he had the sense that everyone in the world knew something that he didn't, and as the apparent subject of that knowledge, it disturbed him. He wondered how much of the feeling came from being gone from the house and how much was just run-of-the-mill paranoia. "Have you—" He fell silent, unsure of what he wanted to ask.

Mariah waved a hand at the cheese plate. "Have some camembert, darling. It's quite good, for being made in the States."

"It's brie," Cass said.

Mariah looked from the cheese plate to her sister-in-law. "Are you certain?"

Ulysses took another drink of the wine. It was a pleasant vintage, dry, fruity, and crisp. "Magical bonds," he managed, setting his glass down. "Have either of you—"

Cass patted his arm. Mariah shook her head and said, "Don't be so bourgeois, darling. You're a powerful magician and your lover is a retired god. Of course things are going to be a bit unusual."

"It's terrifying."

"Eh, bien?" Mariah made a dismissive French noise. "It's love. It's supposed to be terrifying."

Ulysses picked up his glass and drank the rest of his wine in one go. "On that note—"

"That reminds me," Cass said. "Mom left something for you."

She ducked into one of the rooms off the kitchen and returned a moment later with a newspaper clipping.

"I hope this is meaningful to you," she said, handing it over.

It was an obituary for Dr. Alfred Barth. Ulysses frowned at it. The old man had been in his nineties when he and Sam visited last spring, clearly not in the best of health at the time. Still, it was a surprise that someone so palpably evil could have just . . . died. The obituary didn't give the cause of death, but listed a next of kin, Julie Stricker.

"It is," he said, folding it. "Thank you." He slipped it into his jacket pocket. "I should be going."

"Take care, nephew," Cass said. "If you come across any more of those spiders, try to catch one for me."

Mariah gave Cass a sharp look, but to Ulysses she just said, "I hope I'll see you again before I depart. I'd like to speak with your young man."

"Sure." He tried hard to sound like he was looking forward to it. In a way, he was. It was just a complicated feeling, like everything else with Mariah.

"Good." She slid off the stool and kissed him on the cheek. "Go safely, my darling."

It was still light out when Ulysses stepped out into the street. He had reached the top of State Street before he heard a shout behind him. When he turned, there was Laz in dark green canvas pants and a neatly buttoned plaid flannel shirt, looking reasonably pleased to see him.

"Did you eat yet?" Laz asked.

"Not really." He raised an eyebrow. "Are we not saying 'hello' anymore?"

Laz opened his mouth and then shut it again and looked at Ulysses carefully. "Sorry, that's . . . I'm still kind of living in Thailand in my brain. Do you *want* to get something? Or are you on your way to . . ."

"To see Sam?" He shook his head. The little part of his mind that always knew roughly where Sam might be found suggested he was still down on campus. Probably still with Ellen. "He has a thing tonight. You want to get dinner?" He glanced back over his shoulder, as though the house could still see them from blocks away. "Aunt Cass and Mariah are drinking wine together back h—back at Gooseberry House. I just came from there."

"As if I needed another reason," Laz said. "Is Nick's still open?"

They went to Nick's.

It was a townie bar on State Street that also served a selection of foods ranging from burgers to spanakopita. It had been there practically forever, and nothing about it ever changed: black and white vinyl floor, dark red vinyl booths, jukebox in the corner playing Country Joe and the Fish. It was quiet when they walked in.

They slid into a booth. Laz pressed his lips together when he recognized the music but was otherwise silent as they examined the menu.

"Thailand?" Ulysses asked eventually. "Is that where you were stationed at the end?"

"Yeah." Laz kept his eyes on his menu. "A base in Udon Thani, in the northeast."

"How was that?"

Laz fidgeted, and then finally looked up. "I learned Thai. Warm weather all year round." He shrugged. "I don't know, U. It was a war, not a vacation."

Ulysses felt abruptly guilty. "Sorry."

Laz shook his head. "Would you think I was crazy if I said I miss it?"

He sat back and tried to really look at Laz. Thin, careworn, sitting stiffly as though his back was hurting him, but all that was only tarnish on top of his old intensity. The je ne sais quoi that had made Laz becoming a pilot make some kind of sense was still there, staring back at him. "No, I don't think that's crazy," he said quietly.

"Are you fellas ready to order?" the waitress asked, coming over. She was a pretty blond girl with long, frizzy hair, and she looked at him with narrowed eyes. "Sorry, you look really familiar," she said, tapping her chin with her pen. "Do I know you?"

Ulysses shook his head, but she snapped her fingers.

"The Sett! My girlfriend and I consoled your"—she glanced at Laz, who looked mystified—"your *friend*, Dio. You'd wandered off." When Ulysses looked perplexed, she rolled her eyes and said, "Dionysus."

Ulysses still couldn't quite place her, but he did land on a hazy memory of women at the next table over who were studiously minding their own business for the few minutes he'd gotten to spend with Sam. Across the table, Laz was mouthing "Dio?" as though Ulysses had an explanation. "You're the one who got sick?" he hazarded.

"Yeah!" she said, and then looked a little embarrassed. "Is he okay? We saw him running from someone, and then he didn't come back."

"He's fine," Ulysses said. "We—anyway, he's fine."

She stared at him for a long moment before she nodded.

"What's your name?" Ulysses asked.

"Galadriel." She gave him a slightly challenging look, and he smiled as benignly as he could.

"I'm Ulysses, and this is my brother, Laz."

She nodded, finally. "I'll tell my girlfriend Dio is okay. She'll be relieved."

"Groovy," Laz said dryly.

Ulysses rolled his eyes. "It's good to meet you." He reached up to shake her hand.

She gasped when their hands met, eyes going wide and stunned like she was seeing a ghost. Ulysses froze. Something crackled around them, between them, cold and ozonic, sharp like an electrical current. It stung, but he couldn't let go, couldn't glance away from the expression on her face, at once intent and full of fear.

Ulysses started to speak, but she put her free hand on his head, startling him into silence. If they'd been on stage, Sam would have dimmed all the lights around them and put them in a spotlight. It felt like *someone* did. "Beware," she said.

"What?"

"Beware," she said again, voice quiet but intense. "Listen:

Knowledge soars; beware what sinks.
Protect the ivory and ink.
The withered skin, lost breath won't blink.
Spare the wine, there's blood to drink."

Ulysses was silent, trying to shake off the silken tendrils of the moment. Galadriel removed her hand, a dazed expression on her face. "I . . . sorry. I don't know what—" She cleared her throat. Laz, thankfully, was silent.

"Are you okay?" Ulysses asked, struggling out of his seat.

"I'm fine." Galadriel took a half step back and clutched her notebook like a shield. "Goose walked over my grave. Are you gents ready to order?"

When she'd run back to the kitchen, Laz sat back, arms crossed. "Does this sort of thing happen to you a lot?"

"More than you'd think." Ulysses ran his hands through his hair. He could still feel the echo of her touch, the burning web of magic across his unsteady nerves. Abruptly he missed Sam, missed him more than seemed real or fair considering they'd just seen each other a few hours ago. Sam had been through this before; Sam would understand. Ulysses wanted to reach into the bond. Instead, he fished out a pen and scribbled the prophecy down on the paper placemat in front of him, not that he was likely to forget it.

When he looked up, Laz was watching him, amber eyes unreadable. Ulysses tapped his pen on the table. "You have a question," he said.

"I think I have a lot of questions," Laz told him, voice flat.

"Start with the most pressing."

Laz nodded slowly. "Are you okay? Are you safe?"

Ulysses frowned at him. "What do you mean?"

Laz gestured covertly toward Galadriel and leaned forward. "Your boyfriend is a god, and *that* just happened. What the hell, man?" he hissed.

Oh. Ulysses considered a couple of responses before settling on a simple, "I'm safe." He hesitated. "I mean, you heard what she said. Maybe I'm not. But Sam isn't the danger."

Laz sat back and rubbed his jaw. "All right." Ulysses couldn't tell if he was totally convinced. "If you're sure, I'll support you."

Ulysses did not especially appreciate the way that was phrased, but it was coming from a good place. "Thanks," he said gruffly. "What's your next question?"

For a while, Laz just ran through a bunch of nervous tics—tapping, glancing awkwardly around, playing with his lighter. "My visions have changed," he said finally, all in a rush.

"Technically, not a question." Laz groaned, and Ulysses waved a hand. "What do you mean by changed?"

A different server came back with two bottles of beer, set them on the table, and left again. Where was Galadriel? He couldn't see her. Was she okay?

Laz picked his beer up, turning it in his hand to look at the label. "The visions happen sometimes when I have those episodes." He didn't look up. "Like at the car dealership. It's like I'm running away from something and I go through a door in my head."

"And you see things?"

Laz nodded tightly. "Sometimes I see shit that happened back in. . . ." He looked at his hand on the bottle and took a deep breath. "Sometimes I see the future. Not like I used to. It's more complex."

Ulysses wasn't sure what to say to that. "Has it happened other times when I was there?"

Laz nodded. "That night in the Sett. I saw Sam being chased."

Ulysses reached for the other bottle. It was a dark beer, with a bitter coffee flavor to it, the glass damp with condensation. He wrapped his fingers around it. "When did this start?"

Laz didn't answer. Ulysses rolled his eyes. "Was there an incident, or was it just out of the blue?"

"There was an incident," Laz ground out. "I was still back there." He glanced over one shoulder as though making sure they were alone. Or—no. He was looking toward the scars on his back.

"I see." Ulysses rolled the bottle between his palms, trying to focus. "I don't know if I have any advice. I can look into it." He took a swig of the beer. It fizzed bitterly down his throat. "As talents go, foresight is not that rare. I'm certain a fair amount has been written on the topic. Comparatively, anyway."

"Ah, academic magic," Laz said, pursing his lips.

Over by the bar, Ulysses spotted Galadriel, drinking a glass of ice water. Her face was animated when a coworker asked her a question. She looked recovered. He hoped it wasn't just an act.

Ulysses let his head rest against the back of the booth. "For what it's worth, I don't think you're going crazy. I think this is probably a common reaction to whatever it was that happened to you. A reaction to war, basically. Mix that in with any sort of magic ability and of course *something* is going to happen."

Laz greeted this with narrowed eyes, but he didn't get up and leave as Ulysses had feared.

"I'm serious. Wars mess people up. You've heard of shell shock? Returning soldiers after World War I rendered jumpy and unable to function? It's clearly on a spectrum with what you've got going on." He didn't wait for Laz to acknowledge this but rushed on. "I'm sure that if the government hasn't admitted that a lot of returning vets have similar issues, it's because they're lying about the whole war to try to placate people."

A lot of emotions flitted across Laz's face. Eventually, his features settled into a wry grin. "You look tired, man."

"Thanks," Ulysses grumbled.

"I mean, you really light up when you say that shit now. Is this what they've done to you? You gotta care about everyone now?"

"I don't do it because I have to," he said.

Across the bar, Galadriel leaned toward the window to the kitchen, and a plate got shoved through at her. Laz looked at her, then at his watch.

"The Siegel–Schwall Band is playing at the Webster Street Inn tonight. You wanna go?" Laz spread his hands invitingly.

"I shouldn't," Ulysses said. "I have research to do."

"Might do you good to blow off some steam," Laz suggested.

Someone was coming across the room now, carrying their order. *Protect the ivory and ink* indeed. "Sure," he said finally, and took another gulp of the beer. "Why not?"

He still wasn't sure it was a good choice, but Laz's wild grin made him feel that at least it wasn't a terrible one.

Chapter 15

S AM WALKED HOME FROM campus, guitar case slung over one shoulder, knowing Ulysses wouldn't be there and hoping he would be anyway. He was somewhere to the northeast, as far as Sam could tell. That was the downside of knowing where Ulysses was all the time—Sam knew where he was.

He only bothered to turn on one light in the apartment, the one on the bedside table; it painted the room with a low yellow glow as he hung up his suit jacket and vest, unknotted his tie, and unbuttoned the shirt that had given him so much trouble that morning with all its fiddly buttons. Everything felt too quiet with Ulysses gone, too empty. Sam sighed, found a T-shirt and pulled it over his head.

It wasn't until he'd finished changing clothes that he realized he was going out again. He pulled on his shoes and an old corduroy jacket and clattered back down the stairs on autopilot. It was that time of early evening that was no longer twilight but not fully dark either, when the sky still seemed to glow; he had a brief glimpse of the moon, getting on toward full, sailing between the buildings as he walked back up to the Square.

There were people—students and non—walking around in twos and threes, side by side or holding onto hands or arms. Most of them had a slightly tense, skittish look to them. These were the ones who were choosing to stay after the bombing, still nervous about their decision. Others had left, afraid of what might happen next; Edith had mentioned enrollment was down. He wanted to ask Ulysses what the city felt. Was the damaged building like a lingering ache to it? Did cities think of themselves like that?

He wanted to find Ulysses.

Sam circled the capitol, not paying too close attention to where he was wandering, and found himself in front of the Webster Street Inn. Music was spilling out onto the street through the open door. He paid the cover charge without asking what the act was and got his hand stamped with smeary purple ink to prove it.

A wide space immediately past the door housed the dance floor and stage. Past that was the bar on the left and a row of booths down the right side, and then tables in the back. It was the same old place, down to the band posters on the walls. He'd been back to the Webster Street Inn a handful of times in the year since he'd nearly started a riot while dancing there. It was still Harry and Ellen's favorite dive, which made it hard to avoid. They probably felt like inviting him back was a way to emphasize that he hadn't done anything wrong and no one blamed him for what had happened. Which he knew, but walking in still put him on edge. There was a band setting up on stage; he seemed to have arrived as the opening band finished its set.

He looked around at the crowd. There were more people than he'd seen here since that night. Most of them were trying to get to the bar for a refill before the main act took the stage. That was fine. This was all fine.

He took a breath.

He spotted Laz, who was watching the stage from a position along the side wall with crossed arms and an expression of mild annoyance and didn't appear to see him. Sam moved as far to the rear of the crowd as possible to skirt around toward the back. And then suddenly he was face to face with Ulysses.

Neither of them was exactly surprised to see the other. How could they be? But Ulysses grinned. As Sam stood there trying to decide what to do, Ulysses leaned forward and said, "What are you doing here?"

His voice was low, applied almost directly to Sam's libido rather than his auditory nerves, making him shiver. Ulysses was doing it on purpose, too, eyes flicking from Sam's eyes to stare at his lips momentarily, then back up.

"I came to find you," Sam said, because it was true, and because he couldn't remember any other words.

Ulysses grabbed his hand and sparks flew up Sam's arm. "Let's find somewhere a little quieter," he said, and led Sam through a crowd that seemed to part before them. They ducked down a back hallway, up a flight of stairs, and through a door onto the fire escape. The door clicked shut behind them.

"How did you know this was here?" Sam asked.

"Curiosity and snooping, mostly."

Ulysses looked down at the alley for a moment; Sam looked at Ulysses. "If you had a coat of arms, that would be your motto: Curiositas et exploratio."

"That's a very medieval way to translate that, but I like it." Ulysses turned to him. "Is that my shirt?"

"I—oh." The 13th Floor Elevators wasn't a band Sam was familiar with, but then again what else could that name possibly have referred to? It was a little short in the torso. He tugged at the hem and laughed. "Sorry."

"It's fine. Looks good on you." Ulysses sounded distracted, like he was having the conversation with Sam while directing most of his attention elsewhere. Something was going on; it wasn't a spell the way Sam understood spells. If anything, it was the opposite; he felt a subtraction of magic, rather than a build-up. He found himself leaning away unconsciously, although the feeling wasn't painful, just discomforting. He had a sense of pressure, somewhere deep in the bond, that grew and grew until it burst painlessly against him. Sam rocked back on his heels, but before he could figure out what had happened—"Want to help me test something?" Ulysses asked, then pushed him up against the dirty brick building and kissed him.

Sam didn't know if it was a greeting or a promise, didn't know if he cared. He tried to force himself to relax, worried that if he put a hand on Ulysses or deepened the kiss, Ulysses might realize what they were doing and stop. Sam didn't know if he could bear that.

But Ulysses didn't stop, pushed a little closer, hooking his fingers into Sam's belt. The feeling was exciting, arousing, like electricity shooting through his body. Sam realized suddenly that he wasn't feeling the bond move. He had braced himself for the weird duality of sensation, but it wasn't there. He was alone in his skin. Even the sparks from earlier were dull where their skin met, almost absent. With the knowledge came relief, but also a quiet sinking feeling he couldn't put a name to.

When Ulysses finally let him go, he said, "What have you done?" He tried to keep his tone light, not let his eyebrows draw together. Almost succeeded.

"I've been learning some new tricks." Ulysses looked up at him, proud, a little worried. "It's all right, isn't it? No side effects?"

Sam kissed him again. He tried to take his time, this time, cupping Ulysses's face with his hands, wishing he could figure out how to convey the weird bundle of emotions he was feeling, joy that Ulysses was trying to fix the problem and guilt that he found it necessary in the first place. Ulysses pressed closer, grinning against his mouth. It was hard to remind himself that they were outside and entirely exposed when all he wanted to do was let Ulysses pin him against the bricks and be remade in his arms.

They had to part eventually, reluctantly; Sam was as aware of his own ragged breathing as of Ulysses's dark eyes, the gentle fingertips and callused hand on the back of his neck. Sam leaned forward, pressing his forehead to Ulysses's shoulder, inhaling the slightly piney scent of his shampoo.

"We should probably talk," Ulysses said when he straightened up again. "A lot has happened."

They eventually settled down on the stairs to the next level up, Sam a step below Ulysses so he could rest his head on the other man's leg. It would have felt a little pathetic how much he wanted to touch Ulysses except clearly Ulysses was feeling it too, and played with Sam's hair as he told him about seeing his mother and Cassandra, the prophecy he'd gotten from Galadriel.

"Busy night," Sam said when he'd finished.

The sound of a bass riff rose up from the building behind them. Ulysses smiled, a little grimly. "I know."

"Protect the ivory and ink, though," Sam continued, tapping one long finger on Ulysses's knee. "That's interesting. It sounds like an old book, doesn't it?"

"It does," Ulysses admitted. "But I couldn't think of a specific volume off the top of my head that would need to be protected and also has ivory on the cover. Can you?"

Sam shook his head. "I'll look around. And Edith might know."

"I appreciate it." Ulysses still looked troubled, but at least some of the tension in his body seemed to be bleeding away.

"I can call the archivist at Wisconsin General too, if you give me those other names again." Sam turned so he could look at the other man's face. "You look tired. Want to go home?"

Ulysses closed his eyes. "More than anything."

The door they'd come through had locked behind them. By the time they got down from the fire escape and back around to the front of the bar, the place was hopping. Another fifty people had shown up since Sam had walked in the first time, dancers crowding nearest the band, drinkers by the bar, and appreciators of the blues everywhere else. Ulysses grabbed Sam's elbow and tugged him to an open spot along one wall near the dance floor. Everyone was moving, gyrating to the beat, but in a normal, nightclub way. Everything was fine.

He wasn't Dionysus anymore.

Eventually, Sam spotted Laz in the middle of the crowd. He was dancing with a short, black-haired young woman. Laz was a decent dancer and the two of them seemed to be having a good time. Sam nudged Ulysses in the ribs and nodded in his direction. It was too loud for Ulysses to say anything, but Sam caught the amused look on his face.

Laz spotted them on a turn, and Sam saw his gaze slide from Ulysses to Sam and back. No telling what that meant. When they came around again and his dance partner noticed Sam, a surprised expression flitted across her face. He'd seen her earlier, when he was sitting with Ellen at the Union; she was part of a group of five women watching them, whispering and giggling. One of them had whispered, "Hi, Dionysus," before her friends dragged her away.

Sam bit his lip.

Dionysus had collected followers—maenads—more or less at random; anyone who was nearby got drawn into his orbit. Dionysus was also gone. There was no way the women at the Union could have been exposed, contaminated. But he was still unsettled.

As the song ended, the woman leaned into Laz and said something. He laughed. For a moment, he looked very normal, young and happy. Unguarded. She took his elbow, and he made his way through the crowd back toward them. When they arrived, Ulysses leaned forward to speak almost directly into Laz's ear. Sam watched a few emotions—suspicion, maybe, or regret—flit across the younger man's face before he nailed everything down. That was the face of an officer, eyes lively but expression strictly controlled.

The woman bowed to Sam with her palms pressed together in front of her. It was a courtly gesture, somehow familiar but foreign. "Nice to meet you," she said when he leaned down. "I'm Manaow."

Sam nodded. "Are you, perchance, friends with Buttercup or Galadriel?"

She grinned. "I met Buttercup first."

Sam smiled and tried to return the bow, which made Manaow giggle. He glanced over at Ulysses; he and Laz appeared to be carrying out an argument mostly through gesticulation. Laz wanted them—wanted Ulysses, anyway—to stay until the end of the set. In a few moments, Ulysses, ever the peacekeeper, was going to look at Sam pleadingly and ask if he'd mind, and then they'd wind up with another night of a drunk Laz sleeping on their sofa. He sighed.

The band had swung into another number, and even Sam was tapping his toes. He looked at Manaow, who was watching the band and the crowd, and felt his apprehension evaporate. What could possibly go wrong? He said, "Would you like to dance?"

She took his hand.

Ulysses took his elbow while they walked home, as though they were Victorian gentlemen out on the town. Laz ignored this, pacing slightly ahead of them, smoke curling up in his wake like the exhaust of a passing train. He bounded up the stairs at the Baskerville ahead of them, then kicked off his boots at the door while Ulysses fussed around retrieving blankets and a pillow.

Sam went into the bedroom and shut the door. He'd left the windows shut during his brief return earlier, and the place was stuffy from the heat of the day, so he distracted himself by opening them. When Ulysses finally came in, Sam was stretched out on the bed shirtless, letting the breeze wash over him.

"Did you see the paper?" Ulysses unbuckled his belt and pulled it off, wrapping it around his hand. "Barth's dead." The buckle clunked as he set it on the dresser.

Sam grunted. "Couldn't have happened to a nicer person."

The mattress dipped as Ulysses sat down on the other side. He smelled like beer and cigarettes; Sam knew he wasn't much better off himself, and they should probably both drag themselves into the shower. Instead, he shut his eyes. "Is this going to happen frequently?" Sam asked.

"Which part?" There was a rustle, presumably Ulysses pulling off his shirt, and a soft noise as he dropped it on the floor.

"Your brother on our sofa."

He opened his eyes in time to watch Ulysses shift, throwing a leg over Sam's hips to straddle his supine form. "He's going through something," Ulysses said. "Maybe several things."

Sam put a hand on Ulysses's hip. He looked good in the soft light of the bedside lamp, and Sam's fingers itched to touch him again. "And he's going through them here," he said, knowing how bratty he sounded.

"He just needs somewhere to be that isn't Gooseberry House for a while. You'd do the same for any of your siblings," Ulysses said mildly.

Sam pressed his lips together. He wanted to snap that of course he wouldn't. He'd barely even been in a room with any of his own siblings for months. Instead, he took a breath. "I'd do it for Celeste," he muttered.

Ulysses's face softened. "Then give Laz a chance too."

"Fine." Sam sighed and sat up, forcing Ulysses to sit back on his heels. For a moment, they were face to face. Sam inhaled, knowing that if he leaned just a little bit farther forward, he could put a hand on Ulysses's shoulder, draw him closer, lay claim to him in some way.

Instead, he passed a shaky hand over his face. "You should get some sleep," he said. "I'm going to go shower."

Ulysses sat back so he could get up. He felt the other man's blue eyes burning questions into his back until he shut the bathroom door between them.

Chapter 16

S AM WAS UP BY five, cursing his body's inability to just chill out ever in his life. Ulysses was still asleep as Sam crept around the room finding clean clothes to run in. Luckily it was too dark to make out his face. Sam didn't want to see if he still had that hurt, confused look.

Laz was still on the sofa, also sleeping, apparently peacefully. No sense disturbing him, either. Sam found his sneakers in the dark and shuffled out into the hall to put them on.

Vikram found him sitting on the floor of the hallway, one knee drawn up, forehead resting on it.

"We don't have to go," he said, startling Sam.

"No, no." Sam climbed to his feet. "Sorry, I was just—" He made an expansive gesture that Vikram hopefully took to mean 'woolgathering' rather than 'rethinking every damn choice I have made in my entire sorry life.'

"You're certain?"

"Never more so." Which, in retrospect, sounded a little deranged, but what the heck. A run would help him feel better. He bounced from foot to foot, waiting for Vikram to capitulate. Which he did, of course, and quickly. The man was an obsessive; he and Sam both knew it. That was why they were there.

Once outside, they stood for a moment on the dark sidewalk while Vikram turned his wrist this way and that, trying to catch the dial in the lamplight. Then at some silently agreed upon moment, they set off up the hill toward the capitol.

Sam felt physically a little off, but that faded as his muscles remembered that they liked running. By the time they were jogging along Capitol Square, he was looser, warmer, and more mellow, but something was still strange. It took him a number of blocks, running near silently, half-listening to Vikram's quips as they went, before he identified it. He could no longer feel where Ulysses was. He'd grown accustomed to that thin thread stretched between them in space, holding tension between self and other. And now it was just . . . gone. He was alone.

He tripped on an uneven spot in the sidewalk and went down hard, encountering the ground with one knee and both hands. Vikram exclaimed, already reaching down to help him to his feet.

"Are you okay?"

It was still too dark for Sam to see his stinging palms. "I'm fine." He pushed his body back into motion, ignoring his knee's protests.

"I was just thinking how sure-footed you are in the dark," Vikram said with a laugh.

"That must be what got me," Sam agreed.

They jogged along for another block before Vikram said, "I think I've remembered where I know you from."

"Oh?" Sam asked weakly, wondering if he could get away with another fall, or perhaps just teleport back to the apartment and not have to go through with the rest of the conversation.

"The biology building at MIT," Vikram said. Sam could tell he was waiting for some sort of response, but didn't offer one. "That was you, wasn't it. I was a little confused, because you seem so much taller now, but—"

"I've grown a bit since then," Sam said.

Vikram made a skeptical noise. "That's unusual. You must have been . . . twenty-two at the time?"

"Twenty," Sam said. "I was twenty. It happens."

"I see." There was a long and not very comfortable silence. Finally, Vikram said, "I don't know if you're aware, but you're pushing the pace."

"Am I?" Sam snapped, and then felt like a dick. "I'm . . . sorry. Sorry." He slowed down, or tried to. Everything was still jittering through him; his body couldn't tell the difference between the conversation and the running and assumed he needed to escape from bears or demons or something.

"It's fine," Vikram said easily. "Look, I brought it up because I wanted to apologize. And not leave you feeling like the other shoe was about to kick you in the neck."

"You . . ." Sam slowed further, unable to run and process this simultaneously. "You what?"

"I feel bad. I overreacted, in retrospect. What was I shouting at you? 'Your reputation will be stained if this gets out'?" They were underneath a streetlight on Sherman Avenue; they hadn't even made it to Tenney Park yet. Sam looked at Vikram, whose angular face was annoyingly earnest. "I've learned a lot since 1965."

Sam didn't know exactly what to say to that. Or any of it. "Thanks," was what he eventually, uselessly went with. "I'm . . . glad you've had an opportunity for reflection." Sam wanted to add that he wasn't the same person he'd been in 1965 either, but that felt like letting Vikram off the hook. Still, he felt a lot of embarrassed anger he hadn't even known he was holding onto evaporate. The shame he'd felt for so long at not living up to his own values began to wither.

It was almost annoying how willing he was to let things go. Was it just that Dionysus was terminally easygoing? Or that Sam didn't want to fight?

They started moving again. Sam asked a few questions about his upcoming classes, mostly to keep Vikram from asking any of his own, but he barely heard the answers. Instead, his head was churning.

The idea of fighting at all brought up memories of lying in bed as a child, listening to Howard and Francie scream at each other in the kitchen, their voices audible but unparsable, their anger and frustration all too palpable. Sam didn't want to fight like that, had actively tried to arrange his life so he never had to. But if he didn't say *something*, what would happen?

Ulysses probably thought he had solved the problem with whatever he'd done. If Sam said he didn't like it, what would happen? Maybe things were going to end badly whatever happened. Maybe it was in the nature of things to end badly. Maybe—

Vikram said something with the intonation of a question, and Sam tried to replay the last few minutes of conversation to figure out what he'd missed. "Sorry, what was that?"

"You recognized me, didn't you?" he asked. His friendly features were concerned, sympathetic. "And you didn't mention it. That morning I asked you guys to come to dinner."

Sam very nearly missed a step again. "I . . . yeah. Sorry. I probably should have."

They were nearly back to the apartment, and Sam still felt twitchy and out of sorts. If Vikram noticed, he didn't mention it. "I understand why you didn't." After a moment, he added, "I told Sita I knew you slightly from Boston. I didn't tell her why. And I won't tell Ulysses either."

Sam hadn't actually thought of hiding the truth from Ulysses. Now that it had been dragged out, the moment stood too proud in the wreckage of his past to pass by in silence.

"Where are you going?" Vikram asked as they reached the building's front door and he didn't stop.

"I'm just going to go around the capitol again once or twice. I'll see you around."

By the time he got back, Vikram had long since vanished back into his apartment. Laz and Ulysses were awake, judging by the voices in the kitchen. Sam didn't stick his head in, just went through to the bedroom and got into the shower as fast as he could.

Ulysses was waiting for him when he emerged from the bathroom, leaning against the headboard, reading. He had already showered and dressed in a white T-shirt and jeans; from where Sam was standing, he could smell familiar Ulysses scents of coffee, aftershave, and bleach, and beyond that the distant lake through the open window, the diesel train exhaust from the tracks down that way, cars from the traffic only just beginning to pick up, and now he knew he was anxious and in another minute he was going to be communing with the dresser, which was made of beech and practically humming to itself and he really needed to get it together.

He forced himself to take a deep breath and focus on the sensation of his lungs inflating within his chest, the thick green rug under his feet. Ulysses shifted, setting his book on the nightstand, and Sam could feel his attention. He turned away and busied himself with finding a pair of briefs and an undershirt in the dresser. Ulysses waited while he pulled them on and then rubbed at his hair uselessly with the towel.

Finally feeling like he could speak with a level tone, Sam turned back and opened his mouth.

"What happened to your knee?" Ulysses asked.

"I tripped." Sam looked down. "I must have scraped it when I fell." There was a sizable wound on his kneecap, very slowly oozing blood. How had he managed to shower without seeing it? Without *feeling* it?

"Didn't you notice?" Ulysses got up and went into the bathroom, coming back with a washcloth and the little box of first aid miscellany. Gently, he took Sam's arm and guided him to the foot of the bed.

"I . . ." He cast his mind back. "It stung. I was thinking about other things."

Ulysses knelt down and inspected the wound. "What happened?" He picked up the washcloth and carefully dabbed at it, and this time Sam did feel every angry nerve ending.

"Something felt off. And then I realized I couldn't find you anymore." He took a deep breath, then hissed at something Ulysses did. "It was like you were just gone."

"Gone from your head, you mean?" He sounded curious rather than angry. Sam wasn't sure how he felt about that.

"It was a bit of a shock." Ulysses was opening a jar of salve rather than looking at him, so he added, "I guess I didn't realize how important that sense was to me. The knowing." Ulysses's fingers brushed Sam's knee, bringing a rush of awareness back to his body.

He heard Ulysses exhale. But all he said was, "And you didn't notice last night because we were together."

"I guess." Sam couldn't quite keep the sadness out of his own voice. "I know you wanted to find a solution to get rid of the bond."

"I don't know if we can get rid of it entirely, but a way to turn it as far down as we can." Ulysses was carefully taping a piece of gauze over the scrape. "I think it would be better for both of us." Then, a little more slowly, he added, "At least, it would be better for me." He looked up at Sam. "If it wouldn't be better for you . . ."

"That's a problem," Sam said. "A pretty damn insurmountable one, I'd say."

Ulysses stood with surprising speed and leaned into Sam's space, a disapproving look on his face. "Nothing is insurmountable, Sam. We just haven't found the answer yet."

Sam's heart kicked up like he was still out running. "We can't have it and not have it," he said, knowing that he was babbling and not caring. He felt naked. He was, he supposed, or nearly so, but it was possible to be naked and not feel half as raw and exposed as he did.

Ulysses said, "Ssh," and kissed him.

Sam made an involuntary sound of outrage and kissed him back. It went from reassuring to hot and wet and filthy in the span of a minute, and he slid a hand around to Ulysses's lower back to pull him closer. The magic between them was muted, almost indiscernible, and he *hated* it and wanted Ulysses in what felt like equal measures.

The frustration must have been mutual. Ulysses grabbed the white cotton of Sam's undershirt in one fist, clutching the back of Sam's neck with his other hand just shy of too hard. Sam leaned backward, pulled him along until Ulysses was a comforting weight above him, pressing him into the mattress, reminding him where the edges of his body were. When Sam grabbed Ulysses's hips and arched up against him, he gasped, breath hot on Sam's neck.

Sam was no longer thinking much. Had he ever thought anything? It had been six days since he'd really gotten to touch Ulysses, and he was going to fly apart from it. He rucked up Ulysses's T-shirt and dragged his fingernails along the exposed skin of his sides. Ulysses made a noise, maybe said something Sam couldn't quite parse, and grabbed one of Sam's hands away, pinning it to the bed, as a second thought twining their fingers together. With his other hand, he reached down to adjust them both. Sam bit back a curse at the brush of Ulysses's knuckles against his dick, tried and failed to stop himself rolling his hips up against the hand, because of *course* he was already hard, of course his body was taut like the string of a bow.

He planted a foot and flipped Ulysses onto his back, and Ulysses let him despite being strong enough to prevent it, watching wide-eyed, his breath shallow. Sam chucked the clothes he'd just put on and settled with one knee on either side of Ulysses's hips. Ulysses ran his hands up Sam's back, murmuring something soothing into his ear when he bent forward. Sam wasn't interested. He pulled back, yanked Ulysses's shirt up, and licked a wide stripe down his taut stomach. He felt Ulysses inhale at the sensation. "You're so frustrating," he muttered against Ulysses's skin, and Ulysses laughed breathlessly.

"Not the first time I've heard that."

Sam wasn't sure whether he wanted to laugh or cry, so he settled on reaching down to jerk Ulysses's belt open. "What percentage of your former lovers," he began, fumbling with the button of his jeans.

"Most of them. Not usually something that comes up . . . *during* sex, but"—Ulysses tried to lift his hips so Sam could slide his jeans down—"you've always been surprising." Between Sam's clumsy hands and Ulysses's, they managed to get the jeans partway off. Far enough. Sam closed his hand around Ulysses's cock, hot, velvety skin around an iron core. Ulysses's control over whatever he was doing to the bond faltered when Sam stroked him, so he did it again. It was like a wave breaking over his head. Sam bit the spot where Ulysses's neck met his shoulder hard enough to bruise, felt it himself, and meant it, dizzy with reciprocated, reflected desire before the duality ebbed away again.

Sam kissed Ulysses, making some soft noise against his mouth when Ulysses gathered both their erections into his hand, stroking them. He kissed the side of Ulysses's mouth, the corner of his jaw, buried his face in the warm cave his neck made against the bed as their hips rocked together. "I just don't—I can't—" he tried, not even sure what he wanted to say.

"Sam." Ulysses's voice was raspy, halfway ruined. "It's okay. I've got you."

For a moment, with their foreheads pressed together, Sam felt somehow weightless, like a pile of silk veils about to blow away.

He came hard, almost painfully. Reached down and wrapped a shaky hand around Ulysses, stroked him once, then again, and felt his muscles tense as he followed Sam over the edge.

Sam collapsed clumsily onto the bed, feeling still entirely at sea, and wobbly and boneless to boot. Ulysses looked down at the mess they'd made of his stomach and started to laugh.

"Is, ah . . ." Sam watched the other man sit up enough to strip his shirt over his head and wipe himself off with it, then had to wait a moment for his brain to reconnect with the thought he'd been having. "Is Laz still here?"

"He's showering," Ulysses said, and added, "in the other bathroom," somewhat unnecessarily. He glanced around, but apparently not finding a clock in his direct line of sight, gave up. "Hopefully he's still showering. I lent him some clothes."

Sam nodded and let himself be pulled over and cuddled against Ulysses's side. His brain was fizzing quietly; he couldn't quite decide if what they'd just done was a mistake or not, couldn't remember what they'd been trying to prove or disprove or why it was important to spend so much time making himself miserable.

"Jesus, you don't stop," Ulysses muttered, looking over at him. His thoughts must have been written all over his face, Sam realized, or Ulysses was still feeling him somehow. He rolled over onto his other side. Ulysses didn't try to prevent it, just draped an arm over his waist, pressing his face into the back of Sam's neck. He was cool against Sam's burning skin. "Look," he said after a while. "Maybe this feels weird because it's new. Can you try living with it for a few weeks and see how it goes? That will give me some time to come up with other solutions."

It was a reasonable approach. Caring. Sympathetic to his concerns. Sam hated it immediately and had to bite back his impulse to say so. "Sure," he said instead, quietly. He'd been an entire, whole person for most of his life. Surely he could deal with this.

He watched Ulysses get up, rearranging his remaining clothes. He stooped to pick up Sam's underwear and handed it back to him. Eventually Sam forced himself to get dressed again, trying to remember that feeling alone was not the same as actually being abandoned.

Chapter 17

B Y THE TIME ULYSSES had cleaned himself up and found a new T-shirt, Sam had managed to throw on a suit, kiss Ulysses on the cheek, and rush out of the apartment like it was a radioactive exclusion zone. Ulysses had never seen him move through his routine so quickly. He shut his eyes and stood for a moment with his forehead pressed against one of the bedroom windows. It was good, perhaps, to periodically be kicked in the ribs by life.

Possibly he shouldn't have kissed Sam. Shouldn't have instigated that. But he couldn't bring himself to regret it. He missed Sam more than he had words to tell. He should have pulled back. It was ridiculous that he didn't have more self-control, especially given how few days it had been. Touching Sam was only going to make mental shielding more difficult. But he couldn't not do it.

Things had been much easier in the days before his research and his personal life had become severely intertwined.

He wondered abruptly what Dr. Parvati Ranganathan would have to say about all of this. Where was she, anyway? Was she haunting someone else in her spare time?

"Ulysses?" called Laz from the living room.

"Coming." He forced himself to straighten his shoulders and unclench his fists.

Laz was sitting stiffly on the living room sofa, cradling a coffee mug. When Ulysses came out, he stood up, ramrod straight as though he was reporting for duty. He was wearing Ulysses's jeans and Sam's corduroy jacket over an old Pete Seeger T-shirt that had been washed so many times the picture was flaking off.

"Is it chilly out?" Ulysses asked, and found his voice was steady.

Laz shrugged. "It's always cold here."

Ulysses glanced out the window. It was one of those sunny, beautiful mornings when the autumn was just beginning to assert itself. He opened the front hall closet and stared into it for a full thirty seconds before grabbing his leather jacket.

"Ready?" he asked Laz.

Laz picked up the paper bag of his clothing from the previous night and tucked it under his arm. He hadn't surrendered the mug yet, and Ulysses wondered if they'd ever see it again if it left with him. "What's wrong with your neck?" Laz asked abruptly.

Ulysses turned and looked at himself in the mirror. There was a red half-moon of tooth marks just visible at the base of his trapezius where his T-shirt was pulled askew. Thanks, Sam. But he didn't exactly object to being marked, either. It was—complicated. And it was nothing he wanted to tell Laz about. He shook his head. "I must have scratched myself or something." He pulled the collar of the jacket up until the spot was no longer visible. "It's fine. Let's go."

They paused in the hall while Ulysses locked the door. Laz produced a pack of cigarettes and a lighter, juggled around the various items he was carrying until he had a cigarette in his mouth, then reversed the process.

Before Ulysses could decide if he wanted to point out the no smoking sign, the door across the hall opened and Vikram emerged.

"Good morning!" He glanced at Laz, then back to Ulysses. "Going to campus? Can I offer you a ride?"

Ulysses blinked and then forced himself to smile. "I'm going to walk Laz home, actually. But . . . would you like to grab lunch later?"

"I should have time."

"I'll stop by your office," Ulysses said.

Outside, walking up the hill toward Capitol Square, Ulysses was pretty sure Laz was staring at him, waiting to ask a question. "When are you starting that job?" he asked before Laz could.

"What job?"

"The one you interviewed for." Ulysses glanced over at him.

Laz shrugged. "Next week, maybe. Week after. I don't know." He scratched the back of his head, squinting in the early sun. "Carla was a little ambiguous about it."

"Did she actually hire you?"

Laz shrugged again. "You know how it is."

Ulysses didn't. "You have to sign some papers, usually," he suggested.

"Ah," Laz said unenthusiastically. "Papers." He took a long drag on his cigarette. "Hey U, are you happy?"

"What?" He had to stop so he could turn fully toward Laz.

Laz's short hair made his eyes look very large, and his face was very young, despite the stubble on his jaw and deep rings under his eyes. "You just . . . all these things. Finished your doctorate, won a Dee, got a big prestigious job, fell in love, for god's sake. Are you happy? Or do you worry that you've . . . you know, you've reached a height you'll never get back to. Like maybe the most exciting part of your life is over and that's it for you."

They were not actually talking about Ulysses's life at all, that much was clear. He reached out and gently patted Laz's shoulder, because Laz seemed to cry out for physical contact but would probably never allow Ulysses to hug him. "If all I ever do for the rest of my life is teach undergrads and have coffee every morning with Sam, that will be just fine. Will I be secretly disappointed that someone will write an encyclopedia entry about me that says, 'His later work never lived up to the promise of his early stuff? I don't know. Success is a complicated thing." He frowned at Laz.

"I don't think I believe you," Laz said, cocking his head to one side. "You'd get bored."

"Right now I could do with some more boredom in my life." He sighed.

At that, Laz raised his eyebrows. "What's up?"

Ulysses started walking again, and Laz followed. "Beyond finishing all my syllabi? There's that portal thing in Vikram and Sita's apartment, the bastard who tried to kidnap Sam, and I'm still tying up loose ends from last spring." He decided not to mention the ongoing friction with Sam. His brother wasn't going to help him look at that objectively.

"Need anything?" Laz offered.

He took a breath to decline and then hesitated. Laz needed something to do. "Actually, yeah. Interested in finding someone for me?"

Laz rolled his eyes, evidently aware of what Ulysses was thinking, but he nodded. "I can do that." He hesitated and added, "I did a little of that kind of thing back in Thailand."

"What, tracking people down?"

"Yeah, sure."

He didn't say more, and Ulysses decided not to ask. Instead, he nodded and fished the obituary out of his inside pocket. "The next of kin listed here. Can you find her?"

Laz snorted and pocketed the clipping. "Anything you want me to ask her?"

"No, just find her for now. I need to figure out if she's amenable to answering questions or not."

Laz looked skeptical of the whole endeavor, but nodded. "I'll come by when I know more."

They parted company at the top of State Street, leaving Ulysses alone with his thoughts as he walked toward campus. The problem was that alone with his thoughts was not necessarily where he wanted to be.

In retrospect, he couldn't believe he hadn't considered that their experience of the bond might be asymmetrical. It was the mistake of a first-year epistemology student. Worse yet, the asymmetry was probably entirely predictable. Sam had been the first of them to feel the bond; Ulysses remembered Sam wandering across Madison to find him, Sam feeling his visions, Sam . . .

He stopped, heedless of the other pedestrians who grumbled and swerved to flow around him. Was he wrong? Sam had once argued that Ulysses being able to find him on Madeline Island constituted the beginning of the bond. But what if it were earlier? The first time Sam had taken him out to meet Harry and Ellen, Ulysses had found the other man walking alone near Bassett Street. At the time, he'd said something like, "It's my job to find people," trying to come off as cool in front of his lover. But now he wondered.

Back in motion, he tried to quickly run the film of their relationship through his mind. How many times had they done that trick? More than either of them was aware, it seemed.

He cracked his knuckles idly. What would it mean if the bond had always been there, or at least almost since the first time they'd made love? Certainly that it wasn't just a matter of finding the right spell to . . . turn it off, and then everything would go back to normal.

What did it mean that the bond was changing? Or had it always been changing, and he was only noticing now because it was moving faster than it had been?

Too many questions he couldn't answer.

He paused next to Memorial Library on the State Street side, looking up at the fourth-floor windows. He hadn't been in Sam's office enough to be quite sure which one was his, although he knew the general area where it must be. It killed him just a little that a day or two before, Sam would have known that he was out there.

He turned away, shaking his head, and noticed a couple of men standing farther down the street looking up at the same windows. One of them had pale skin, light hair, sunglasses, and a dark suit; the other was older, with a long beard and a blue cardigan over a white shirt and dark slacks. They were talking quietly to each other, but fell silent as Ulysses got close. He walked on past, trying not to let on that he'd noticed them.

He could still feel their eyes on him as he crossed Park Street and went up the hill.

S AM HAD BEEN TO two committee meetings already and remembered nothing from either of them. He looked down at his notes and felt like he'd been writing down the details of someone else's fever dream. Then Edith found him wandering vaguely through the storeroom, looking for books with ivory on their spines. She looked concerned as he retreated to his office. The library was trying to tell him something, but he couldn't hear it over the rushing pulse of his regrets.

He'd no sooner sat down in his desk chair but the phone rang. Sam stared at it for a moment, startled, then lifted the receiver.

"Remind me. The DCI agents who visited you, what did they look like?"

It was Ulysses, his tone casual but slightly tense. It reminded Sam of when they'd first met, the way Ulysses had desperately been trying to keep the investigation businesslike, and against all reason he found himself smiling. "A short white woman with reddish brown hair and a taller Black man. Why?"

"When I walked past the library, there were a couple of guys outside watching the windows. Neither of them matched those descriptions."

Sam glanced out his window now but saw no one remarkable, just the flow of students back and forth to different parts of campus. "Neither of them looked like the guy who chased me?"

"No." Ulysses exhaled roughly. "One of them had a long beard and a blue sweater. The other was just your standard square in a suit."

The guy who'd chased him could also be described that way. "I'll keep an eye out," Sam promised. Something about the phone, the remoteness, made it easier to smile as he spoke. This was an investigation, like old times. "I called the hospital. They didn't have records for anyone named Landover or Garcia, but if they were trainees the records would be held by the medical school, not the hospital records department. I can put in a request over there. I'm still waiting to hear back from a friend at the Historical Society, but I'm not optimistic."

"Damn." There was an audible creak, Ulysses leaning back in his chair. "Although. What if they're not dead or retired yet?"

"If they were residents twenty-five years ago, it's possible," Sam said. "You should check the current faculty."

"Sam . . . you don't think they've been continuing the experiments all these years, do you?"

There was despair in Ulysses's voice, and Sam ached for him. "A secret cult of magicians creating god children for nearly twenty years after Julius Sterling's demise?" he said, trying to keep his tone light. "No. Who could do it? You understand the ritual, but you wouldn't be able to do it, and you're the strongest magic user I know. And Ekaterina would know if there were anyone more powerful around, wouldn't she?"

"But would she tell us?" Ulysses grumbled.

Sam had another thought. "What we *might* have is a second generation of god children. If I'm one of the oldest and I'm twenty-five . . . Ulysses, Howard had three kids by the time he was my age."

"Well, that's terrifying," Ulysses said. They were both silent for a moment, and then Ulysses cleared his throat. "Do you ever think of having children?"

"Not since I understood that it would probably require kissing a girl," Sam said, and enjoyed the snorting noise Ulysses made into the phone. "What about you? You dated women before."

Ulysses made a musing noise. "I like kids," he said at last. "But the last woman I was with was not interested, and now . . ."

There was another silence, during which something ungenerous in Sam bristled at the implication that Ulysses would have—with *Livia*. These thoughts were interrupted on Sam's side by a knock at his office door. "Sam," Ulysses started to say, "I—"

"Sorry, I gotta go," Sam said, and hung up.

It was Greenspoon and Robinson. The latter was carrying a briefcase; his companion looked sour, but Sam thought that was possibly just part of who she was.

"Mr. Sterling," she said. "We got your note. Is it all right if we sit down?"

"Of course." Sam gestured to the empty chairs on the far side of his desk. Robinson sat and folded his hands calmly, while Greenspoon fidgeted. "I have a transcription of the first document prepared. I thought I should do that much, at least."

Greenspoon took the paper Sam had carefully typed and stared down at it. "Thank you." After a moment she looked up. "We have more documents."

Sam stared at her for a moment. "I—all right?"

"I know you mentioned a conflict of interest—"

"This document was written by someone who was tracking my father's movements around Madison in late October last year," Sam said, trying to keep his bewilderment in check. "That's a pretty serious conflict of interest."

"Yes." Greenspoon sighed. "The problem is, we haven't been successful in finding anyone else who knows this particular type of shorthand."

Robinson cleared his throat. "There is some urgency in getting these things transcribed—"

"As you say," Greenspoon interjected, "these are documents about living individuals, and if they're in danger, we need to be able to warn them. If they are possible subjects of our investigation, we need to know that too. You've cleared our background checks. If you're willing to continue your work . . ."

Sam wasn't sure what to say to that. "I'm happy to help. May I see the new documents?"

The duplicates were not great quality, but they were clear enough that he could see the swooping shorthand interspersed with Aklo. The glyphs they'd been using to write Sterling appeared again, and others he couldn't immediately translate but felt very worried about.

"When do you need these?" he asked.

The agents glanced at each other. "As soon as you can manage."

Sam nodded. "It'll be . . . I don't know, a week?" He flipped through the sheaf of paper. "This is—it's a lot of stuff."

"Thank you," Greenspoon said, getting to her feet.

Robinson followed suit. "I think you already have our card. Please get in touch with us if you need anything."

Sam was deeply buried in the task, assisted by the department's copy of *Cultic Languages and Scripts*, 5th ed., when Ellen arrived around noon.

"I have decided to claim you for lunch today," she announced as she breezed in. "Unless Ulysses is making the trek over and you have very important and mystical things to accomplish, in which case I claim the right to have lunch in your office, since that woman at the front desk definitely knew I was sneaking food in here and I don't want to walk back past her so soon." She sat down in one of the guest chairs, dropping a collection of tote bags and a long blue raincoat on the other. "Sorry, I'm still jet lagged. I've been up drinking coffee since four a.m. and I don't know how I'm going to make it through my afternoon meetings." She exhaled loudly and then noticed what he was doing. "What's going on?"

Sam shook his head. "The usual."

"Clearly not, Sam." She sat forward. "You look awful. What's going on?" She looked around and abruptly bounded out of her seat, shutting the door to his office. "Is it Ulysses?"

"It's . . ." He shut his eyes. "It's hard to explain."

Ellen snorted. "I've fought demons and plant zombies for you. What could be harder to explain than that?"

Sam considered those things fairly straightforward. Even the words "plant zombies," unfamiliar though they might be in that combination, certainly brought to mind an image. "All right. I just don't want to talk about it right now."

Ellen stared at him for a long moment and then nodded slowly. "What are you working on?" She leaned forward over the desk, then got up and came around, bending over his shoulder.

"It's written in an old Victorian shorthand. Someone needed a transcription."

"And they asked you?" Ellen reached out and pointed, finger hovering just above the page. "They're using that thing. Aklo."

He looked up to see her face crinkled in disgust or horror. "It's a kind of a substitution cipher for cultists." Sam tapped his pencil on the desk. "Or a shibboleth, I guess."

"What's a shibboleth?"

"A linguistic marker that members of a group can use to recognize other members of said group that non-members wouldn't understand, or be able to say.

Like how people who grow up in Wisconsin know how to pronounce the name of the town 'Mazomanie' correctly." He stared down at the document for a long moment. "It's paranoia, really."

"What do you mean?"

"This is a letter about Hugh's movements around Chicago before the cult killed him, and some recommendations for where and when what they refer to as 'the ceremony' might be most effective." He tapped the page. "If you were a little paranoid about your mail being intercepted, you might use a cipher or an obscure old shorthand. But if you were really paranoid that someone would find your letter and replace it with one of their own, or that the people writing to you might come under pressure from authorities to entrap you, you might devise some rules that only you were aware of to indicate whether you were receiving an authentic letter or a compromised one. Hence the Aklo."

Ellen looked at him, her mouth a skeptical line. "This sounds like a Ulysses problem."

Sam shook his head. "Everything is, these days."

Ellen raised an eyebrow and went back around the desk. "Do you know what I did this morning?" she asked conversationally. "For three hours, I debated this question with the other postdocs in my department: If you got one of those four-prong lawn sprinklers that spins around in a circle, and you put it at the bottom of a tank of water, and you made it suck the water in instead of spitting it out, would it go around in the opposite direction?"

"What did you come up with?" Sam asked.

Ellen tossed him a sandwich wrapped in brown deli paper. "When we broke for lunch, the jury was still out. Ernie has gone to the hardware store for supplies."

Sam stacked his papers haphazardly to one side. "Does any work actually get done in your department?"

Ellen turned her seat slightly so she could put her feet up on the other guest chair. "I think you'd like it a lot less if it did," she said thoughtfully. "Anyway, if you can give me literally anything else to think about for a few minutes, I'd be grateful. Which is to say, I'm listening."

Sam opened his mouth to say that he still didn't really want to talk about it—

—and found the entire story spilling out of him. Every sorry little bit of argument, all the useless ideas he'd been turning over in his head for days.

"Wow," she said when he was finished. "That's pretty heavy."

"Yeah." He finally unwrapped the paper and looked at the sandwich. Hummus, tomato, cucumber, and onion. He was not especially hungry, but it smelled good.

"Just to get this straight . . . you guys discovered you had some sort of magical bond back in April? And you didn't talk about it again until now?" She shook her head.

Sam put his forehead on the blotter. "What did we need to talk about? It was fine. Things were fine."

"Mmm." When he looked up, she was making a sympathetic face. "I'm sure you'll figure it out. It's obvious that Ulysses loves you."

Sam exhaled and sat up. "I don't have any doubts there. It's everything else."

Ellen nodded, tucking a stray lock of hair behind her ear. "You know," she said conversationally, "there's quite a nice conference room at the top of Van Vleck. If you can get him over to this side of campus, I can accidentally lock you guys in there for forty-five minutes. I bet that would be long enough for you to figure this out."

Sam found that he was smiling, despite himself. "I don't know if we're quite ready for that," he said. "But thanks."

"Let me know," Ellen said. She sounded glib, but he didn't miss the concern on her face when she thought he wasn't looking.

They talked about other things. Ellen finished her sandwich and carefully folded the paper; Sam picked at his. "I didn't ask before, but where did all those papers come from?" she said finally.

"The DCI pulled them out of Sterling Hall." Sam looked at the remains of his sandwich fretfully. "Howard is mentioned in some of the documents I already transcribed."

Ellen's eyes went wide. "I thought you were just being paranoid." Then she covered her mouth with one hand. "I heard two guys talking about trying to get some files back from the Army Math offices at Sterling Hall yesterday! They were all cagey about it, too."

Sam sighed. "I mean, from what you said before, half the math department was probably in and out of Army Math at one point or another. And I'm willing to bet a bunch of you are awkward. No offense."

There was a long silence. Ellen was looking up at the ceiling, a slight frown on her face. "I have a plan to figure out if they're part of your cult or not," she announced, getting to her feet. "Don't worry."

"Um," Sam said.

Chapter 18

ON SATURDAY, ULYSSES SLEPT in. It wasn't as though he had that much of a choice in the matter; his body, fed up from a full week of bad sleep, gave up on him around two in the morning and just switched his brain off. The next thing he knew, it was nine thirty, and he was groggy but conscious again.

Sam wasn't around. Ulysses stumbled into the kitchen and put the percolator on. He'd left the copy of *Magical Bonds: A Historical Overview* Dr. Lesko had lent him on the kitchen table, and now he sat down and tried to figure out where he'd left off. It was not an exciting book. He'd read parts of it before and found it tedious, and now he had to go back and make sure he hadn't overlooked something important in his rush to prove to himself and Sam that nothing was wrong. *How to Improve Your Mental Shielding*, the other book Dr. Lesko had lent him, was also crushingly dull, and the typeface had given him a headache. It did have the twin virtues of being incredibly short and fairly useful; he'd been able to execute the basics relatively quickly.

Not that it had proven to be a great or popular option thus far.

When the percolator boiled, he took his coffee back into the living room and sprawled across the sofa with the book. Sunlight spilled through the windows. It was a beautiful day outside, and he proposed to spend it lying on the sofa reading about rituals for connection among the Rus in the ninth and tenth century.

He missed Sam. They should be doing something together, renting a boat to row to Governor's Island, or going to an apple orchard, or just sitting together up on the roof talking while he pretended to do research.

The previous evening had been depressingly like living with Virgil and Mariah just before she went back to the continent for keeps. They'd both come home late. When they spoke to each other, Sam's voice was normal, and he seemed to forget he was hurt long enough to engage with Ulysses, like he had on the phone. But when they fell silent, it was like Ulysses was having his eyes clawed out. A chasm had opened between them that he couldn't find a way to reach across. Eventually he'd retreated to his office to read, and Sam had spent an hour or two noodling around on his guitar in the living room and then gone to bed.

Sam's key scraping in the front door's lock brought Uclysses out of his reverie. The other man, dressed in his running clothes, looked sweaty and tired, but his skin was luminous from the exertion. When he straightened up from untying his shoes, his gaze skittered over Ulysses and he looked . . . resigned? Trepidatious?

It was terrible, and Ulysses was abruptly exhausted. "It's after ten," he said quietly. "Where did you go?"

Sam looked slightly perplexed. "Around the lake."

Ulysses put his book down and got to his feet. "Which lake?"

"Mendota." Sam was looking at him, head cocked to one side, like he was trying to figure something out.

Something about his gaze made Ulysses's heart race unpleasantly, but then Sam had always seen through him when it was important. "It's got to be thirty miles around that lake," he said, frowning. "What time did you leave?"

"Around six."

"You ran for four and a half hours?" He stuck his hands in his jeans pockets, looking down at his bare feet. Absurdly, he had a dark bruise on the top of one of them that he couldn't account for. It was livid blue against his pale skin. Sam's feet were sock-clad, probably sweaty and gross. He shuffled slightly closer to Ulysses as the two of them stood there.

"I just kept turning left."

Ulysses said, "Why?" Sam looked confused, and he sighed. "Sam, just tell me if I've messed things up so badly that you don't want to be here anymore—"

Sam shook his head. "It's not that." He opened his mouth to say something more, and then stopped. Ulysses waited.

After a moment's further consideration, and with no additional explanation, Sam closed the distance between them and kissed him.

Ulysses had kissed Sam since he'd figured out the rudiments of the mental shielding thing—actually, Ulysses generally tried to kiss Sam as much as possible. He liked doing it, and he thought that Sam needed to be reassured that he was human and loved, and if someone as good-looking as Sam was willing to kiss him, Ulysses thought he ought to take advantage of that fact. It was different, now that he'd managed to turn the volume down on the bond. Not *bad*.

He hadn't fallen in love with Sam because he was a god, or because kissing him was different from kissing anyone else, but because he was Sam, and he was absurd and bewildering and beautiful and willing to show Ulysses all of his feelings even when he was terrified. But the other stuff, Sam couldn't put that away any more than he could stop being that person. Which was probably the worst part of this, that in order to protect himself, Ulysses had made Sam feel like he had to try.

Ulysses missed the bond too. Not the overwhelming, all-seeing rush of it, but the quiet sense of knowledge and connection. But they couldn't have that anymore.

Ulysses pulled back, pressed his index finger to Sam's lips. "Sam."

"Mmm?" Sam opened his eyes. They were very green, and they looked slightly worried as they traversed Ulysses's face.

Sam's body was angular, bony where they pressed together. Sam was right; having to abandon this would be awful. He was frightened for good reasons. Ulysses was frightened too. "I'm sorry," he managed.

Sam hugged him.

For a moment, Ulysses had a dizzying sense of being underwater, as though he'd lost all sense of which way was up. He could feel the pressure of Dionysus—of Sam—against his shields, like a wave poised to break over his head. The worst part was that he wanted it. He would drown, and happily. *Come death and welcome.*

It wasn't much of a strategy.

He held fast, and after a moment the feeling receded. Ulysses took a deep breath, and exhaled. "We need to find a different solution to this," he muttered.

Sam gently kissed his forehead. "Yes."

Ulysses made himself tip his head back and meet Sam's eyes. "You're more patient than I deserve."

Sam raised an eyebrow. "Probably, yes. But I'm not sure 'deserve' has anything to do with it."

Ulysses rested his forehead against Sam's chest. Sam smelled of fresh sweat, slightly salty, and of green growing things. It should have been gross, but it wasn't. He placed a hand on Sam's hip, feeling the flex and play of muscles as Sam shifted from foot to foot, and weighed his next question, because he'd gotten this wrong so many times already. "What do you want?" he asked after a long moment.

Silence. When he raised his eyes, Sam was gazing down at him, considering. "In the bond?" he asked. At Ulysses's nod, he shrugged. "I want things to be like they were before the bond went haywire."

"Sam, I don't know why it happened," Ulysses said. "What happens if I can't fix it?"

"Then I want to be here with you," Sam said. He said it like it was simple, and maybe it was for him. Ulysses put his free hand on the side of Sam's face, ran a thumb along his cheekbone.

"I don't know what to do," he murmured. The difficulty was that he didn't have any other ways to protect himself except to stop touching Sam altogether, and that didn't seem realistic when Sam kept looking at him with a halfway feral mien, like he was going to eat Ulysses alive.

"I trust you," Sam said, his mouth practically on Ulysses's already.

Ulysses was not certain that demonstrated good judgement on Sam's part, and he was even less certain that there was going to be a great way to solve the problem, but then Sam was kissing him.

His back hit the wall hard when Sam pushed him into it, and then there was a jumble of sensations: Sam's mouth on his; Sam's hands on his sides, pushing up his shirt; Sam biting his shoulder. Ulysses could practically taste the other man's desire on his tongue. Sam pulled back enough to strip Ulysses's shirt off over his head, and then he was mouthing at Ulysses's neck.

"Sam," Ulysses managed. "How can you . . . how can you just . . ."

Sam's hands were between them, unbuckling his belt. "What?" he murmured, sliding to his knees.

Ulysses tried very hard to marshal his thoughts. "You just believe I can—"

A knock on the door cut him off.

Sam groaned and sat back on his heels. Ulysses looked down at him, bewildered by how pretty he was, how perfect. "The timing is astonishing," Sam muttered, getting up. Their visitor knocked again.

Sam brushed his lips against Ulysses's and stepped away. Ulysses was abruptly dropped back into cold reality with as much ceremony as if he'd been thrown into the lake.

He heard Sam speaking to someone, and before he could put any two thoughts together, Laz was pushing his way into the apartment. He looked around until his eyes lit on Ulysses.

Ulysses, who was still braced against the wall as though he couldn't stand up on his own, shirtless; he hadn't even gotten his belt done up again. Ulysses crossed his arms in front of his chest and glared at his brother.

"What are you doing here?" he managed after a moment, surprised that his voice sounded normal and steady.

Laz's gaze darted around to Sam, who was between him and the way out. Ulysses could see the exact moment Laz decided he was not going to ask questions, because his shoulders went back, and he suddenly stood an inch taller than before, body tense. Captain Lenkov, reporting for duty.

"I told you I'd come by when I found Julie Stricker," Laz said. He was looking at an unoccupied spot in the middle of the room, and Ulysses took advantage of this to fix his pants and cast about for his shirt.

"How did you find her?" he asked. The shirt had made it to the sofa. He crossed the distance and snatched it up.

"I went to her father's funeral and then followed her home." Laz finally made eye contact and looked confused at Ulysses's expression. "What?" He turned around and looked at Sam, who shrugged minutely.

Ulysses pulled the shirt over his head. "It's clever, I'll give you that. She didn't notice anything?"

"I don't think so," Laz said. He fidgeted, touching the wooden beads he wore around his neck with one hand, then caught himself. "I can take you to her if you'd like."

Ulysses nodded slowly.

"What are you thinking?" Sam asked.

"Just remembering the time we had getting any information out of Barth," Ulysses said. "Hopefully, his daughter is more cooperative."

"After being raised by Barth?" Sam lounged against the wall. "Her father was at least fairly immobilized by age and disability."

Ulysses cracked his knuckles, left hand first this time. "Julius didn't see fit to bring Howard in on what he was doing."

"Howard was aware. So perhaps it wasn't for lack of trying."

They stared at each other, something tense hanging in the air between them. "It's a fair point. We'll be careful."

Sam didn't quite wince, but he made an unhappy face. "What are you suggesting?"

Ulysses took a deep breath. "Stay here, take a shower, get some rest. Talk to Sita if you get a chance. Laz and I will go over to Stricker's and see if she can be persuaded to give us access to her father's papers." He leaned past Laz to grab his coffee cup off the end table and drained the remainder in one go.

S AM MADE HIMSELF SCRAMBLED eggs and toast and sat at the kitchen table with *Slaughterhouse-Five* propped open against his mug. Then he showered, forcing himself to keep his mind on what he'd been reading and not spiral out about Ulysses, the bond, the cult, the—

When he was clean and dressed, he sat down on the sofa and dug the Army Math documents out of his satchel. The one he'd been transcribing was a memo from early October 1969: *Dionysus S. Sterling was reportedly seen leaving the Lenkov compound early on the morning of October 25th wearing borrowed clothing. Ekaterina Lenkov is unlikely to rouse herself to intervention; Virgil Lenkov is no*

threat to our plans. The grandson, Ulysses Lenkov, is
an unknown. Clever but focused primarily on ghosts
rather than the living. Skilled but less powerful than
his grandmother. He could be useful to keep Sterling
alive until the god arrives.

Someone must have clocked Sam the first night they'd slept together.

Sam remembered the first time Ulysses had kissed him, and then all the other times between then and now. Vonnegut had written about an alien book consisting of feelings and ideas that, when all were read simultaneously, created a full picture of a life. Sam tried to hold even a year's worth of kisses in his mind at once and couldn't.

A year ago, knowing that some malevolent group was keeping tabs on his movements would have shamed him to the point of paranoia. Now, he was a little surprised to find that he didn't care that they knew about his relationship, except insofar as they were dangerous and he wanted to protect Ulysses.

A year gone. Not so much time, and yet he had been changed.

There was another knock on the door. He looked at it suspiciously, but there was no particular menace to the sound. When he got up and opened the door, it wasn't Vikram as he'd half expected, but Mariah, in a wide-brimmed blue hat, carrying a potted plant and a bottle of wine.

"Ah, Samuel," she said. "How delightful to see you." She handed him the plant, and he stepped back automatically to admit her.

"Ulysses isn't here," he said. "He and Laz have gone out—"

In the absence of a hall table, she handed him the wine bottle too and spent a moment taking her hat off. "That's all right. I'd hoped I'd run into you." She had a bright smile and a French accent.

"Would you like something to drink?" he offered automatically. "Coffee, or tea? Or—"

They both glanced at the bottle of wine and she laughed. "Coffee is fine, thank you."

She followed him into the kitchen and stood in the doorway, watching him empty the grounds out of the percolator and refill it. "Every time I come to America, I'm beset by coffee on every side," she remarked, shaking her head.

"But France is so close to Italy," Sam pointed out.

"Close enough to appreciate good coffee without being able to replicate it ourselves," she said. "It's the same thing with tea. Has la belle dame, my mother-in-law, ever made you tea?"

Sam shook his head.

"Real Russian tea is a delight, but difficult to produce here." She settled into a chair. Sam turned to the cabinet and sorted through the cups. Francie would certainly have—well, she would have told the housekeeper to put out the best china. But Sam and Ulysses didn't own good china, so Sam selected the best mugs and hoped that Mariah was too genteel to make any arch observations about them.

When the coffee was brewed and poured, and he'd offered cream and sugar, he sat down in the chair across from her. "I'm not quite sure why you're here," he admitted, and then closed his mouth and waited.

"I wanted to meet you, darling," she said, turning the mug in her hands. "You are important to Ulysses. I'd like to get to talk to you properly. So tell me about yourself."

Sam took a breath. "I'm a librarian at—"

"No, darling. I don't want to know what you *do*." Mariah sipped her coffee. "I want to know who you *are*, independent of commerce."

He nodded. "I'm Sam. And . . . I like the theater . . . and I'm not sure a recitation of my hobbies is going to answer your question any better than a recitation of my curriculum vita."

"I see." Mariah looked down into her coffee. "Let me tell you a story."

She told him how she'd met Virgil. She had been a twenty-two-year-old art student at the Sorbonne when the newly arrived Virgil caught her eye. He was nineteen and spoke a rather formal, halting French, but when he smiled he'd been so vital and intense, how could she look away?

"He used to come out to where I was practicing plein air painting along the Seine and watch what I was doing." Mariah smiled to herself. "He was an economics student, but so interested in art. I started taking him to galleries and shows with me."

Sam murmured something congenial. It was hard to picture the Virgil Sam knew pursuing her. But then, he didn't think he'd even seen them interact.

"We married in 1938, when the war still seemed far away." She shook her head at the memory. "By the time of Celeste's birth at the end of 1939, the situation was different. France was at war."

Ekaterina and Mariah's parents had agreed that the best thing for everyone was to evacuate, and they had moved the entire group to England.

"From there, while Virgil finished his degree, Ekaterina managed to find the magic department at the University of Wisconsin, and she's been here ever since." She smiled. "Tell me about your history."

Sam didn't really want to offer the story of how he and Ulysses had met in exchange. He was pretty sure she'd already heard it from Ulysses, or a version of it Sam didn't want to contradict. Instead, he said, "My parents also met around that time." She raised her eyebrows, inviting him to continue. "My mother was studying at Radcliffe, and my father was a student at Harvard. They took a class on mathematical logic and set theory together. They spent the entire semester arguing, then got married the following summer."

"How delightful," Mariah exclaimed. "What was your mother studying?"

"Philosophy." Sam glanced to his right, as though he could see through the refrigerator and the wall behind it. "I have some of her books, actually."

Mariah smiled. "Are they still together?"

"No. My mother died when I was born."

She nodded, keeping her eyes on his.

Sam slipped his coffee. "The thing is, Howard—my father—never talked about any of this when I was growing up. Last year, Ulysses had to steal—" He hesitated, but she just laughed. "He got ahold of some letters they had exchanged during their courtship. Everything I just told you, he found in there and showed to me." He gave her a crooked smile.

"There, you see? Now you have told me about yourself." She drank the last of the coffee and set her cup down. "You are a romantic, I think. A bit nostalgic. But that is all right, because Ulysses is also a romantic." She cocked her head to the side. "You are also very loyal to your loved ones."

Sam frowned. "How do you take that from my story?"

"You chose to tell me a story in which my son was lovely, rather than the story of how you met, in which he was a bit of a dick."

Sam laughed.

"Will you come and visit me in Paris?" she asked, taking one of his hands. "Force my son to travel. I think it will be good for him."

"I'll see what I can do," Sam said.

"Thank you." Mariah got to her feet and gestured to the plant. "It needs a lot of sunlight but not much water. After it blooms, cut it back a bit. Cassandra can help if you have any questions." She opened her purse and withdrew a small satin bag. It was dark blue and quilted, closed with a drawstring at one end. "Would you give this to Ulysses when he gets home?"

"Yes, of course."

He walked her to the door and watched her put her hat back on, carefully adjusting it for dramatic effect. "You're not what I expected, Samuel," she said after a moment. "But I'm glad he met you."

Then she was gone.

Chapter 19

J ULIE STRICKER LIVED ON the far west side, in an area where Ulysses's near-encyclopedic knowledge of the city ran out and he was reduced to following turn-by-turn directions Laz provided, letting the bike roll slowly along the streets until Laz patted his leg and indicated that they'd arrived.

"It's the Tudor-style one," Laz said, leaning forward to speak quietly into Ulysses's ear. Ulysses checked their speed even further and idled past, trying to get a look at it. It didn't look like anyone evil lived there. It didn't feel especially distinct from the rest of the city either. They were west of the Arb, east of Midvale, winding past a handful of houses that had survived the decades since the 1930s more or less intact among the more recent constructions.

Ulysses parked around the corner under a tree. Laz slid off and stretched, rubbing his back.

"Hey," he said, when Ulysses didn't immediately follow. "Are you—that is, maybe it's none of my business, but . . . you seem . . ." He rubbed the back of his neck.

"I'm fine," Ulysses said, running a hand over his hair fruitlessly.

"Are you?" Laz squinted at him. The younger man didn't have any particular intuitive powers, as far as Ulysses was aware, but he looked concerned. Ulysses sighed.

"Things are weird right now," he said. Laz stayed silent, staring at him, and he added, "I'll be all right."

"The thing is, you don't look all right," Laz said. "You look kinda drugged out, honestly. And I know that's not it, because I know you, but I'd be lying if I said I'm not worried."

Ulysses leaned forward and looked at his face in the bike's side mirror. He saw dark purple circles under red-ringed eyes. His skin looked unusually pale and slightly sweaty, and his hair was going in all directions. "Terrific." He looked back at Laz, who was still eyeing him. "Look. Sam and I have this magic bond. At first everything was fine, and then stuff got weird, and now we're trying to figure out how to manage it." He took a deep breath, hoping Laz would be happy without too many details. The whole situation felt like a missing tooth, not painful but annoying and disconcerting.

Laz cleared his throat. "That's . . . because of Sam being Dionysus?"

"Yeah, probably."

"Why are you staying, then?" Laz looked away. "I know Sam's hot, but . . ."

Ulysses stared at him blankly, more confused than offended by the question. "Why would I leave?"

Laz's expression suggested he was being especially incomprehensible. Finally, not knowing what else to do, Ulysses set the kickstand and slid off the bike. "Do me a favor, okay? Spend a little time getting to know him before you go asking questions like that."

He set off up the street before Laz could put together a response.

The house was done in a half-timber style, a tradition that must have arrived in the state along with all the German immigrants in the nineteenth century. Ulysses stood at the end of the front walk looking at the building for a moment. It was very tidy, with window boxes full of mums on either side of the door and rose bushes that had already been cut back and covered for the fall.

Arriving at the door of someone who had just lost her father a week earlier to demand access to his papers was probably not the sort of thing good people did. And how pathetic was it that the best lead for information on the cult might be in the effects of a cantankerous ninety-year-old who had been out of the game for years. But that was where they were in the investigation: driven by desperation and fear. It was really a great feeling, as good as having to explain to his brother why he didn't want to dump his boyfriend.

Laz trailed him up the front walk. Ulysses looked at their reflections in the glass of the door while waiting for someone to answer the doorbell.

"We're disreputable bastards, aren't we," he muttered.

Laz laughed. "I blame you. I used to be entirely reputable. You're a bad influence."

"Me?" He pulled a hurt face. "I'm an upstanding member of the community. I have a job and everything."

Laz snorted. "I think that's just some last ditch attempt at rehabilitation."

The door opened and a woman in her mid-fifties looked out at them. She had short, permed blond hair and wore a dark jumper dress over a dark blouse.

"Mrs. Stricker?" Ulysses asked, sobering.

She nodded. "May I help you?"

"My name is—" He hesitated an instant; her father had known Ekaterina, and the Lenkovs had a certain notoriety that he was not anxious to highlight. "My name is Alexis Sterling. I'm at the UW. I'm sorry for your recent loss." He paused awkwardly while she bowed her head in acknowledgement. "I know the timing is very poor, but I'd like to talk to you about your father's papers, if that's possible."

She glanced over at Laz. "And you are?"

"Karl. I'm Karl. Nice to meet you." Laz managed to hold out a hand and look endearingly dorky.

Julie Stricker gave them both a tight smile and opened the screen door. "Please, come in."

She didn't take them farther into the house than the front room, which was sun-dappled. The thick carpet was the sort of bright white color that only happened when no one actually walked on it, and the furniture was so scrupulously clean that Ulysses felt guilty sitting down. There had been a parlor in Sam's childhood home that neither he nor his siblings were permitted in; this had a similar air, although the house was quiet, with no sound of children in it.

"So," Mrs. Stricker said, lighting a cigarette, "tell me about your research. You're a medical student?"

Laz glanced sideways at him and didn't say anything.

"I'm a historian, actually," Ulysses said. "I'm really interested in the evolution of obstetric practices during the early to mid-twentieth century as a result of changing feminist beliefs about childbirth." He was suddenly glad he'd spent all summer listening to Celeste's rants on the topic, although he could never tell her.

"And your interest leads to my father because . . . ?"

"He was running a very busy practice in the '40s and early '50s," Ulysses said. "I hoped you might have some of his treatment notes and potentially his reference materials."

"All of his medical records are held at the hospital archives," she said, taking a drag on her cigarette.

"Yes, but he was also involved in cross-departmental research. The hospital doesn't have those records, but you might."

"Mmm." Stricker was holding her cigarette in a way that obscured her mouth, so he couldn't make out her expression. "I do have some of his notebooks from that period." She fell silent, studying him. "You're going to have to be specific. I can't allow you to just go digging through these things."

"Uh—" Ulysses had a sudden cold feeling, but he was in too deep to stop. "I know he collaborated with a biologist named Julius Sterling who was interested in fertility."

"Julius Sterling," she repeated, pressing her lips together. "No relation, I suppose?"

"Afraid not." Ulysses tried to look harmless. "I'm not related to the Sterling Hall Sterlings either."

"Mm." She took a drag off the cigarette, then got up and opened the window a crack. "I don't have those, I'm afraid."

"No?"

She shook her head, still looking out the window. "Anything related to their collaboration would be stored with Sterling's papers, I believe." He watched her reflection smile brittlely at the window. "Or my father destroyed them. He destroyed a number of things in his final days, I'm told."

It sounded like she was telling the truth, but Ulysses didn't quite believe it. Quite aside from his own feelings about burning information, the Barth he and Sam had met had seemed to be suffering from neither guilt nor shame. He'd recognized Ulysses as a Lenkov and Sam as—well, Dionysus. He could have confessed then instead of flinging insults, but he didn't. And he didn't seem overly hung up on his legacy. Why else did people burn things? "Are you sure?" he asked uselessly. "There's no notebooks, no diaries, no—"

"I'm afraid not."

The Barth had been a dried up, bitter old man, and Ulysses could suddenly believe that he'd burned his notebooks out of spite. He'd had something he didn't want other people to have. That was it.

She didn't turn back to them. "I think you and your friend had better go."

He got to his feet. "Did you ever hear him mention anyone he was close to that I could check with?" he persisted. "Maybe a former resident. Dr. Landover's name has come up a few times, or Dr. Garcia?"

Julie Stricker did turn back then and looked carefully into his face. "Where did they come up, those names?"

"Just talking to people Dr. Barth knew during his career." Ulysses shrugged.

"Interesting." She shook her head. "I'm sorry to disappoint, Mr. Sterling. Or is it Doctor?"

"Mister," Ulysses said slowly.

She nodded and led them back to the front door. "I have to go make a call," she said. "I'm sorry I don't have longer to chat. How lovely to have met you both." She paused, just before turning, and added as an afterthought, "He did talk about a Dr. Ranganathan at times." She pursed her lips. "I don't know if that's any help. He was babbling about that toward the end."

Ulysses thanked her.

When they were alone, Laz looked askance at him. "That was definitely worth the trip," he muttered.

Ulysses shushed him and dragged him back around the corner to the bike.

"Do you think she's telling the truth?" Laz asked.

Ulysses shook his head. "I don't trust her."

"She sure saw through that pseudonym," Laz said, leaning against the motorcycle. "Alexis Sterling. Really?" He shook his head.

"I couldn't say Lenkov!" Ulysses said.

"You couldn't say something nondescript like Green?"

"Do I look like a Green?"

"You look like a mess." Laz exhaled loudly and stepped aside. "What now, o fearless leader? Want to try and find that person she mentioned, just in case it wasn't a red herring?"

Ulysses threw a leg over the bike. "Yes. We're going to do exactly that."

⇝⇝⇝ ⇜⇜⇜

W HEN SAM HAD MOSTLY recovered from Mariah's visit, he went across the hall and knocked on Vikram and Sita's door.

Sita answered. "Sam." Her expression wasn't exactly the happiest he'd ever seen, but she didn't look annoyed by his appearance either. "Vik has gone out."

"That's okay," he said. "I actually came by to talk to you."

She stepped back, apparently unsurprised. "Is it my turn?" At his look, she added, "Ulysses went by Vik's

263

office yesterday and quizzed him on his entire life from birth. He didn't tell you?"

"That sounds about right," he said. "He had to go do something, otherwise he'd be here himself."

"You work with him?" At his nod, she said, "I guess I shouldn't be surprised. You burst in here to fight that . . . thing . . . right alongside him." She looked at him. "You look hungry. Come in the kitchen, I was just making rotis."

He followed her. The kitchen smelled delicious, and there was a pile of rotis already made and cooling under a towel. "Help yourself." She gestured toward the far end of the counter. "There's butter if you want, or I have some chutney." There was a little pop as she turned on the burner under a large cast-iron pan.

"That sounds delicious."

"I meant to thank you," she said, picking up her rolling pin and attacking a new lump of dough. "For agreeing to run with Vik. He's very happy to have someone to talk about running with who isn't me."

Sam mumbled around a mouthful of roti. "We mostly don't talk about running," he admitted.

"Still." She held a hand out over the pan to judge how hot it was and then dropped the roti in. "I'm guessing Ulysses is also grateful."

Sam nodded. "He tries, but it's not really his thing."

She smiled to herself. "Vik wants to go do that Boston Marathon again in the spring. If you're not careful, he'll drag you along with him."

He watched Sita carefully flip the roti with her fingers. She had a practiced way of grabbing the hot dough for just long enough, then snatching her hand away. "That would be fine." He tried to remember how far a marathon was. What was distance between Marathon and Athens? Twenty-five miles? No, the race was more than that. He'd spectated at the damn thing five years ago. At the time, it had seemed like a lot of nonsense. "How have things been since that night?"

She shook her head, but her expression didn't change. "Fine, mostly. I mean, it's been quiet. I think we're both waiting to see if the other shoe will drop." She took a deep breath. "I've been jumpy. Something's—it's not quite right, you know?"

Sam nodded. "Have you seen any of those spiders around?"

"No." Sita stared down at the surface of the roti, watching it bubble and puff in the pan. "They seem to have gone, thank goodness."

"Had you seen them around before that night?"

She turned her head, fixed him with a stare that made him feel very silly. "If I'd seen spiders of that size before, we would have called an exterminator. Or moved out." Apparently satisfied, she pulled the roti out of the pan and tossed it onto a plate, then dropped in another piece of dough. It sizzled. "Any other questions?"

"Tell me about your namesake." He took another bite of the roti.

"My mother?" Her innocent, curious expression caught him off guard before it crumpled into laughter. "What do you know about Hinduism?" Seeing his confusion, she shook her head. "The word is kind of a catch-all. When the British colonized the region, they decided that all the traditions were variants of each other . . . denominations, I guess you'd call them." She waved a hand. "Sita appears in the tradition that follows Vishnu as their primary deity. She's his consort; sometimes as an avatar of the goddess Lakshmi, sometimes as a goddess in her own right. She appears in an epic poem called the *Ramayana* in which she is found in a furrow in the earth, marries Rama, goes into exile with him, is kidnapped and rescued, and finally is asked to prove her purity by walking through fire." She shrugged, flipping the roti in the pan. "It's a good read, if you like that kind of thing. At any rate, my maternal grandmother was a follower of Vishnu who named her daughter Sita, and then my father named me in her honor."

Sam considered this in silence while she flipped the roti. "Do you ever feel like you just know things about people?"

She gave him an odd, guarded look. "What do you mean?"

"You meet someone for the first time and you . . . know things about them you can't explain."

Sita said, "That sounds a little mystical for me," and forced a smile that didn't reach her eyes. "Are you going

266

to tell me about my rising sign next, or what phase of the moon I was born under?"

"Sorry," Sam said. He watched her flip the current roti out of the pan and drop the next one in. "Let me ask you this, then. How much did your father talk about your mother when you were growing up?"

"That's quite a change of topic." Sita frowned at the pan. "Why?"

He shrugged and picked up another roti from the pile. "My mother also died when I was born, and when my father remarried, my stepmother forbade all mention of her. It was weird to grow up feeling like I didn't have a mother."

Sita nodded. "My father liked to talk about her. Maybe that's why he didn't start dating again until I was nearly an adult." She flipped the roti, not looking at him. "It felt like a lot to live up to. He remembered her as a saint, and I was a real human person with real human problems he had to deal with."

"Did he ever talk to you about how she died?"

"Not more specifically than telling me that she died during childbirth." Sita pulled the fresh roti from the pan, brushed it with ghee, and dropped it on the pile. "I assume she died of postpartum hemorrhage. Maybe undiagnosed preeclampsia."

"Mm." Sam thought about blood magic and shivered. "I didn't learn until I was an adult that my mother was sacrificed."

Sita turned, rolling pin in hand. "You mean they had to choose which of you to save, and they chose you?" She hesitated, clearly trying to choose her words carefully. "That's not actually how it works in the delivery room."

"No, that's not what I mean." He took a deep breath. "Around the time I was born, there was a . . . a group of conspirators at Wisconsin General engaged in a secret, unethical experiment to create children who could be consecrated to and later inhabited by gods in some sort of power exchange."

Sita stared at him. "And your mother . . ."

"Was probably sacrificed as part of their rituals." He looked away. Thinking of his mother's death had never bothered him especially; he'd never met her, had no memory to mourn. But laying the situation out so starkly felt indelicate. Sita, meanwhile, was frowning more and more as she considered this.

"Your implication is that my mother . . . died in a similar situation?"

"That's my guess." He sighed. "Well, Ulysses's and mine. We've been looking into this for a while." He ate the last of the roti and dusted the flour from his fingertips. "Questions?"

Sita rubbed the rolling pin, frowning at a little knot in the wood. "I have so many."

Before she could ask any of them, there was a ruckus in the hall, the sound of two people shouting in Russian, and a knock on the door.

Sita glanced at him.

"It's all right. They're debating . . . Bruce Springsteen, I think." She wrinkled her nose, lips turning up at the edges, and Sam laughed. "Whenever you've had a chance to think it all over, we're happy to talk. Either of us. Ulysses is actually a world expert in the topic of gods."

"Only in Madison." She turned off the burner and led him back to the apartment door.

"Sam!" Ulysses exclaimed from the hallway. "There you are. I need your help. Sita, we're having a séance tonight. Would you tell Vikram?"

"We're what?" Sam said.

Sita stepped aside to let him out. "Vikram should be back in a few hours. Is there anything we can bring?"

"Wine," Laz said promptly. He was carrying a large paper bag that smelled of beeswax and herbs.

Ulysses snorted. "You don't need wine at a séance."

"Yeah, but it's nice to have."

Sam followed Ulysses and Laz back into their apartment. "Mariah was here this morning," he announced when there was a break in the conversation.

Both men swung around to look at him. Laz smirked; Ulysses raised an eyebrow. "What did she want?"

"To talk." He pulled the blue bag out of his pocket. "She wanted me to give you this."

Ulysses took the bag and stared hard at it. After a moment, he opened it, looked in, and pulled the drawstring shut again. "If you looked inside here, I'm really sorry."

"I didn't. What is it?"

269

Ulysses cut his eyes over to Laz and said, "She's just trying to be helpful. Or drive me crazy. One of the two." He stuck the bag in his pocket. "We can talk about it later. Come on, we have a séance to prepare for."

Chapter 20

ULYSSES AND LAZ PREPARED the apartment for the séance, cleaning, setting out candles, burning dried plumeless thistle and bits of myrrh in a little metal dish on the dining room table. Most of it felt like received Victorian spiritualism to Ulysses, but it was what Babushka had done.

Sam wrinkled his nose at the smell. "What exactly are you trying to accomplish? You talk to ghosts all the time."

"It's different when you're summoning them." Ulysses held a glass of water over the rising smoke. Soot began to gather on its base. "If you call a spirit, you have to make sure you get the right one."

Sam watched curiously for a while, then wandered off to the kitchen. Ulysses found him there later, washing dishes over the sink while various pots bubbled on the stove. He studied the long line of the other man's back, skinny in a soft white T-shirt. Sam looked less argumentative than at any point in the last week, which was good. Ulysses took a dish towel from the counter and stepped up next to him, picked up a pan that wouldn't fit in the drainer.

"Are you ritually purified or something now?" Sam asked, glancing sideways at him.

"No," Ulysses said. "I just took a shower so I could be fit to receive company." Up close, Ulysses could feel the tension radiating off him. "How is it for you?" he asked. He set the pan down and grabbed blindly for the next thing Sam had finished washing, a coffee mug.

"I don't know," Sam said, giving him a sidelong glance. "I feel like a junkie, to be honest. I spent twenty-four years of my life without this—I don't even know what to call it, the extra sense, the magic. And now, after six months . . ." He sighed. "This can't be easy for you."

Ulysses shrugged. "When you're not touching me, I feel like an unresolved chord."

Sam made a muffled, frustrated noise. "How am I supposed to go about my day and act *normal* when you say things like that?"

"How am I, feeling like that?" Ulysses set the mug down and took up the next one. "I know exactly what you mean. But if I let go, the bond would drown out everything else in my brain."

Sam nodded. "And this has gotten worse?"

"Yeah." He stared at the mug. It was a fat handmade thing Sam must have picked up at some craft fair along the line, glazed in brown at the bottom and blue at the top. "A lot worse."

"Well," Sam began, and then fell silent for a while. "I'm a lot more concerned than I was before."

Ulysses elbowed him gently, closing his eyes as his arm brushed Sam's. "This isn't forever."

Sam shut the water off and turned fully toward him. "At this rate, how much time do we have before the bond becomes entirely unmanageable?"

Ulysses put the mug down, looping the end of the towel around his hand. "I don't know. It's not like a bomb with a timer on it. I would have to have an idea of what's causing this and what the end state will be to try and make a prediction." He sighed. "We still have another week before classes start. That's long enough to figure it out."

"I hope so." Sam swayed a hair closer, his pale eyes fixed on Ulysses's. "Ellen gave me a lecture about how to divide up household chores with you in an egalitarian way," he added, one edge of his mouth quirking up.

"This is definitely not quite what I expected, moving in with you," Ulysses admitted. "But it hasn't been all bad, has it?"

Sam leaned forward and kissed him. Ulysses had a few seconds of heart-wrenching joy and the sense of something pressing *hard* against his shields, and then Sam pulled back, mumbling, "Sorry."

"Sam." He had one hand pressed against Ulysses's chest. Ulysses could feel the heat of his skin leaking through the fabric. Ulysses reached up and covered

Sam's long fingers with his own. "Don't. It's all right,
I—"

Behind him, the door swung open and Laz said,
"Your friends are here. Stop doing . . . whatever that is."
Ulysses turned to see Laz eyeing them skeptically. Then,
to Sam, he said, "What are you cooking?"

His tone wasn't perfect, but Sam seemed willing to
accept the overture. "It's just lentils and rice."

"Oh," Laz said, sounding a little surprised. "Well, it
smells nice." And he turned and fled.

The dining room was a quiet, cool, east-facing space
with a large bank of windows, a table from Sam's
last apartment that took up most of the space, and
a freestanding liquor cabinet Ulysses picked up at a
secondhand store over the summer. Sam had a couple of
plants on the windowsill, including the hydrangea Aunt
Cass had given him nearly a year before and a new one,
some sort of orchid. Mariah must have bought it as a gift;
it was too fussy for Sam to have picked it out himself. Not
his style.

The seating plan presented some issues. The table was
a rectangle, which felt awkward to join hands around.
Ulysses eyed the entire room while Sam opened a bottle
of wine. A qualified Victorian mesmerist would probably
have made everyone stand for the summoning, but that
seemed even more awkward and tiring than making them
sit for an extended period. And if Sam had run some
absurd distance that morning, Vikram probably had as

well; neither of them looked exactly enthusiastic about standing around even now.

"All right," he said eventually. "We'll leave the far end seat open for our guest. Sita, take the first chair on the left, and Vikram, on the right. Sam, you're next to Sita, and Laz, you're on my other side next to Vikram." He watched them all move to their positions. "Vikram, what was your mother's favorite drink?"

"You mean alcohol?" Vikram asked.

"However you choose to interpret the question is correct," Ulysses assured him.

Vikram frowned at the empty chair. "Gin and tonic."

"All right." He glanced at Sam, who nodded and set the open wine bottle and five glasses on the table. Ulysses looked at Laz. "Can you light the candles?"

Laz pulled out his lighter and moved around the room. They'd purchased a lot of candles. Probably too many. There were long tapers and short pillars, a few on every surface.

"Babushka would just light these like—" Laz snapped his fingers.

"Yeah." Ulysses turned and tugged the curtains shut. It was twilight outside, but he didn't want any distractions. "I can't do that one. Can you?"

Laz shook his head.

Sam, returning, set the cocktail at the far end of the table. "I can."

"Bullshit you can," Laz said.

275

Sam shrugged easily, sliding into his assigned chair. "We'll never know, I guess."

Ulysses took the chair at the head of the table, directly opposite the drink. Vikram and Sita poured themselves glasses of wine and sat on opposite sides of the table.

"Sorry," Vikram said after a moment. "Can you explain exactly what it is we're doing? All I heard was séance."

"We're going to try and summon your mother's ghost." He looked at Vikram's face in the candlelight. "She knew something about what's going on. She was trying to tell me. I hope she's still willing to." Vikram was a good-looking guy, with sharp, inquisitive features and dark eyes, now watching Ulysses carefully. He was easygoing, maybe a little naïve, but he'd somehow become Sam's friend. Probably Ulysses's too, if it came to that. And Ulysses felt bad, absurdly, for deciding to do this thing without asking Vikram if he felt up to seeing his mother again.

But after a long moment, Vikram just shook his head. "I thought her spirit was going to go—somewhere else."

"I did say that." Ulysses sat back, crossing his arms. "That's usually how these things work. But instead, she came over here."

"She was a bit rude to Ulysses," Sam stage-whispered to Sita. "On more than one occasion."

Sita covered her mouth, somewhere between embarrassment and laughter. "Oh no."

"But she's not here now," Vikram said, looking around the room as though Ulysses had been concealing her all the time.

"Not at the moment, as far as I can tell." He watched Sam pour two glasses of wine and pass them down to him and Laz, then pour the last of the bottle into his own glass. It was exactly the type of light white wine that Sam usually picked, citrusy and slightly sweet, cool on the tongue. Ulysses smiled down into the glass. "I've never had to recall a ghost," he added. "Usually they just come to me when they want."

"What do we do?" Vikram asked. After a heavy moment, he added, "Do we need a Ouija board?" and both Sam and Sita giggled.

"All right, calm down." Ulysses looked at the four of them. Everyone was watching him with varying degrees of interest and skepticism, but there was no open hostility. That was good; mindset and intention were important. "Join hands." He got to his feet to retrieve a slip of paper and a dish he'd left on the windowsill. When he turned back, everyone had—except Laz and Sam, who were eyeing one another across the table with mild distrust. Ulysses bent over, drawing a sigil on the paper.

When he'd finished the small, swooping shape, he rolled it up and muttered the activation word under his breath. Something crackled to life in the room, sweet-smelling but sharp like a claw, quiet in a way that demanded attention. Ulysses could see Laz notice it, his questioning gaze upward. Sam seemed to feel it too. Of their guests, Vikram didn't move, and Sita . . .

Sita's eyes were wide. She had also noticed the opening of the ritual. That was interesting.

Ulysses thrust the paper into the flame of the nearest candle and held it there until it caught, then dropped it burning into the dish in the center of the table. Then he sat down again, taking Sam's hand in his left and Laz's in his right. "Think about Dr. Parvati Ranganathan."

Touching Sam for a ritual was very different than touching him for sex, or reassurance, or just in passing, or any of the thousand reasons he found his hands straying toward Sam's body during the average day. Even with his shields, Sam's power was like cayenne pepper on his tongue. Belatedly, he wondered if Sita could feel any of it, or whether for her touching Sam was the same as touching anyone else. He couldn't decide if the thought made him jealous or not.

Instead, he closed his eyes and tried to recreate the woman's face in his mind. He pictured the old-fashioned way she'd worn her hair pulled back, the suit coat she'd been wearing the last time she'd accosted him, the lines of her face, brown skin, gray hair, a posture so similar to Vikram's and yet entirely distinct.

After a while, someone cleared their throat. Ulysses opened his eyes to see the woman herself sitting at the end of the table.

"So now you are ready to listen to me," she said, giving him a pointed look. Glancing around at the others, she sniffed. "Interesting group you've got here." Her gaze focused on Sita and Sam. "Please stop this calling, all of you. With these two in your circle, I'm sure the entire cosmos can hear your summoning, and that's not good. You don't want too many beings to know that there's a door open." She gave Ulysses a cold, knowing look.

"Thank you for responding so quickly," he said, pulling his hands back.

Sam murmured an exclamation when Ulysses released his hand, staring hard at Dr. Ranganathan. "Why can I still see her?" He reached out and grabbed Ulysses again, then let go, frowning.

"It's the spell," Ulysses supplied. "Everyone can see her right now."

"Mum, how are you?" Vikram said.

Dr. Ranganathan looked over at him, her expression a little tender. "Ah, Vik. I had hoped to keep you out of this, you know."

Vikram sighed. "I appreciate that, but I can handle it. I'd like to know what's going on."

"Mm." She stared at him, then looked down at the gin and tonic. "I assume this is for me?" she asked the room, and before anyone responded she picked it up and took a sip. Or—she didn't lift the actual glass, but she lifted . . . the idea of the glass? Its spirit? He'd seen the trick done once or twice, and it was always a little troubling. Beside him, Sam hissed quietly and grabbed his hand again under the table, and Ulysses wondered how it looked to him. "Ask your question, Dr. Lenkov," she said, looking across the table at him. "Your time runs thin."

"Tell me about the cult." He tapped the index finger of his empty right hand on the table. "I know you were there at the same time, but you weren't a member of the conspiracy."

"No. They never would have admitted me, not that I would have joined in any case. I was too foreign." She sniffed. "The 'cult,' as you call it, predated my arrival in '39. I don't know exactly when they got started, though Barth and Sterling had known each other for years by the time I met them. Thick as thieves, those two."

"Do you think Barth named his daughter after Julius?" Sam murmured to Ulysses.

"Possibly," Dr. Ranganathan said. "At any rate, I was an attending physician in the pediatrics department when the first death happened." She folded her hands in front of her. "The woman hemorrhaged during the fourth stage of labor. It happened more than it does now, but still not what you'd call frequently. In this case, the woman was Indian, her daughter just a few months younger than my own child. I grew curious as to whether the obstetrician, Barth, who was by then fairly well-known in some circles, had somehow mismanaged the case."

"Was the child—" Ulysses glanced at Sita.

Dr. Ranganathan frowned at him. "Of course it was." She glanced over at Sita and her face softened. "Did your father ever talk to you about any of this?"

Sita shook her head. "He never spoke of her death."

Ulysses's mind was moving along a different track. "Why did Barth think Sita was dead too?"

"Dr. Barth came to ask about her some hours after the birth." She looked over at Sita. "You had aspirated something and had to go to the NICU. Barth came to see me later and asked you. I was already suspicious, but I told him the truth—that you'd suffered a respiratory arrest."

Sita nodded with what seemed like a great deal less upset than Ulysses thought that information would have provoked in most people. On the other hand, the incident in question had happened nearly thirty years ago; perhaps it didn't feel quite as concerning when she'd lived through so much since then. "Did I die?"

"Perhaps." Dr. Ranganathan shrugged. "What is death?"

Sam muttered, "Shouldn't you know?" and Laz snickered. Dr. Ranganathan looked at them sharply.

"If there was later some confusion about the identities of who lived and who died, that was nothing to do with me." She looked fierce, suddenly. Protective. "If Barth was not motivated enough to seek out further information, that's his problem."

It was Sita who spoke into the silence that followed this declaration. "But you hated me. You forbade our marriage and haunted our apartment for *nine months.*" Vikram reached out across the table and took her hand again.

"I didn't want my son getting mixed up in whatever nonsense Barth was part of. I had too many questions. For example, did her father know what had happened?" Dr. Ranganathan looked at her drink, swirled the remaining liquid slowly. "It wasn't until a few days ago that I managed to speak with Barth and clear up a few points that had been bothering me for years."

"What did Barth say about her mother's death?" Ulysses asked, trying to get back on track. "At the time, I mean."

"That there'd been a delay in blood typing her, he'd administered a vasoconstrictor but she'd already lost too much blood." She took another sip of the gin and tonic. "I resolved to keep a closer eye on him, but they didn't try again for almost two years."

Sam shifted in his chair and sat back. "My mother," he said quietly.

"She had developed preeclampsia during her pregnancy. It's a serious condition that causes raised blood pressure, and can lead to seizures and death. She was young, but it's not unheard of." Dr. Ranganathan shut her eyes for a moment.

"That must be how Julius convinced Barth to let him use your mother as the sacrifice," Ulysses said quietly. Sam glanced over at him, eyes wide. "She was already dying, so why not."

"Why would they do this?" Sita asked. Her head was bowed, eyes shut.

"A convoluted way to become more powerful and long-lived in the process." Parvati Ranganathan sighed. "The magic is very esoteric, or so I am given to understand, but much of it is based on work that goes back centuries, if not millennia."

"Given to understand?" Ulysses asked.

She nodded. "That was also around the time that I met Ekaterina."

Ulysses wondered again why Babushka hadn't told him herself. But she'd sent him to Ranganathan. He tried to wrap his head around all that and then gave up. There was too much else going on. "That's when she and her group started to investigate the two of them?" he guessed.

"At first we didn't know of Julius Sterling's involvement. That was something she discovered later on. He tried very hard to disguise his presence. But I was the one who figured out that some of the residents were also in on it."

Ulysses nodded. "And those residents took their knowledge when they left for attending positions elsewhere."

Dr. Ranganathan tapped the side of her nose. "None of them were as powerful as Barth or Sterling. Especially Sterling. That's why your grandmother wasn't worried about them. None of them would have been able to replicate his experiments. But some of them stayed here, and those have never forgotten their experiences." She shot Ulysses a pointed look. "I'm sure if someone tried to convince you to stop, you would right away, without qualm or complaint."

Ulysses ignored the dig. "And the other two names she gave me, Garcia and Landover?"

"Garcia was our informant. She was peripherally involved until she had a crisis of conscience." Dr. Ranganathan tapped a finger on the table soundlessly. "She later married and moved away. I'm not sure where she went. As for Landover . . ."

"He's still here," Vikram said suddenly. "I know him. He's not a—well, he's not that kind of doctor. He works in the meat science lab." His eyes were wide. "We play basketball on Tuesday mornings at the Red Gym."

Ulysses nodded, then remembered their audience. "Let's talk about that later."

Dr. Ranganathan shook her head. "I forbid this! You need to keep him out of danger, not—"

"I'm trying!" Ulysses exclaimed. "I'm trying to keep *everyone* out of danger. But I can't if I don't know who we're up against, and everyone in your generation seems content to bury their secrets and never speak of them again, so I don't know where I'm supposed to find out—" Sam touched his shoulder and he subsided.

"Try harder," Dr. Ranganathan said. She drank the last of her cocktail. "I must go now."

"Mum, why didn't you tell us this earlier?" Vikram's face was shuttered, but Ulysses could imagine everything he was feeling.

"Without having met him," she gestured to Sam, "would you have believed me?" She looked at Vikram and smiled wanly. "I just wanted to protect you. Perhaps someday, you'll understand. I did what I could with the information I had at the time."

"Mum—" Vikram's voice was rough, cracking.

"I hope you can forgive me. Both of you." Dr. Parvati Ranganathan looked at Sita. "Take care of him."

During that speech, she'd been fading, and at these last words she vanished entirely. As she went, every candle in the room flared suddenly and went out.

There was a long silence. Finally, Laz said, "Yeah, it's a bit of a cheap trick, isn't it."

Sam laughed.

Chapter 21

T HAT TUESDAY, AUTUMN REALLY began. They'd been enjoying a run of warm, sunny days, the nights cool but not cold. And then suddenly, Sam rose at five thirty to find that the apartment was chilly and damp; outside, it was raining and forty-five degrees. The streets glistened wetly beneath the streetlights as he went around and closed the windows.

Ulysses stirred when he came back to bed, mumbling something before he rolled over, burrowing under the covers to press himself against Sam.

Sam put a hand between his shoulder blades and Ulysses twitched. "You're cold," he said, partly into Sam's shoulder.

"Sorry," Sam said, feeling more amused than apologetic. "The temperature dropped overnight."

Ulysses opened one eye. "It's still dark out. What godforsaken time do you call this?"

"I was supposed to meet Ellen for tennis," Sam said mournfully. "But it's raining."

There was a longish pause, and Sam thought Ulysses might have dozed off again. "When?" he asked eventually. "Do you want a ride?"

"Across campus on a motorcycle in the rain? That's not going to keep me dry."

Ulysses shook his head marginally. "No, but it will get you there faster. And you'll have the thrill of riding around on a motorcycle." He moved just enough to look at Sam with both eyes, sleepy but mischievous.

"There is that." Sam moved his hand up Ulysses's back to his neck, threaded his fingers into the other man's thick hair. "Are you going to play basketball with Vikram this morning?"

Ulysses made an equivocal noise. After a while, he said, "For all we know, Landover has turned good and this is nothing."

"Yes," Sam said, "that seems likely." He traced the edge of Ulysses's ear with one finger and watched him shut his eyes. "If history has taught us anything, it's that sometimes evil people just stop being evil and it's fine."

"History," Ulysses said dismissively. He pulled back finally, rolling onto his side and propping his head up on one elbow. "Are you doing anything tonight?"

"What do you mean?"

Ulysses shrugged. "We could go out."

"Are you asking me on a date?" Sam said.

"Am I not allowed to now?" His eyes were half-lidded but bright. Sam couldn't quite read his emotions, but his face seemed almost wistful. "We haven't had much of a chance to spend time together lately."

"We hung out yesterday," Sam said, and Ulysses snorted.

"Not the same." He rubbed his face with his free hand, fingers rasping against the stubble on his jaw. "We should go out to dinner, maybe see a movie or something. Any good shows right now?"

"There were a few Ellen wanted me to spy on," Sam said. "But it's a Tuesday."

"A movie, then," Ulysses said. "I'll come by the library after work. We can go out and pretend to be normal people for a while."

Sam laughed. "I'm not sure I know how to do that anymore, but all right. If that's what you want, I'll try."

"Yeah, yeah," Ulysses said. "You wait. I'm gonna order a bunch of suits from Monkey Wards and join the Rotary Club and never have to worry about magic cults again."

"I'd love to see you at a Rotary Club meeting," Sam confessed. "Getting into fights about whether the Junior Chamber of Commerce should take a role in the redistribution of profits from local businesses to help the proletariat . . ." Ulysses was laughing now. Sam leaned forward and kissed him, feeling his smile against his lips.

Sam's office phone was ringing as he unlocked the door, and he dropped his tennis bag on the floor and crossed the space in two great strides to get to it. "Sterling."

"How's it going?" It was Ellen's voice, too bright and loud.

"It's . . . Ellen, what are you doing?" She could only just have gotten to Van Vleck from the tennis stadium, way out on the west side of campus.

"I was thinking about those papers the DCI brought you," she continued. "Those weird Aklo ones."

It took him a long few seconds to connect her strange tone and their prior conversation. She'd said she'd had an idea about drawing out some of the math people, but. . . . "Oh, no," Sam groaned. "I teach you about shibboleths and *this* is how you repay me?"

"Are you going to take them over to show to Ulysses? I feel like he has a right to know that he's mentioned in them."

Sam sighed. "I'm going to see him tonight," he said after a pause, hoping that was the kind of response she was angling for.

"This evening? That sounds good."

"Ellen, I'm going to kill you."

"He can handle it," she said sweetly. "I'll see you later."

"Thanks," he said, and dropped the receiver back into its cradle. And then he had to think about what he was doing.

Ellen was ridiculous, but she was also right about something. The documents shed little light on the group's current plans except by extrapolation—they'd been tracking Hugh, and then they'd killed him, so Sam could make certain assumptions upon seeing his own name in the records. There were others mentioned besides Ulysses that he ought to tell. Hugh he could write to, but there was someone in town who should know. He'd put it off, but it was past time he did it.

Sam checked his watch, then reached for the phone and dialed a number he still knew by heart.

ULYSSES FOUND A CROWD waiting in front of his office when he arrived at eight thirty—a woman who looked vaguely familiar, a guy named Leo Ma who had started as a grad student two years after Ulysses and was still finishing, and Laz. He checked his watch, just to be sure he hadn't totally forgotten what week it was and missed class somehow.

"All right," he said, finding that it was still the fifteenth of September. "Guess I'm popular today. Who was here first?" He opened the office door and went in. There were—he counted—thirteen books stacked in one tall pile in the center of a blotter that had been clear when he left the night before. He dropped his satchel in the corner and wrestled off his damp leather jacket.

Leo stuck his head in. "Dr. Lesko said you need a grader for the Magic 101 section you're teaching."

"Did she?"

"I did," Dr. Lesko shouted through their adjoining wall. "And you do."

"All right," Ulysses said, and scrawled his name on a form Leo shoved in front of him.

He was sorting through the books when the Black woman came in and sat down. She was tallish, wearing a green turtleneck and slacks, and he got the sudden feeling that he'd met her before.

"Are you . . ." He stared at her for a long moment. "Are you one of Sam's friends?"

She squinted at him. "Oh, you're that guy who was sitting with Dio."

He shut his eyes. "Dio. Yeah." When he opened them again, he found his gaze straying to the portrait of him and Sam at the corner of his desk, Sam's annoyed, charmed expression. "What's your name?"

"Buttercup Diaz."

Ulysses nodded. "I think I met your girlfriend the other day. Galadriel." He hesitated. "Is she doing okay? She had an odd moment in the restaurant."

"She's fine."

"Does she—" He hesitated and flexed his hands, unsure what he wanted to ask. "She's got some magic blood in her."

He saw his meaning dawn on Buttercup's face. "Yeah. Her grandmother—yeah. She's in the dance program." She finally sat down in the vacant chair he waved her to. "Dio okay?"

"He's fine." He found himself looking at a book called *Ancient Greek Rituals of the Home and Family* that

E. H. LUPTON

had been at the bottom of the pile. "You didn't come here to lecture me about him, did you?"

"No. Unless you've got something to say about Galadriel." She met his gaze and held it.

"Absolutely not."

She nodded decisively. "I'm here to ask if you would be willing to sit on my committee."

"In what department?"

"Comparative literature."

That was a new one. "What's your dissertation on?"

"The changes in magic manuscripts and marginalia as a result of the crusades around the time of the twelfth-century renaissance." She hesitated, looked nervous, and added, "In Italy."

He blinked. "That sounds fascinating. What is my role here?"

"I need someone who can make sure I'm interpreting the magic stuff correctly." She took a deep breath. "I've got a grant to go Padua for a semester starting in January, so my plan is to do as much preparation as I can now, then go do my research, write everything up over the summer and next fall, and defend in December next year."

He cast about for a pen and made a note on the blotter. He'd never had appointments more than a few weeks in the future, and now he needed to remember things more than a year away. "Sounds good. Do you need me to sign anything?"

When she was ready to head out, she paused in the doorway, and he abruptly asked, "Does the phrase 'ivory and ink' mean anything to you?"

Buttercup shook her head. "No. Some sort of book?"

"I guess it must be." He shook his head. "Let me know if you need anything. Or if you want to talk about courses or—" He waved a hand.

"Thanks." She bit her lip and looked at him like she wanted to say something else, but couldn't find the words. "You're not a bad guy," she said finally, all in a rush.

"Okay?"

She shook her head. "I'll see you around."

He pressed his fingertips to the ridges of his eyebrows when she stepped out, wondering if it was too early to have a headache. He should have picked up another cup of coffee after the basketball game, just to emotionally cushion him for having to deal with students.

Laz came in a few minutes later, carrying a cup of coffee he must have scavenged from the lounge. And, like he was reading Ulysses's mind, he had an extra, which he set on the edge of the desk.

"What brings you here?" Ulysses asked, once he'd drunk half of it.

Laz sat down. He was looking very pleased with himself. "I got curious after our discussion on Saturday, so I did some digging. Any guesses what Julie Stricker does?"

Ulysses shook his head. "Other than refuse to help us out?"

"She's an engineer." Laz raised both eyebrows. "She's interested in the industrial applications of spider silk." He held up a hand. "But it gets better. There was an article from three years ago—she was working with a biologist to breed spiders for better silk."

Ulysses's chair creaked as he leaned back. "Shit."

"We should go to the cops." When he looked back, Laz was practically vibrating with excitement, and Ulysses sighed.

"What do we know?" Ulysses asked. "A couple of names. Sam's got some documents suggesting that he and I were being tracked. It's almost nothing."

"The spiders. You saw them yourself!" Laz set his mug on the edge of the desk. "That definitely looks like some kind of illegal magic hybrid."

"It looks that way, but we don't have one to show anyone." Ulysses shook his head. "If we want law enforcement to wrap this up, we need a smoking gun."

Laz shrugged. "We could do more research on Stricker. Or that guy Landover. How was he, by the way? Did Vikram introduce you?"

Ulysses shook his head. He'd been worried about the game, because although he did quite a bit of running, it was almost always when he was being chased by something. When he arrived, he realized he had nothing to be concerned about. Vikram's group consisted of about seven guys, most of whom did nothing more vigorous on a day-to-day basis than put a couple of bottles in an autoclave. Landover was average height, stocky, bearded, with graying dishwater hair and unremarkable eyes. Ulysses had the feeling he'd run into him somewhere before, but he wasn't that distinctive looking. He played less aggressively than some of the men, but he'd made a few three-pointers. "He's just a guy," Ulysses told Laz. "Exactly the type you'd expect to be playing pickup basketball with a bunch of biologists and meat scientists. He didn't react to being introduced to me." He'd watched Landover throughout the game, trying to be subtle. If the man had noticed, he hadn't let on. "He was clocking Vikram," he added. "I don't know why."

Laz looked amused. "Really, you don't?"

"Vikram's married!" Laz shrugged. Ulysses sighed and rubbed his face. "Consider whether he was at the game in the first place to keep an eye on Vikram, because of his mother's connections to Babushka."

"Maybe." Laz drummed his fingers on the arm of his chair. "If they're that paranoid, we should do something to draw them out. If we freak them out enough, force them to act before they're ready, we gain an advantage."

"That's true." Ulysses sipped his coffee, turning the heavy ceramic mug in his hands. "But what are they preparing for? What's their objective?"

"They're trying to reach the god children, right?" Laz tilted his chin back. "Does it really matter why? It just seems like we should stop them from doing that."

"Yeah. But how do we stop them if we don't know what they're doing it for?" Laz made a skeptical noise and

Ulysses waved him off. "How do we get ahead of them if we can't predict where they're going? We know about exactly three god children, and none of them have any power. I haven't been able to trace any of the others."

Laz scrubbed a hand over his short hair. "What are our options? I could tail Stricker, see if she's up to anything. Or Landover." He shot Ulysses a look and added, "We could go talk to Babushka."

Ulysses considered this. "Let's do that tomorrow, when I can bring Sam along. I'd like him to hear what she has to say."

"All right." Laz sounded mildly irritated, but he didn't try to argue with him. "What do you want to do for now?"

"Can you find out what Julie Stricker is doing with her time on a day-to-day basis?" He cracked the knuckles of his right hand one at a time, then started on his left. "I think that might be useful to know."

"As you wish," Laz said. He got to his feet and mimed a sarcastic little bow, then left, taking his coffee cup with him.

><<

TRUE TO HOWARD'S WORD, the car was outside within half an hour of Sam's call. Sam had been waiting impatiently, occasionally turning around to glance out at the street below, and when the heavy black sedan prowled up to the curb he got to his feet.

"I'm stepping out for a moment," he told Edith, who waved a hand without looking up from what she was working on.

Downstairs, he slid into the passenger seat. "No chauffeur?"

"I assumed you'd want privacy." Howard had driving gloves on with his dark suit, which gave him a little touch of absurdity, as though he were a cat burglar out for lunch. "You sounded nervous on the phone."

Sam shrugged. "Last fall," he began, and then broke off, thinking about everything that had happened.

"I remember it." Howard sounded wary but not upset. Someone behind them honked and he glanced over his shoulder, put the car into gear. "It was about this time, wasn't it?"

"What?" Sam watched Library Mall slide past.

"When you met your—when you met Ulysses." Howard took a left onto Park Street.

"It was in October." Sam looked over at Howard, saw him nod minutely. "Eleven months ago."

Howard shifted into third gear and passed a Chevy, sneaking through the light at Dayton just before it turned from yellow to red. "I'd wondered."

Sam raised an eyebrow but decided not to take the bait. "Last year, did you know you were being tracked?"

"I had my suspicions." He looked at Sam out of the corner of his eye. "How did you come by that information?"

"The Department of Criminal Investigation asked if I could help translate some papers they found in Sterling Hall. Your name was in them, as were your movements." Sam looked out the window; they rolled past Madison General Hospital, passing people walking along the sidewalk, chatting, smoking. "And ours."

"I see." A few seconds passed. "Sterling Hall is—engineering?"

"Physics. And the Army Math facility."

"Have you run into a woman named Julie—oh, what was her married name?" Howard's fingers clenched around the end of the shifter. "She used to be Julie Barth."

"Stricker," Sam said. "Yeah."

"Be careful of her."

Sam bit his lip. "Is she dangerous?"

"I don't know. I could never . . ." Howard shook his head. "Don't assume she's a pushover or an innocent."

"All right." Sam took a deep breath. "What aren't you telling me? Is there something going on?"

Abruptly, Howard pulled the car into the far left lane and made a quick U-turn, tires squealing, engine roaring. The car fishtailed on the wet pavement, and Sam swore and clutched the door handle. When he looked over, Howard's face was grim, focused on the road ahead of them. "Try again."

"How do we stop them?" Sam heard himself ask. "They stalked us. They *killed* Hugh. They tried to kill Sita.

Ulysses has been caught in the crossfire more than once. Is there a way to protect everyone?"

Howard was silent for a few blocks. "I'm not a good person to ask about that." His voice sounded slightly choked.

Sam raised a shaky hand and pressed it to his face. His palm was sweaty, his fingers cold. "Because you don't have an answer, or you won't tell me?"

Howard didn't reply. They rode the rest of the way back to the library in silence. It wasn't until Sam had one foot out of the door that Howard said, "Dio—sorry. Sam?"

"Yes?"

Howard's face looked thinner than it had a year ago. The rainy light seemed to press against his cheekbones, leaving the flesh beneath them shadowed, slack. His hair was grayer, too. "It was good to see you."

Chapter 22

D EEP IN THE TAIL end of the afternoon, when all the
meetings were done and Edith had left for the day,
Sam wheeled his desk chair into the rare books stacks
and sat down.

He'd spent a lot of time thinking about the problem
of "ivory and ink." It was clearly a reference to a
book of some sort. Unfortunately, there was no catalog
information for cover embellishments. Some books with
especially elaborate covers did have that noted in their
records, but it wasn't consistent, and there were also
plenty of books that hadn't been cataloged yet. Even
Edith, with her near-eidetic knowledge of the collection,
had no ideas.

Sam decided to ask the library.

Ulysses had once contended that the library building
itself was not especially intelligent, but the books were.
When Sam thought he was talking to Memorial, most
of what was answering him was the collection. If that
was true, the rare books stacks would be the best place

to commune with it—not necessarily the books that had been in the collection the longest, but the oldest books.

He'd seen Ulysses do the rite of communion twice. It didn't seem all that complicated; he sat with his eyes closed, and after a while, the building talked to him. Or—the gestalt that was Memorial Library spoke.

Sam sat down, hands folded, and waited.

There were a lot of problems with his plan, Sam realized after what felt like half an hour but was probably a lot less. First of all, Ulysses had described the early stage as a gradual clearing of the mind, and Sam was decidedly having trouble with that. Almost as soon as he forced his body to stop moving, his thoughts took off, and he found himself conjugating Russian verbs or recalling odd lines of poetry he'd memorized long ago. Second, sitting still without moving was extremely frustrating.

He pressed the heels of his palms into his eyes and wondered how he'd ever made it through two Ivy League degrees. He had vague memories of sitting in a study carrel in Widener for hours, until friends came and reminded him to eat. Where had that gone?

He got up and started to pace. At least if he was moving up and down the shelves, he could clear his mind. And maybe the library could indicate somehow if he got close.

A phone was ringing out in the main room somewhere, maybe the extension in his office. He ignored it, pacing the room like a detective searching for a clue. He had the feeling the library was trying to tell him something, but he didn't know what it was, just a steady, mounting pressure at the back of his throat.

The shelves holding the magic collection were at the back of the room, near the door. As Sam paced along the line of grimoires and codices, his attention was caught by a volume bound in black leather with onyx pressed into the spine in a pattern that made him uneasy. But there was also something about the book next to it.

It was an octavo, not large, bound in dirty off-white leather. The flag stuck in the top suggested that it had been earmarked for conservation but not yet sent down to their basement lair. He took it off the shelf; there was no ornamentation on the front, and no title stamped on it. The paperwork sticking out of the top said *Grimoire c. 1852*, which was unhelpful. He flipped it open and looked at the first page, which was blank. The following page was covered with tightly printed words in Aklo and Greek.

All right, so—it had been rebound at some point, probably. Books in the 1850s were often bound with gold embossing on the cover, or complex reliefs beneath the leather to add texture and interest. Who would have rebound it without putting the title—He shook his head. It had clearly been well-used before it came to the library. Who had—

Someone behind him cleared their throat, and Sam jumped. When he turned, he saw a man in a cheap black suit. He had pale skin and pale hair, and he was looking at Sam with a wary expression. "Mr. Sterling?"

"Yes?" When the man didn't say anything for a moment, Sam added, "Are you here from the DCI?"

"Yes."

"What happened to Alberts and Richardson?" he asked, hoping the fake names fell from his lips undetectably. Sam found he was clutching the spine of the book and forced himself to relax his fingers. The library was still poking at him, and he did his best to push it away. "They've been my main contacts with the department."

The man nodded. Sam didn't like his eyes, which were cold. "They're busy. Asked me to come and see if you were available."

"And you are?"

A brief hesitation. Sam wouldn't have noticed it if he hadn't been looking for it. "I'm Mr. Thatcher."

Sam tried to smile benignly, didn't quite make it. "Just let me lock up."

He turned to put *Grimoire c. 1852* back on the shelf and heard the door open again. No footsteps, but the guy had moved quietly before. Would it betray his suspicions to look over his shoulder? He reached out for the shelf, curled his fingers around the edge where the support was—

"That won't be necessary, Mr. Sterling," said a new voice. Sam recognized it, then wondered why and turned to see the man who had chased him outside the Sett.

"Oh," Sam said, voice thin. "What are you—" He groped behind him until his fingers found the onyx book. "You shouldn't be here."

"Neither should you," the man said. "But I'm glad you are." Sam flung the book at him.

There was a moment of confusion as both men leaped out of the way and Sam sprinted for the emergency exit. He could hear hard shoes clacking on the steps behind him as he descended, not falling over his own feet only by the grace of—Well.

He burst through the door at the bottom of the stairs and collided with a man in a blue cardigan. Sam reeled backward, noted the man's graying beard—why was that detail important, where had he—and then he saw the revolver the man was holding trained on him and froze.

"Dionysus Sterling, I presume," the man said. A moment later the man who wasn't Thatcher came clattering through the door and slid to a stop right behind Sam. The bearded man raised a sardonic eyebrow, but addressed Sam when he said, "If you would come with us."

Sam scowled. "What if I refuse?"

Beard sighed deeply, as though offended by Sam's entirely unoriginal resistance. "I don't think that's an option you want to explore." The door opened and shut again behind Sam. The man with the gun seemed unimpressed with the new arrival. "Did you get it, at least?"

Sam looked around. Thatcher was holding a book—but not the onyx one, he had—

The grimoire. Sam tried not to let the horror he felt show on his face.

"Very well." The man with the gun gestured to a large, low-slung saloon car. "Mr. Sterling, after you, if you please."

ULYSSES HAD NO SOONER settled back with the book on the Greeks than Laz called, letting him know Stricker hadn't left her house all day. Interviews with her neighbors had unhelpfully suggested she kept to herself. Laz was going home to change out of his wet clothes.

At five, Ulysses left, feeling like a radio tuned between stations. It was still drizzling. Sam had been right about the experience being rather unpleasant on a motorcycle, but he barely noticed.

The most efficient route back to Memorial Library was to take Observatory Drive, a long, hilly avenue that ran all the way to the Union. In good weather, it was a fun thoroughfare to race along, but the wet pavement slowed him down. There was still construction on the corner with Park Street where they were putting in the new library, and he had to slow further to skirt it.

Ancient Greek Rituals of the Home and Family had been left for him by Dr. Lesko, who was no doubt trying to make a point about something. Magic for ancient

Greeks had been primarily temple-based. Temples were one place where the world of the gods and the world of men collided. Not the only one—curse tablets were one example of non-temple magic. But there was also regular, common magic. Rituals that happened at home. Every culture had things like that, folk beliefs and traditions that were often submerged magical rites. What was she trying to tell him?

Or what, ultimately, was Dionysus trying to say?

Ulysses parked the bike next to the library on the State Street side and went in. The librarian on the circulation desk smiled in recognition and waved a few fingers as he passed.

He took the elevator up—the wonky elevator, the one he'd once been trapped in with Sam when the library left them a message. It was on the fritz again, climbing from floor to floor with excruciating slowness, the lights flickering. Ulysses frowned and patted the wall as the bucket of bolts ground to a stop on the fourth floor and the doors whined open.

He went through the entrance into special collections and breezed in to—

Silence.

He stopped in the reading room and looked around, fingers tightening on the strap of his shoulder bag. From where he was standing, he could see through into Dr. Pearlman's empty office. That wasn't surprising; she often arrived earlier than Sam and left earlier too. Ulysses had taken advantage of that once or—anyway.

Sam's office was farther down the hall, and he couldn't even see if the door was open or not.

There was a difference between the silence of someone working and a place with nobody in it, some indefinable quality to the way the air was moving. But if Sam had left, and Dr. Pearlman was gone, he would have locked the door. That was department policy, and Sam was very strict about it.

A phone began to ring. The sound was strident, and it made his nerves jangle in sympathy.

Ulysses waited for a moment, the breath between rings, and then the library grabbed him so hard it felt like he'd been slapped. He tripped and scuffed his chin on the low pile industrial carpet.

Something was wrong past the pain in his head.

Ulysses scrambled to his feet and ran to Sam's office, which was empty. But the phone was still ringing, so he answered it.

"Oh my god, Ulysses." It was Ellen, her voice tight with suppressed panic. "I've been trying to get Sam all afternoon. Is he with you?"

"No." Ulysses looked around, as though he might find Sam hidden among the old books and cards and papers. "What's going on?"

"There were a couple of guys in the next office I thought might have been involved with Sam's cult. I thought—anyway, they were whispering together, and then they headed out pretty damn fast." There was a noise in the background. "I've been trying to warn Sam that they might be planning something for tonight."

"I just got here." Ulysses looked around, carried the phone over to the window and peered at the street below. He saw rainy late afternoon light, students, yellowing leaves already dropping to the pavement. Nothing to explain why his body was twitching with fight-or-flight energy. "I'm going to go check the stacks, see if I can find him."

A long pause. "Okay. I'll—Christ, I'm halfway across campus. Do you want me to come over there?"

"It's fine. I'm sure he's still around, just stepped out. We were supposed to go to a movie." Ulysses tried hard to force himself to believe that, or at least to sound like he did. "I'll keep an eye on him tonight."

When he was off the phone, he tried the stacks. They were empty, but the pressure from the library was stronger. Something had happened, and now he knew where Sam had been.

He went back to Sam's office, taking careful, measured steps, because he wasn't panicking. He stood behind the desk and looked at Sam's blotter, his papers, his books. The office reeked of Sam, like green and rain and something else, deeper and more beautiful and strange.

He picked up the phone.

Laz answered after several rings, sounding tired, like Ulysses had caught him napping. But he didn't have much time to feel bad about it. "Is Sam with you?"

"No," Laz said curtly. "Why would he be?"

Ulysses didn't have an answer for that, except that he'd really hoped—"Something is wrong. I just got to his office, and he's not here. The library is upset about it, too, so I think whatever happened was bad. We need to find him."

"Where are you?" Laz asked after a moment's silence. "I'll pick you up."

SAM WOKE UP GRADUALLY to ringing in his ears and the lingering scent of sweet acetone. He felt like he'd fallen down a flight of stairs while he'd been unconscious, but his head was clearing, and although he was nauseated, there were no hallucinations when he opened his eyes in the too-bright room. So. Could be worse.

He didn't remember being drugged. Or—he remembered getting into the car, one man on either side of him. Then a handkerchief that smelled acrid and slightly sweet pressed to his face. He'd struggled, but . . .

He was in a small lab space in some sort of building with galvanized steel walls, reclining in a dental chair that was bolted to the floor. Whoever had grabbed him—the cult, probably—had strapped him down. The thick leather bit into his wrists, his ankles, the edges of his ribcage. It was annoying, but also he was vaguely flattered that they thought he might be able to put up any sort of fight after being etherized. His shirt and tie were gone, leaving him in his thin undershirt.

Aside from him in the chair, there was a long workbench down the center of the room and counters along the perimeter. He could see some equipment: microscopes, a small refrigerator, and other things that he couldn't make sense of. Twisting as far as he could, he spotted a glass case in the corner that appeared to be half full of wood chips.

Oh. Oh no.

There was a rustling noise, and a large spider emerged from somewhere at the back of the tank to peer at him through the glass.

Okay, it probably wasn't peering at him. That was definitely the fevered imagining of an unwell mind. Spiders didn't stare at people.

How many more were there that he couldn't see?

Another question: how long had he been out? It didn't feel very long, but. . . . There were no clocks in his line of sight, and they'd taken his watch when they removed his jacket.

Eventually he shut his eyes. Something was making a whispering sound. No, it *was* whispering. He just couldn't make out the words. He strained his ears.

Before he could get too far in that direction, the door opened and a handful of people filed in: a woman, the man with the beard and the gun, Thatcher, not-Thatcher, and a handful of others he didn't recognize. His memories swam behind his eyes. The woman looked familiar, but he couldn't place her.

She was clearly in charge, though, and that more than anything led him to the conclusion that this was Julie Stricker. She came forward and looked him over, eyes dispassionate. "Dionysus Sterling, at last." She smiled tightly. There was something about the way she said his surname that gave him pause, but he wasn't clear-headed enough to figure it out. "When Shapiro here said you'd gotten some of our papers, I had to move our plans up a bit." She gestured vaguely at not-Thatcher, and he felt just a little bit grounded, to have a name to connect with that punchable face. She went on, "I have to admit I've been wanting to meet you for quite a while."

Sam shrugged as best he could. "I'd love to shake your hand."

"Oh, don't trouble yourself." She picked up a little otoscope from the workbench and shined it into his eyes. The bright light made him wince and try to flinch away, but whatever she saw pleased her. "Get samples from him," she said to the bearded guy. "It'll be interesting to study."

"I'd like to wait to get the blood sample until the ether is out of his system."

Stricker considered this and shook her head. "As far as I'm aware, ether is magically inert, so it shouldn't be an issue."

Beard went around behind one of the benches where Sam couldn't see him.

"What did you want us to do with him after that?" Shapiro asked. He was eyeing Sam nervously. "We can't just kill him and dump the body. There'll be questions." He fidgeted. "His old man is a big shot, isn't he?"

"He is." Stricker stared at Sam for a long, silent moment, an expression Sam couldn't parse on her face. "We're going to hold onto him for the time being. See if we can draw the other one out."

She turned and left. Most of the group followed her, leaving Beard and Shapiro behind.

Beard was moving around the room, in and out of Sam's field of vision. But Shapiro stayed where he was, and Sam kept his eyes on him. He looked sweaty. Maybe he was new and just confronting something ugly for the first time.

"You know what they'll do to you if you hurt me," Sam said softly. "My father will hunt you to the ends of the earth, and that's not a patch on what my boyfriend will do."

"Your *boyfriend*," Shapiro scoffed. "Let him try. I'm not afraid of him."

Sam tipped his head to one side, and while he did it flexed one arm to test the wrist strap. It held. "Hey, why have you been keeping tabs on Vikram?"

"Why have you?"

"I'm not the one joining his pickup basketball game."

Shapiro blinked, but before he could speak the bearded man came back from wherever he'd been rummaging. "That was me, actually." He—Landover—glanced at

Shapiro. "This guy couldn't hit a three-pointer if they were about to set his grandmother on fire."

"Fuck you, that's not true. You got lucky—"

Sam let them bicker for a minute, then cleared his throat. "What's the endgame in all this? Why do you want a demigod so badly?"

Landover gave him a long, flat look, then turned to his companion. "Grab me a vial for blood."

Shapiro opened a drawer and pulled out a couple of vials and a needle. "Tissue too? Hair?" He opened another drawer and stared down into it.

"We can do some hair," Landover said. "I don't have a dermal punch." He shuffled forward and took a small pair of scissors and a bottle from the drawer the other man seemed perplexed by.

"Hey," Sam said. "Why are you doing this?"

"Boss says to," Landover said, coming toward him with the scissors. Sam tried to lean away and flinched when Landover cut off one of his curls. He dropped it into a sample jar and screwed the lid back on. "Don't squirm, or I'll have to knock you out again."

"Why is she the boss?" Sam asked. Landover swabbed the inside of his elbow with something cold. Even though Sam was expecting it, the tourniquet pinched, and he tried to jerk away in the other direction.

"She's just the boss," Landover said. "Her old man was the boss and he passed the torch. That's why."

"Did she design those spiders?"

Landover looked at the cage in the corner. "That was a joint effort."

"Pretty illegal, isn't it? If that ever gets out . . ." Out of the corner of his eye, he saw Shapiro coming back, holding a bottle and a rag, and felt his pulse kick up unpleasantly. "Who's the *Twenty Thousand Leagues Under the Sea* fan?"

"Thatcher," Shapiro said. He glanced over at Landover. "You ready?"

Sam heard the sound of sloshing liquid and opened his mouth to say something reasonable and calm. "Please, you don't have to etherize me," he said instead, somewhat horrified at how high and tight his voice sounded to his own ears. "You can still let me go and walk away from all this. I won't come after you." He thrashed against the straps, trying to twist his legs free, get his head out of the way.

"I'm not sure you're in any position to bargain," Landover said. "Just hold still and this will all be over soon."

"Not really an inducement," he said, just before the rag came down over his nose and mouth again.

Julius Sterling could have dealt with the two of them. Sweaty-handed lackeys. But Sam didn't have any power, and he didn't have a sigil, and he couldn't think of a way around that. He needed Ulysses. He needed—he needed Dionysus. But he didn't have Dionysus. Or he had—what the hell did he have? He was—he wasn't—

"Is he out yet?" Shapiro asked, his voice echoing badly, and before Sam could follow his thoughts any further, the world hurried away again.

Chapter 23

ULYSSES HEARD THE CAR coming down State Street before he saw it. Laz had bought the red GTO with the convertible top, and it had a guttural engine noise that was surprisingly distinctive. Or perhaps Ulysses had just been straining his ears, waiting for the moment the muscle car would stop in front of him.

"How are we going to find him?" Laz asked without preamble as he got in.

Laz was still wearing Sam's jacket. Ulysses swallowed around an unexpected lump in his throat as they pulled away from the curb. "The thing is . . ."

Laz took the idea that Ulysses could somehow sense Sam's location in stride. "All right, so tell me where to go."

"Just a minute."

Ulysses thought briefly about the jacket. Celeste could have used it and a pendulum to set up some sort of resonance to lead them to its owner. But they didn't have time to go see her, and he was no good with fiddly charms like that. No, the simplest option was the one he'd been avoiding. The one he really, really wanted to exercise.

He closed his eyes and let the bond flower open.

Everything lurched sideways as the connection came rushing back, every cell in his body tingling with it. It was like getting pins and needles in his liver. It was like turning into a cloud. Ulysses must have made a noise as he lurched sideways, because Laz twitched and said, "What the fuck, man?" Ulysses felt Laz's hand on his wrist, fingers gentle but reaching for his pulse.

"East," he managed, pulling his limbs back into his seat. "Go east."

Laz spared him another glance, but turned left onto West Johnson. "Got it."

They drove through the drizzle, Laz weaving through the evening traffic as he followed Ulysses's somewhat wonky directions around the capitol and out toward the edge of town.

"It's odd," Ulysses said as they changed lanes to head toward Northport Drive. "This is the same area Livia took me to. She said there was a power nexus nearby."

Laz frowned. "Sensing them is not one of my talents, but can't *you* tell?"

"I can't." It was a fact Ulysses was unhappy about for a number of reasons. "But you've been away. Does Madison feel any different?"

Laz was quiet for a moment. "No. Well, maybe." He made a frustrated noise. "Don't ask me; I'm too close to all of this. I honestly couldn't tell you if what I feel is a result of actual differences or wishful thinking on my part or . . . I don't know."

"You don't *know*?"

"Is this what you want to talk about right now?" Laz growled. "Yes, I miss Thailand like I'd miss my own hand if it were cut off. I couldn't tell you if that feeling, that yearning, is why Madison feels different, or if there's something—" He turned sharply onto the road that ran past the airport, tires squealing in protest, and shifted into fourth gear.

"Is it that bad, being back?" Ulysses asked quietly.

Laz glanced at him, back at the road. "No. Except for how much I seem to have missed in the last few years."

And, well, what exactly was he going to say to that? "I appreciate you doing this," he said finally.

"What the hell, U. He's family."

They were coming up to a bunch of old buildings—warehouses, barracks, things left over from World War II that looked derelict now, covered with broken windows and rust stains.

"We're close." Ulysses sat forward in his seat. "There. The Quonset hut."

Laz took the car out of gear and let it decelerate gradually. "We're really close to the base," he mused. "I wonder if they know what's going on."

Ulysses watched the long steel building as they passed it, the weird half-cylindrical shape, a relic of a time he didn't remember. "It looks abandoned." He shut his eyes to focus on what the bond was telling him, but he hardly needed to. Laz parked a ways away, and they got out. "Do you know anyone at the base?"

"Sure. Buncha people." Laz went around the car and opened the trunk. "Here," he said, tossing a sheathed knife to Ulysses and pulling out an ax for himself.

Ulysses recognized the ax and decided not to say anything in almost the same moment. "I have a knife," he said instead, offering the sheathed one back.

Laz scoffed. "That little flip thing? Take this one. At least if you have to cut someone, they'll notice."

Ulysses decided not to argue the point. "Think you could raise the alarm with them?"

"Yeah," Laz said. He pulled a pack of cigarettes out of his coat pocket and started to tap one out. "If I go over there, are you gonna wait for me to get back before you go in?" He stuck the cigarette between his lips, shifting his weight over one hip challengingly.

"Go quickly, how about," Ulysses said.

They stared at each other. Laz was the first to look away, focusing his eyes on his lighter as he held it up to his cigarette. "Don't do anything I wouldn't do, okay?" he said, and went back around to the driver's side of the car.

"I feel like that gives me some latitude," Ulysses told him. "*Is* there anything you wouldn't do?"

Laz looked pensive for a moment. "I reserve the right to answer that question on a case-by-case basis," he said, and then got back into the car and roared off.

Ulysses waited almost a full minute after he'd gone before turning his attention toward the Quonset hut. He felt like he'd leveled out; the earlier disorientation from the bond was gone, and he was tense and ready for action. There was no way he could see to sneak up on the building, not walking across what was essentially a big, flat field south of the airport. If anyone was watching, they would see him. He had no way to know what was inside, and no way to prepare himself. But he'd also decided that there was nothing that could stop him. So he tucked the knife into the pocket of his jacket and went.

The door was white, its paint peeling; it was unlocked, which surprised him, and opened onto a hallway that seemed to run the length of the building, with doors on either side. There were only periodic overhead lights to throw the gloomy interior into sharp relief. Ulysses crept along slowly, trying to prevent the soles of his boots from crunching on the old, mildew-stained linoleum. He could hear every move he made echoing off the roof that curved above him, higher than he would have thought, and dark. Some of the doors he passed had windows into dim storage rooms. He didn't stop to look in; the bond was practically singing now, and every step he took felt like he was a wave rolling closer to the shore.

The building was about a hundred feet long, although walking down the hallway it certainly felt longer. It should have been like crossing Library Mall. Instead, he felt like he was covering the entire distance from the magic building to the library. He made it seventy-five feet or so before something made him stop.

The nearest door, on his right, was solid and white, no window. He leaned forward and put his ear to it, but if anything was happening inside, he couldn't hear it.

It was interesting, actually—the whole structure was extremely quiet. Was it empty? Was a spell of some sort in use? He didn't think that even a god could soundproof a corrugated steel building.

He tried the handle. Again, no lock. Ulysses tried not to think about that too much. Possibly whoever was behind this didn't really believe anyone was going to come looking for them. Possibly, well . . .

It was a large room and it smelled wrong. Sour, like bad magic. There was another door just past the entrance, part of a protruding section of wall that suggested a closet. He stepped past and into the main space. It was clearly a lab of some sort, although he didn't really want to think about why someone might be hiding a lab there. And then he saw Sam, and Ulysses wasn't paying attention to anything else as he ran across the room.

Sam was in an old medical chair of some sort, strapped down and unmoving. He'd been stripped of his suit coat and his shirt, leaving him looking thin and pale in just an undershirt. Ulysses crossed the space between them in a handful of steps and put his hands on his shoulders. "Sam!"

The other man twitched awake, eyes wide, pulling at his restraints. "What—*Who*—" he rasped. His voice sounded rough.

"Ssh," Ulysses said, "It's me."

"Oh my god." Sam's eyes darted around the room. "Are you real? Am I dreaming you?"

"I hope I'm real," Ulysses said. "I don't know what I've been doing with my life if I'm not." He put a hand on Sam's cheek until the other man's panic subsided. Ulysses started unbuckling the strap pinning Sam's left arm. "Laz went to go raise the alarm."

"How did you get in here?"

"I walked in."

Sam blinked. "Ulysses, it's a trap."

"Maybe," Ulysses said. The leather tongue of the strap pulled free of the metal frame of the buckle and he rubbed the spot where it had touched Sam's wrist, his fingers shaky. "Maybe they all stepped out for a minute."

The other man snorted. "They knew you would come. Stricker said as much."

"I gotta be me," Ulysses said. He went to work on Sam's right arm while Sam undid the strap across his chest. "Did they hurt you? Are you okay?"

"I'm—I think I'm fine. The drugs have worn off." Sam got to his feet and then immediately swayed forward, knees buckling. Ulysses's stomach dropped, but he managed to catch him before he went over. "I can't quite feel my feet," Sam said. "That's a problem."

"It'll be fine," Ulysses said, hauling him upright. Sam threw his arms around Ulysses, half seeking balance, half hugging him. "Do you know any of the people who grabbed you? Can you identify them?"

"Yeah," Sam said. "Hey, here." He tried to turn around, facing the rear of the lab. "We gotta—"

"This way." Ulysses tugged him toward the door. "We don't have much time."

"They've been talking to me." Sam's eyes were wild, his hair going in all directions. "They want me to let them out."

"What?" Ulysses steadied him as he tried to lurch away. "Who?"

"The spiders." Sam wrenched away and stumbled over to a bench.

"What are you talking about?" Ulysses grabbed for his arm.

"I think I have my balance back," Sam said, wobbling dangerously but staying more or less upright. "Let's—"

The door opened. Ulysses reached into his pocket and pulled out the big knife as Julie Stricker walked in, followed by Landover, who was holding a gun. Sam took one lurching step toward Ulysses and grabbed the back of his coat, hissing a warning that was lost when the woman spoke.

"Ah, Mr. Lenkov, we meet at last." She folded her arms in front of her. "You *are* Ulysses Lenkov, are you not? Not . . . what was it? Alexi Sterling?"

Sam made a strangled noise. Ulysses did his best to ignore it. "It's *Dr.* Lenkov." He glanced at Sam, who had gone white. "I assume you two have met."

When he looked back, Stricker smiled. "I introduced myself."

Sam was—not terrified. Something else, something wrathful, something determined. "She's been quite a host," he gritted out.

"Put down the knife, Dr. Lenkov. I'd be so sad if Dr. Landover here had to shoot you."

Ulysses eyed Landover. He had seemed like such a normal guy when they'd been playing basketball. Aside from the gun, he still did. "Has he ever shot anyone before? How confident does he feel about it?"

"I guess we'll find out," she said. "What an exciting day for all of us." There was a shuffling noise from the hall. She glanced behind her, then turned back, smiling more broadly. "And I think it's about to get even better."

More men came in. One, pale and tall, he'd seen outside the library; the other, brown haired, in a suit, had chased Sam across the Square. They'd tied Laz's hands behind his back. The pale one had the ax in one hand. Both of the men looked bruised. There was blood trickling down the side of Laz's face, but he seemed otherwise uninjured. Ulysses met his eyes for a moment and he shrugged.

"How are you feeling about that knife now, *Doctor* Lenkov?" Stricker asked. "If you could set it on the bench next to you and step away? Thank you. Hands where we can see them. You too, Mr. Sterling. No sudden movements."

The men holding Laz gave him a shove and he stumbled across the room, knocking into Ulysses before he could steady himself. "Sorry," he muttered.

"It's all right," Ulysses said.

Sam tried to lean forward and nearly fell over. "Are you good? Did they hurt you?"

"What should we do with them?" Landover asked. He sounded as uncomfortable as he looked.

"Lock up the Lenkovs," she said, handing him a key ring. "I believe Mr. Sterling is ready for phase two."

Landover looked over and nodded at the pale guy. "What do you think about harnessing some of his power for a spell to wipe the other two's memories?"

"Sure," said the pale guy. "We could do that." He glanced at the shorter man. "Go grab me *In Capiendis Monstris.*"

"No problem." He handed the ax to the pale man and left.

Stricker was still looking at the three prisoners. "All right. Please put your jackets and anything in your pants pockets on the bench to your right. I'll also take your belts and shoes."

Ulysses and Laz grumbled their way through the process. Sam swayed dangerously when Ulysses let go to tug on his shoelaces. He reached out and touched his knee to steady him, unsure how much was artifice and how much the lingering effects of the drugs he'd been given.

"Ulysses," Sam muttered when he was standing again. "I don't like this."

"It's going to be fine," Ulysses said. He could feel Sam's fear, sharper and spicier than his own, burning on the back of his tongue. He looped a hand around the back of Sam's neck. "I'm going to get you out of here, and then I'll burn this place to the ground."

Sam looked at him for one wide-eyed breath, then closed the gap and kissed him, fast and desperate before the suit and Stricker yanked them apart.

Then she unlocked the closet door and shoved Ulysses and Laz in.

Chapter 24

WHEN SAM WOKE, HE was sprawled across a small cot with his head in Ulysses's lap. Ulysses was absently running his fingers through Sam's hair. It was a soothing feeling, the gentle scritch of fingernails against his scalp, the magic murmuring between them. Sam pulled his limbs in to lie within the boundaries of the cot and rolled onto his back, looking up at the other man's face, the cinder block wall behind him. "What did I miss?" He tried to piece together the amount of time since the injection and came up with no answer.

"Not much of interest." He smiled at Sam, tired and tense but real. "How are you doing?"

"They drugged me again," Sam said. He was feeling pretty relaxed about it, though. Whatever they'd given him, it was crooning quietly to the part of his brain the anxiety came from. The thoughts were still there, but with no emotional value, like an unpainted paint-by-number.

He remembered something. "Where's Laz?"

Ulysses gestured with his head, and Sam managed to turn far enough to see Laz curled up in the corner of the cell, against the wall, knees drawn up. "I guess they don't have too much space to keep us all." Sam struggled to sit up to make some room on the cot.

Ulysses scowled at him and pressed him back down. "Just lie still for a while. If you go moving around too much, you're going to get dizzy and probably throw up, and none of us want that."

Sam subsided, primarily because Ulysses was right about how badly the drugs were affecting him when he moved. His heart was racing, and already it was getting hard to locate his hands and feet in space. "They said they were going to do something to me. Take my magic, or . . ." He took a deep breath. Ulysses and Laz were exchanging a look over his head. "I tried to tell them that was absurd, but they didn't listen."

"It's all right," Ulysses murmured. Sam knew that it *wasn't*, that Ulysses was just trying to soothe him, but it helped a little.

"What's the plan?"

There was a long silence before Ulysses shrugged. This time, he specifically wasn't looking at Laz. "They'll be back in a while. Probably another hour or so, when you're good and stoned. We could try fighting them, but we're outnumbered and they have guns."

"*A* gun," Laz said.

"That sounds like a bad plan," Sam said.

Ulysses didn't look pleased by it either. "I don't have a lot to work with."

"What are the chances someone comes to rescue us in the meantime?"

There was a moment of silent communion between Ulysses and Laz. Laz was the one who finally broke it. "My guess, given how magically inclined they seem, is that anyone coming in to find us is going to somehow overlook this little closet, so I wouldn't count on it." He paused thoughtfully. "Babushka would take the place apart piece by piece if she knew we were here, but . . ."

Sam started to nod, but it made him dizzy. He reached out blindly with one hand until he found Ulysses's and twined their fingers together, picturing them as vines growing up a tree together. The sparking feeling of touching him was grounding, familiar. "Ulysses," he said quietly, and then fell silent. There were a lot of things he wanted to say, but not in front of an audience.

Ulysses was looking down at him intently. "Do you remember," he said slowly, "that time you unlocked the library?"

Sam grinned at him. "That was a good night, eh?"

Ulysses's ears turned a little pink, which was the most delightful thing Sam had ever seen. "It was. But the library—"

"Dionysus talked to it," Sam said. "*I* didn't do anything, because I don't have any magic."

Ulysses shushed him. "You *are* Dionysus, though."

"Only as a technicality." He tried to wave his hand and found he was already holding on to Ulysses with it. A brief panic about where his other hand might be resulted in the discovery that it was also clutching Ulysses's shirt where it pulled across his abs. "I'm not the god I used to be."

Ulysses snorted. "What if we were touching?"

Sam blinked. "Why would that change anything? I touch you all the time." He lowered his voice. "That's the whole goddamn problem."

There was a *snerk* from the corner that suggested he hadn't been as quiet as he thought. "Right, right," Ulysses said, sitting forward a little. Sam tried to rearrange his limbs. "But it worked on Julius's tomb, is the thing."

"Yeah," Sam said, "but that had a spell on it."

"But the spell isn't what spoke to you. It was the mausoleum."

Sam inhaled sharply. "Ulysses . . ." he began, and then his thoughts spiraled off in a different direction.

"What?"

"Did you ever really think about how amazing mushrooms are?"

He heard a choked, tired noise and Laz's voice saying, "Oh my god, U, he's so stoned."

Sam shook his head, then regretted it. "No, no. There's a network. Underground. They talk to each other."

"The mushrooms do?" Laz drawled.

"No, like." Sam pursed his lips in concentration. "Trees can talk to each other using fungus as a network. Like a telephone exchange."

Ulysses frowned down at him. "Is that true? How do you know that?"

"I know everything," Sam said loftily. "I went to Harvard. But the point is, Ulysses, what if it hurts you?"

If he was baffled by the sudden change of topic, he didn't let on. "It'll be fine."

"No. No. No, it won't be. You said you were afraid the bond would hurt you. And I know how it makes you feel. I don't want to be responsible for that." Sam took a deep breath, then forgot what he was about to say and fell silent. Against Ulysses's protests, he pushed himself up to a sitting position, but found he was still cuddled up against the other man's body, one arm around his waist, chin on his muscular shoulder.

"Whether it injures me or not," Ulysses said carefully, "it'll be better than waiting here for those goons to come back and do whatever it is they have planned for us. And . . ."

"And?"

Ulysses licked his lips. "I trust you." Then he looked at Sam, bright blue eyes almost electric in the gloom, and said it again. "I trust you."

"Why, though?" He swayed away from Ulysses, his proprioception going haywire, and Ulysses had to grab his shoulder to keep him upright. "I love you, and I don't want to hurt you." He was very clear on that part.

Everything else was rapidly becoming sort of a mush in his head, still there but difficult to fish out without a lot of effort.

Ulysses leaned forward and kissed him very gently. "Come on, Sam, I need you to focus." He slid off the cot and then pulled Sam up as well. Sam slithered, not quite dead weight but not quite able to feel his feet either, and Ulysses staggered backward a pace or two until he hit the wall of the cell. Sam laughed, the room shifting around him like he was inside a die that had just been rolled, and caught Ulysses and kissed him.

It was not quite the experience he'd expected. He could feel himself from Ulysses's side of things, stubble on his skin, the rough and pleasant slide of lips and tongues, his body pressed against the wall . . . but he felt almost nothing from his own side, just the reflection of Ulysses feeling Sam feeling Ulysses. His body was a numb, remote thing, like he was undergoing dental surgery everywhere at once.

"Sorry," Sam muttered, as Ulysses pushed him back upright.

He shrugged, keeping a hand on Sam's hip to steady him. "I've never kissed someone else and had it feel so masturbatory."

"Is it the drugs?"

"Yeah." Ulysses finally stepped back. "I don't know which drug. Probably they gave you acid or something, on top of all the sedatives. The literature posits a connection between hallucinogens and access to latent magic reserves, which I'm sure they're assuming you—"

Sam stopped paying attention. He couldn't feel his body, but he could feel what Ulysses was feeling, the lid he was carefully keeping on his fear so as not to frighten Sam, his pounding heart, a churning tightness in his stomach, icy cold anger. Then there was the soft hum of the cotton that made up Sam's clothing, and beyond that a wild world of Laz's heartbeat, his corduroy jacket, the cement floor and the cold metal roof above them, and the strange smell of the spiders in their cage, a bright swirl of magic around them with an intriguing, sultry rhythm to it. Sam turned to follow it and fell over when the world kept turning past him.

When the universe had settled down again, Ulysses helped him up. Sam kept hold of the other man's hand this time, or Ulysses held onto him. The drugs were singing really loudly now, but he felt like he could burrow into the bond to keep himself from flying off into the atmosphere.

"Sorry," he muttered, watching a slightly pained look cross Ulysses's face. Sam pulled back as best he could, but Ulysses wouldn't let go of his hand.

"You've done worse to me," he said.

Sam looked around, finally focusing on Ulysses's eyes. "When?"

Ulysses smiled patiently. "Focus."

Sam harrumphed and pressed one hand to the door, just above the lock. It probably wasn't necessary, but it made him feel better. Ulysses stepped closer, half hugging him to keep him upright.

"How do I do this?" Sam said, even though he thought he might already know.

Ulysses shut his eyes and leaned his forehead against Sam's shoulder. "Just relax."

So he did.

He took a deep breath of the magic tingling beneath his fingertips. Ulysses was *right there*; his sobriety felt like a bucket of cold water, his roiling emotions a swift push in the opposite direction. Things Sam couldn't put a name to but that he wanted to roll around in.

Focus.

He turned his attention to the door, staring at his hand where it pressed against the white paint. Immediately he could feel the building around them, the soil beneath them, the connections between this structure and others nearby via sewer and water pipes and electrical lines, the way the whole area formed a little organism. The city was a forest. Through the roots, he could feel the Baskerville, Gooseberry House, Memorial, all whispering to each other. He could practically ask the library to vouch for him . . .

Focusssssssssss. He finally managed to collect himself into one zip code. The building was not as friendly toward him as Memorial, but it was there, a sulky presence he envisioned as being below them and yet somehow all around. It was still so young, and it didn't have a library to make it smarter. It didn't really understand the purpose of locks because it didn't understand property or people. From its point of view, people carried things in and then later carried them away. The idea that it might care about what happened to the things was foreign to it. So when Sam asked, as politely as he could, if it would open the lock, it did.

He withdrew and found himself back in his body just in time to press down on the handle and see it open beneath his hand.

Ulysses squeezed his arm; Laz swore. "How did you do that?" the latter asked as they stepped out into the room.

"I asked," Sam said.

"What do you mean—"

Sam shrugged. "I asked the building."

Ulysses let go of his hand.

Time went a little weird.

ULYSSES WAS PLEASED TO find that Stricker's lackeys, obviously not expecting an escape, had left most of their personal effects piled on the lab bench next to the door. They'd taken the ax and the hunting knife, but his little switchblade was still snug in the pocket of his jacket. He pulled on his boots and belt with no small sense of relief, as though rearmoring himself against their foes.

"Sam," he said, "your tie is here, but I don't see your coat." He turned back around to find that Sam had pulled off his shoes and socks and was examining his bare feet with a satisfied expression. "Ah. I'll hold on to it for you."

"This must be yours," Laz said, passing Sam a wallet.

Sam took it, face contorting oddly. "This used to be a cow."

Ulysses turned and went deeper into the room.

"Where are you going?" Laz called out.

"I want Sam's blood back," Ulysses said over his shoulder, stooping to peer into a little refrigerator. "And whatever other samples they took. I'm not leaving that shit here for them." A test tube rack stood on the counter, but all the tubes were empty. He swore.

"They took it out of here," Sam said from somewhere to Ulysses's left.

"How do you know that? Weren't you unconscious?" Laz asked.

"The spiders know."

Ulysses looked over to see Sam with one hand pressed up against the spider cage. A chill washed over him.

Laz, helpfully, said, "Remember that scene in *Crime and Punishment* when Raskolnikov—"

Ulysses groaned. "And what's-his-name says what if eternity is full of spiders?"

"Yeah."

Ulysses decided to ignore this. He went over and took Sam by the arm. "Come away from there."

Laz was by the main door now, ear pressed to it. When they joined him, he glanced at Ulysses and shook his head. "It's gonna be hard to extricate ourselves with him all—" He waved a hand.

"I'm sure you'll figure something out," Ulysses said. "Or we'll get shot, and it won't matter. You ready? On three."

The corridor was empty. He watched Sam turn in a lazy circle before setting off in the direction of the entrance.

"Where is everyone?" Ulysses said under his breath. Laz shook his head.

"This one," Sam said suddenly, stopping in front of one of the doors.

"What's in there?" Laz asked. His tone was gentler than it had been before, probably in acknowledgment of how far gone Sam was. Ulysses could feel him in there, giddily slipping from moment to moment like a brightly colored minnow. They didn't even need to be touching for him to feel it now.

"I don't know." Sam's eyes were wide, almost glowing; he turned and went through the door before either of them could restrain him.

It was an office, nothing special except that Julie Stricker looked up in surprise when they came in.

"You—" she started, halfway to her feet.

Ulysses glanced at his brother, and without another word, Laz was behind her, a hand on her shoulder. "Sit down," Ulysses said calmly. She sat. He fished the switchblade out of his pocket and tossed it to Laz. "For emergencies."

The room held the desk she was seated behind, some shelves, a filing cabinet with a couple of potted plants on top that were gradually dying. Set in both the left- and right-hand walls were doors to the next rooms along the hall, both firmly shut. Sam's suit coat had been dumped in the corner, and the sight of it filled Ulysses with rage all over again when he picked it up.

"What are you going to do?" Stricker asked.

He didn't say anything at first, just draped the coat around Sam's shoulders like a cloak. Then he crossed the room and jerked open the top drawer of the filing cabinet. "I'm going to burn this place to the ground." Sam, peering over his shoulder, grabbed a ledger out of the drawer, making pleased little noises about Al Capone and tax evasion that Ulysses didn't understand at all. "You can stay, or you can leave. I don't really care."

"How compassionate," she said dryly. "I'm sure your grandmother would be pleased."

Ulysses didn't have to look to know Laz's hand was tightening on the handle of the knife. "Want me to nick her for that?" he murmured.

Ulysses raised a hand to stay him without looking up from the files. "Not unless she tries to escape or raise the alarm. We don't need her blood complicating . . ."

Laz cleared his throat. "What is it?"

"They know so much." These files were written in plain English without cyphers, and they were awful. Too many of the papers were too personal. Sam had been right about how close the tabs they'd been keeping were;

they knew more about the god children than almost anyone. Some of what he was looking at had to be transcriptions of the documents Sam had, describing Howard's routines and what Sam had been doing last October, but others—they had information about Hugh, about Sita. . . . "How long have they been watching us?"

"You gotta get that out of here," Laz said. "They have that Freedom of Information Act now. If the cops take that as evidence, anyone will be able to request it as a public record."

Ulysses looked over his shoulder. "It—really, they can just do that?"

Laz's eyes were fixed on Julie Stricker, who was a rock. "I was briefed on it, back in the—before."

There were too many files to carry out with them. When he'd said he was going to burn the place to the ground, he had not been thinking entirely clearly, but suddenly it looked like the best option. He grabbed a few files, things that looked like evidence of criminality while exposing Sam the least, and turned. Stricker was still sitting stiffly in her chair, tapping her fingers on one of the armrests, muttering under her breath. Laz had pulled it a pace or two away from the desk to get her farther from Sam, who was bent forward, drawing something on the blotter in a sure hand. "Why are you—" Ulysses said to Stricker, and then cut himself off and tried again. "Why Julius Sterling?"

She smiled and didn't reply.

He'd been thinking of the group as a cult primarily because that was the word Hugh and Livia had used for them. Not inaccurately, it seemed. "The promise of immortality, I guess. Selfish."

Stricker shrugged, careless of the knife. "We're the same, you and I. Both using the god children for our own ends. You're just convinced of your own righteousness."

Ulysses choked. "Wow," was what he eventually managed. "That's not—no. No!"

She cocked an eyebrow at him, but Ulysses found himself looking away. Looking at Sam.

"Gods care about everyone in general and no one specifically," Stricker said, her voice low. "Humans are the opposite."

"I'll take my chances." He looked over at Sam again. He'd finished drawing a fire sigil on the desk—where had he picked that up?—and was standing a few steps away, looking up into the rafters.

"What's up?" Ulysses asked.

"Just listening to the spiders."

Ulysses twitched and looked upward, but there was nothing there. "What, ah—"

"I think they've colonized parts of the building," Sam said. "Escapees."

Ulysses reached out and put a hand on Sam's cheek. His eyes cleared a bit when they touched. "Hey," Sam said.

"Sam, what's going on with you?" Ulysses whispered.

Sam shook his head. "It's just getting worse and worse," he said.

"The drug is still peaking," Ulysses said. "It's going to take a while."

"The longer it takes, the more I feel like him."

That was a blank Ulysses didn't need filled in. He took a moment to settle himself, because doubtless feeling the full force of his concern and dismay was not going to help Sam with anything. "Let's get out of here," he said.

Sam blinked. "Get the book. Her guys took a book from the library."

Ulysses turned on his heel. "Dr. Stricker?"

She smiled, a thin, chilly expression. "Oh, I have that right here. If you'll allow me to retrieve it?"

Laz glanced at Ulysses and stepped back, keeping his hands at the ready.

Stricker bent down and opened the bottom drawer of her desk, keeping her eyes locked on Ulysses's the whole time, the smile never leaving her face. As she straightened up, it became clear that she was holding a large leather purse. She slipped the strap over one shoulder. "Thank you."

"The book?"

She shook her head. "Not today." And she vanished.

"What the *fuck*," Laz shouted, raising his hands. "How did she do that?"

"I don't know." Ulysses approached the desk cautiously, but Stricker was really gone. The chair was made of wood and was supported by a central pedestal leading down to a wheeled base. Ulysses reached out and hefted it, flipped it over.

There was a sigil carved into the underside of the seat, a twisty, poisonous shape. Laz swore again. "What did she use for a sacrifice?"

"No idea." Ulysses felt numb. "Sam, that book . . ."

"It was an old grimoire," Sam said. "It was . . . the library told me it was important." Ulysses could hear the undercurrent in his words—they'd failed at something important.

The door to the office swung open and a man in a suit came in, carrying a clipboard. "Dr. S," he said, and then looked up and stopped dead, eyes wide. Ulysses recognized him—the guy who'd chased Sam, who'd roughed up Laz. Laz and Sam seemed to recognize the man in the same moment and stepped toward him, Sam growling out the word "Shapiro" like a curse.

Shapiro froze, holding up the clipboard like it was some kind of shield.

"Get out of here," Ulysses barked, and the man didn't need to be told twice.

There would be time enough to think about what the book meant later. Ulysses put the chair down and stood for a moment, gathering himself. Then he looked up. "Laz?"

"Yeah?"

"We're rolling out. I need the knife."

Laz closed the knife and tossed it over. Ulysses flipped it open and took a moment to inspect the blade. It had been well cared-for, respected and loved; it wasn't an athame, but it would have to do. He held up his right hand and carefully drew the blade across his palm, not deeply, but enough to draw blood. Then he pressed his hand to the sigil Sam had drawn.

Sam made a pained noise and took the knife from him. For a moment, he seemed to study it. Then he carefully sliced his own palm and let the blood drip down onto the sigil as well.

Ulysses snatched the knife back and flipped it shut. "We need a sacrifice."

Laz started to turn out the desk drawers, but it was Sam who slid his suit coat off and dropped it on top of the sigil, marred with a bloody handprint. "Clothing of the gods," he murmured, and grinned. "Someone tell my tailor."

"Everyone out," Ulysses announced. He gathered up all the ledgers and papers they'd grabbed in his non-bloody hand and pushed Sam toward the exit with the other.

Ulysses said the words from the doorway. The wooden desk exploded into flames, hard enough to knock him backward.

The spell had been somewhat indiscriminate, and things were burning elsewhere in the building as well. *Good.* Laz was shouting something, trying to pull him off the floor, but Ulysses's ears were ringing and he couldn't make sense of any of it. Sam and Laz managed to pull Ulysses upright, and they started for the front door, dragging him between them.

They piled out the door of the Quonset hut. Laz had parked about fifty feet away, which felt like an endless stretch of pavement to cross. Laz took the papers and jogged ahead, letting Sam focus on keeping Ulysses upright and steady. And then there was a shout from behind them: "Stop right there."

Ulysses's brain clicked back into gear when he turned and saw Landover's bearded face come striding toward them. He was carrying the gun in one hand and didn't seem to notice that smoke was beginning to billow out of the building behind him.

"It's over," Ulysses shouted back. "You've lost."

"I'm not letting you go that easily." Landover raised the gun. "You're going to answer for what you've done here."

"Answer to whom?"

"To me." He'd wondered before if Landover had ever actually fired the gun, but he seemed perfectly at ease now as he aimed.

Beside Ulysses, Sam was frozen, his fingers rigid on Ulysses's arm. Ulysses felt another flash of the rage he thought he had emptied into the fire spell. Was it his? Was it Sam's? Before he could figure anything out, Landover was abruptly arrested by vines.

Vines?

Long, nimble green vines that erupted out of the pavement and snaked up his legs. Landover shouted and nearly fell, but the vines held him fast, pulling his arms down tight against his body. It was Sam who let go and stepped away from Ulysses, but the person who strode across the pavement in the half light and setting sun didn't walk like Sam.

"Hello, Dr. Landover," Sam said. Even from ten feet away, Ulysses thought his voice was peculiarly focused, taut with energy. "It's good to see you again."

"Sterling." Landover frowned at him, then looked over at Ulysses. "Lenkov, let me go. I'm sure we can reach an agreement."

"Mmm," Sam said. "I don't like being held at gunpoint, so I'm not going to do that." Ulysses could hear him smile, and it made him shiver. Sam looked over at Ulysses, then back at Landover. "What *are* we going to do with you?"

Ulysses said, "I have a few ideas," and Sam laughed, a warm, rumbling sound.

From the south, Ulysses heard sirens—police cars, maybe a fire truck. "I could just leave you for the authorities," Sam said, looking in that direction. "But you've acted so badly. *So*—" He broke off, shaking his head, and then took a few steps away and crouched down.

When he got back up, something was standing on his palm. Ulysses could barely make it out at first, despite its size, and then he realized—it was a spider. They were fleeing the fire.

"Sam," he said urgently, but Sam ignored him.

"Hello, my friend," he said to the spider, and then cocked his head as though listening to the creature.

Laz was tugging on Ulysses's arm now, urging him toward the car. More spiders were emerging, but they ignored the two of them, creating a small ring on the asphalt around Sam. It was like they were waiting for something.

"Yes, I think so," Sam said, and lowered the spider to the ground. He looked at Landover. "I'm afraid someone has a prior claim to you. Bon chance."

Almost as one, the spiders started for Landover. Sam watched with quiet interest for a moment, then turned away. Ulysses shut his eyes moments before Landover screamed.

"What are they going to do to him?" Laz asked, not turning around.

Ulysses bit his lip. "Consume his inherent magic, I guess."

"He'll live," Sam said. When Ulysses finally looked, he saw Sam's eyes were half-lidded, but his posture was unusually tall, his skin glowing bronze in the firelight.

Laz said, "Are we just going to leave them here?"

"What?" Ulysses asked, not taking his eyes off of Sam. Something was shifting inside of him, and with the bond so wide open, Ulysses could feel it, like the turning of a wheel, like the dizziness of freedom.

"The spiders."

"Aunt Cass will take care of them. I'll call her tomorrow."

"I think the cavalry is here," Sam said as the first police cars screeched up. "Laz, can you talk to them? I think I need to sit down. Just for a moment." And then he stumbled, and Ulysses caught him.

Chapter 25

I T WAS VERY LATE by the time they finished talking to the police and the military police and—probably some others; Ulysses lost track at some point. He just knew that by the time they were allowed to leave, it had circled around to being early. Laz drove them back across town, Sam curled up in the back seat, moaning quietly to himself. Ulysses sympathized; he'd spent several hours in Wisconsin General's ER going through the same thing. Sam, on the other hand, refused to go to the hospital, so Ulysses took him back home and put him to bed. He didn't know how much time passed before Sam fell asleep, but at least he didn't try to get up and wander as long as Ulysses let him lie with his head on Ulysses's shoulder, one arm thrown possessively across his chest. He was a warm, solid presence, and Ulysses fell asleep to the sound of his breathing.

He woke up late in the morning. Sam was deeply unconscious, which was good, and he didn't stir when Ulysses wriggled out from underneath him, which was also good.

Ulysses found that once he was on his feet, almost every muscle and sinew in his body hurt. He didn't think he'd done anything especially athletic. Maybe it was the basketball game. For a moment, he gave real thought to climbing back into bed for, at minimum, a day or two. But no, there were things to do.

He showered and ate a bowl of cereal. Then, with a pocketful of change, he went down to the lobby and made several calls: to Dr. Pearlman, to the DCI agents whose card he found in Sam's wallet, and finally to Howard.

The elder Sterling's secretary put him on hold for a very long time, but ultimately she did transfer him back.

"Dr. Lenkov," Howard said in a dry tone. "To what do I owe the pleasure?"

Ulysses took a deep breath. "I was wondering if you could recommend a lawyer. We've run into a little trouble with some of Julius's former group, and although I have no doubt that the noble law enforcement agencies that are now engaged in investigating them are . . . fair minded and . . ." He sighed. "I need someone to help make sure they stay focused on the right people, if you get my meaning."

"Yes," Howard said immediately. And then, to Ulysses's shock, he added, "I'm glad you called me. Do you have a pencil?"

Ulysses scribbled down the information and thanked him.

"I'll call him and provide a précis, if you'd like," Howard said. "Just give me your contact information to pass along."

"That's very kind of you," Ulysses said, and found that he meant it. "We just moved, and we won't have a phone again until Friday." He wasn't sure if Sam wanted Howard to have their address, so he didn't offer it. "Tell him I'll call tomorrow morning."

"Of course." Howard didn't say anything for a moment, and Ulysses thought perhaps the conversation was over. Then Howard asked, "Is Sam all right?"

"He's—yeah. He'll be fine." Just being a few floors away from him made Ulysses's skin itch. He didn't tell Howard that part.

"Good." Howard cleared his throat. "Thank you for keeping him safe. Keep me apprised."

"Yeah," Ulysses said. When they'd hung up, he stared at the receiver for a long time. Then he went back up to the apartment and read *Ancient Greek Rituals* again, just to make sure he hadn't missed anything the first two times.

By late Wednesday afternoon, Sam was up, had showered and eaten a bowl of cereal, and was wandering disconsolately around the apartment in a pair of sweatpants and no shirt. Ulysses watched from the sofa over the top of a copy of *Been Down So Long It Looks Like Up to Me* that he was absolutely not following a single word of. After the third or fourth sigh, Ulysses gave up all pretense of reading and put down his book.

"Sam, what?"

Sam looked over at him. "I thought somehow all that was going to fix the bond."

"All . . . what?"

"Being Dionysus, and . . . I grew vines. We did magic together. We took care of the cult." The cops had taken care of the cult, technically, or at least arrested Landover, Thatcher, and Shapiro, but Ulysses didn't point out the nuance there. Sam made a frustrated hand motion. "Somehow I thought it would rebalance things. But I can still feel the bond. It's stronger than ever. I can practically feel you sitting there from over here, which is *unsettling*." He dropped dramatically onto the couch, throwing one arm up over his head.

Ulysses knew what he meant. He'd felt every emotion in that speech marching across him in formation. He dragged his eyes away from Sam's chest. "About that," he said. "I have an idea. We could go now, if you're up for it."

Sam sat up and looked at him. "What does 'up for it' entail, exactly?"

"A walk out to Picnic Point, and then later we can get dinner somewhere nice." He shrugged, trying to act casual and relaxed even though his pulse had started to race the minute he'd even thought about it. "We could ask Ellen to meet us, if you want. There's a new French restaurant that just opened on State Street. I've heard it's quite good."

There was a long silence. "How are we going to fix it?"

"A ritual. I'll explain when we get there."

Sam nodded. "Does this involve dissolving the bond or agreeing never to see each other again? Or both?"

"No."

"All right." Sam got up, stretched, and went into the bedroom.

Ulysses threw a few supplies in his satchel and then went to change as well. He only really had one suit, and he was damned if he was wearing a tie, so that made all of his choices pretty straightforward. He looked fine. A little scraped around the edges, and with one hand still bandaged, but that was life.

Sam, meanwhile, had on a dark brown tweed with a double-breasted vest that made his eyes a brilliant, magnetic green. It was immaculate. He could have met the governor in that suit. He could have met the pope. Ulysses didn't think Sam was all that interested in meeting the pope, but the point stood.

"Is this good?" Sam asked, the corner of his mouth curling up.

"We could cancel the ritual and just stay here," Ulysses said, taking a step toward him.

Sam kissed him, a gentle brush of his lips on Ulysses's, and he was reminded why they needed to do this. There was a certain erotic charge in being able to feel things from Sam's side, but if he had to go the rest of his life feeling every touch from both sides, he was going to go mad. The human brain was not built for such an abundance of input.

"Come on," Sam said, pulling back regretfully. "We don't have world enough or time right now."

"Right." Ulysses straightened Sam's tie. Then he forced himself to take his hands away.

They left the motorcycle at the entrance to Picnic Point and walked the rest of the way. Ulysses tried to remember what the actual date of their last visit had been. October, before Samhain.

"It was the 29th," Sam said, as though reading his mind.

"That was an interesting night."

Sam nodded. "That was the night when everything really began."

"What do you mean?"

"I'd always already been Dionysus, in a sense, but before the geas was gone, I couldn't really feel him. Or feel like him?" Sam tilted his head back, looking up at the light blue of the late afternoon sky. "That was the first night I reconnected with that part of myself."

It was as good an opening as Ulysses was likely to get, he supposed. "How much do you remember from being Dionysus?"

"You mean—"

"Up north, on the island."

Sam pressed a hand to a spot to the left of his breastbone, frowning. "Almost nothing." He lowered his hand. "Why, what did I do?"

"At the time, you called me Ariadne."

There was a long silence. "Ah," Sam said at last. "That's . . . weird." He glanced sidelong at Ulysses. "It *is* weird, right? I'm rather losing track of where the—" He made a throwing motion.

"Where the goalposts are?" Ulysses suggested.

"Yeah."

Ulysses nodded. "It is unusual," he said thoughtfully. "I mean, we've had stranger, to be sure."

They reached the little circle with the fire pit at the end of the point. Sam walked over to the railing Ulysses had once handcuffed him to and gripped the top rail, looking out at the lake.

"There's a bench down there," he said suddenly, and after a moment they found the steps leading down the steep hill to a flat spot with a wooden Leopold bench nearly at lake level. The wind kicked up little waves that broke prettily on the rocks in front of them, the water painted yellow and orange and pink in ripples by the setting sun. "This is nice," Sam decided, settling himself at one end of the bench. Ulysses sat next to him, their knees touching, and pulled the wine bottle out, because he was damned if he was going to do the rest of this entirely sober. Sam watched as he also retrieved a Swiss army knife and opened it.

"I see there's a plan of some sort," Sam said, accepting the bottle while Ulysses put the knife away.

"I wish there was a plan," Ulysses said. "Also, I forgot to pack any glasses. So, you know." He gestured to the bottle, and Sam grinned and took a swig.

"Wow, that's quite sweet," Sam said, handing the bottle to him.

It tasted like blackberry jam, a little bit spicy on the back. "Huh." He looked at the label, which was Italian. "Where'd we get this?"

Sam leaned closer to peer over his shoulder. "Vikram and Sita brought it to the séance. We didn't drink it at the time."

"I don't hate it." He handed the bottle back to Sam.

"Have we started yet?" Sam asked, taking another drink.

"I'll tell you." Ulysses took a deep breath. "What do you know about ancient Greek wedding rituals?"

"Almost nothing." Sam passed the bottle back to him and stretched an arm across the back of the bench. "I assume they varied by city-state and era."

"Yes." Ulysses tried to put his racing thoughts into some kind of order. "We don't know much for sure, although they tend to be a bit grim for women. In Athens, during some time periods, there were some rituals, like bathing and making sacrifices. Then they'd have a party, and the bride would move into the groom's house. Or something like that."

"All right, but we did that, more or less, and the bond didn't go haywire until several days later."

Ulysses was infinitely grateful that Sam understood what he was trying to say. "Yes. Rule zero is that you can't enter a ritual unknowingly. Although consider there to be an asterisk on that last word." He took a swig from the bottle and offered it back to Sam, who held it for a moment, frowning.

"Why is that rule zero? Shouldn't it be rule one?" he mused.

"Rule one is that once you begin a ritual, you have to complete it," Ulysses said.

"Who numbered these?"

"Sam," he said. "Anyway, you *did* enter a ritual. The night that things—"

"I didn't!" Sam protested, fingers tightening on the neck of the bottle. "You just said I couldn't enter a ritual unintentionally. Or is this the asterisk?"

Ulysses licked his lips. "This is a little complicated. You deliberately invoked the name of Dionysus and became intoxicated in their company. Sound familiar at all? And they liked you, felt protective. You qua Sam, meaning the original human, may not have known that you were entering a ritual, but you qua Dionysus did."

Sam huffed out a breath. "That is not a very good bacchanalia."

Ulysses elbowed him. "Talk to your maenads if you're not pleased."

Sam looked at the bottle again and then set it gently on the ground next to the bench. "Accepting this hypothesis for the time being, it follows that later that night, when we had sex . . ."

"There was some sort of ongoing ritual that we got entangled with and didn't exit correctly."

Sam shook his head. "Why wouldn't the ritual just end?"

It was a reasonable question. Ulysses rubbed his jaw. "This is all guesswork on my part, but rule three is that rituals change their participants. They change their status in society, or they change who or what they are. We didn't change that night. We had a fight and then tried to go on as normal."

"What happened to rule two?" Sam picked up the bottle again and took a long swallow.

Ulysses sighed and grabbed the wine back. "We'll get to rule two."

Sam scratched his head, disarranging his curls. Ulysses looked at him in the golden light and thought abruptly of Dionysus striding across the frozen graveyard with a circlet of fig leaves on his head, gorgeous and dangerous in equal measure, the firelight on his skin. Crossing the asphalt toward Landover, all long limbs and graceful motion. "Let me just make sure of this," Sam said. "You're saying that we inadvertently started some sort of ritual that didn't get finished correctly, even though we didn't know we were doing that and we shouldn't have been able to. And that is what made the bond get all weird, and so the way to fix it is to do a new ritual and finish it correctly. Oh, and this ritual should be a wedding, I guess, because we somehow inadvertently did *that* ritual and also didn't at the same time. That seems to be what you're working your way around to." He leaned away from Ulysses on the bench but turned toward him. "Is that all? Did I miss something?"

"No. That's a very succinct summary." Ulysses rolled the bottle between his palms, not ready to relinquish it. After a few moments of deliberation, he took a final swig and set it down. "What do you think?"

Sam groaned and tipped his head back. "I don't want to get married."

"I'll try not to be insulted," Ulysses said quietly.

"No, it's—" Sam sat forward and put his elbows on his knees, face in his hands. "*Don't* take it personally. If I were going to get married, it would be you. But marriage . . . I meant what I told Vikram and Sita that night. It's a holdover from the past, something invented to ensure that one's biological offspring alone inherit one's property."

Ulysses crossed his arms. "I also enjoy history, but I think we can update our definition of marriage to include something that postdates the year 1300."

"You know what I mean, Ulysses." Sam got up and took a few paces along the thin strip of land before turning back. "Marriages are full of unhappy people, and I never wanted any part of that." He took a deep breath. "Also, you said that a ritual has to change the participants. But we already live together. I don't know what you really think is going to change if we do this. A tax break, maybe?"

"The change *can* come from external recognition of the ritual's completion, but it doesn't have to," Ulysses said. "Rituals carry meaning for the participants above all else. Unlike, say, theatrical productions, which carry meaning for the onlookers." He grinned briefly. "That's rule two."

"Of course it is."

Ulysses got up and took a few steps toward him. "I think the more important part of all of this is that if you and I got married, neither of us would suddenly turn into Howard or Francie. Or Virgil, for that matter," he added, at least partly for his own benefit.

"I know that." Sam shut his eyes. "I just—" He inhaled slowly, exhaled. "What do you want?" he asked suddenly.

"What do you mean?"

Sam opened his eyes and looked at Ulysses. "I mean we're talking about this as a way to straighten out whatever mistake we made previously. Whatever mistake *I* made previously, I guess. But what do *you* want? You told Livia you didn't want to get married."

"I didn't want to marry Livia," he said, because it was true and easy to admit. "And I feel like I've already told you, several times now, that I want to be here with you, tusk to tusk for all eternity. I've tried to tell you that whatever problems we run into, we can solve them together." He reached out and grabbed Sam's hands. "I didn't plan this, but I'm not sorry it happened. I want to fix the bond. But I would be glad to have done this even if the ceremony doesn't work, because I want you to understand that I'm not going to leave, regardless of what happens."

His heart was beating so hard that he had no doubt Sam could hear it. The other man, meanwhile, was looking at him with an unfiltered, raw expression, feelings and thoughts flicking through him faster than Ulysses could name them. Finally he groaned again and leaned forward, pressing his forehead to Ulysses's shoulder.

"Sweet-talking bastard," he muttered, just loud enough that Ulysses could hear him. "What am I supposed to say to that, huh?"

Ulysses laughed, feeling shaky with relief. "Tell me to fuck off if you don't want me, because otherwise you're stuck with me."

Sam let go of Ulysses's hands to wrap his arms around Ulysses's waist. "I would not wish any companion in the world but you. Nor can imagination form a shape besides yourself to like of," he murmured. And then, after a moment, he added, "So what does this ritual entail? Are we going to call the watchtowers again?"

"Probably not." Ulysses frowned and took half a step back, because it was getting pretty hard to concentrate with Sam touching him. "It has to be personally meaningful to both of us, and I feel like being outside makes sense, don't you? Watchtowers are usually an indoor thing."

Sam nodded. "Do we need . . . I don't know. Witnesses? An officiant?"

"Do you want those things?" Ulysses glanced back at the steps. "We could go call Laz or Ellen."

Sam followed his gaze, pensive. "For hundreds of years, a wedding was just two people exchanging a vow and sometimes a token in private," he said finally. "That's the important part, right? Besides—" He gestured at the sunset. "We're never going to have a better moment than this."

"All right," Ulysses said, and dug the small blue pouch out of his satchel.

"What's that?"

Ulysses opened the bag and looked down into it. "Rings."

"That's the bag Mariah left for you," Sam said. "How did she—"

Ulysses shook his head. "She's very intuitive, but this seems above and beyond, even for her." He remembered the evening at Gooseberry House when she'd asked if they planned to marry. "Maybe it was just wishful thinking on her part." They were identical plain silver bands, shiny with a rolled edge. He compared the sizes of the rings and their hands and handed one to Sam. "Might have to get them resized, I don't know."

"Oh, that feels odd," Sam said. He held up the ring, turning it this way and that. "Silver?"

"It's tradition," Ulysses said. "More apotropaic magic. Silver is pure, so it protects against all sorts of things. Iron would do too, I guess. I've just never heard of iron wedding rings. Or steel, so it didn't rust?" He shrugged.

"What's the line from that movie . . . 'Forged from the steel of a brave cannon that fought at Stalingrad,' " Sam quipped, and Ulysses laughed.

"That's a bit much, even for my family."

Sam grinned, closing his fingers around the ring. "So we just . . . make a vow?"

Ulysses considered this. "Is there anything else we should include?"

"I still feel a little magical. I could probably grow some flowers if you wanted a bouquet or something," Sam offered, eyes dancing. "But no. I'm . . . this is enough." He looked back at the hill behind them as though the land itself might have something to say about it. "How do we do this?"

"Grab the wine and pour out a libation," Ulysses said without thinking, as though it were a normal suggestion. Fortunately, Sam took it in stride. Raising the bottle for a moment in the direction of the setting sun, he poured a small measure into the lake at their feet. Impishly, he took a swig and passed the bottle to Ulysses, who followed suit. Then, with economical gestures that still felt somehow ceremonial, Sam took the bottle back and set it on the bench behind them.

Ulysses looked down at the ring he was holding. It was warm from his skin and heavy for its size, but just an object. Rituals took meaning from their participants.

All right, what else? Names. Promises. The future. He looked back at Sam. "Ready?"

"No," Sam said. "Not even a little bit. But do it anyway."

Ulysses grinned and grabbed Sam's left hand. "Dionysus Samuel Sterling, you are precious to me. I vow to give you my protection, my assistance, my reverence, and my love for the rest of our days. When you need rescuing, I'll be there. When you need someone to fight for you or a shoulder to cry on, I'll be there." He looked at the ring again. Since he'd been speaking, the breeze had dropped away, as though the place itself were listening to him. "I give you this ring as a token of my promise. Let my life, my affection, and my body be forever entwined with yours." His fingers were shaking when he slid the ring onto Sam's finger, and then he had to close his eyes, because Sam was right that this was a little ridiculous, but also his eyelids were prickling dangerously.

When he opened them again, Sam was staring down at his hand as though he couldn't quite parse what was going on, so Ulysses nudged him. "Ahh," he said, turning wide, bright eyes on Ulysses. "Yes. My turn." He cleared his throat. "O heaven, o earth, bear witness to this sound and crown what I profess with kind event if I speak true. Ulysses Alexei Lenkov . . . I beyond all limit of what else in the world do love, prize, honor you." He paused, staring into Ulysses's eyes now, and Ulysses felt him calm down. "I vow to give you my protection, my assistance, my reverence, and my love for the rest of our days. I shall not be shaken from my duties by tempest or darkness, nor by the stumbling blocks of others, nor by . . . plant zombies or whatever weird, terrible things we run into." Ulysses snorted, and Sam grinned at him, eyes sparkling. "This ring is a symbol of my commitment. Take it, and know that you receive whatever I can give you, body and soul." He slid the ring onto Ulysses's finger, and then leaned forward and kissed him.

Since they'd begun, Ulysses had not been paying much attention to the bond, despite the ostensible purpose of the rite. But he felt it again as it settled around their shoulders in a new configuration, stable and—calm, he supposed. Correct, now. Hopefully less overwhelming. He felt something loosen in his chest, a tension he'd been carrying for a long time, and he relaxed into Sam's touch, hugging him closer. He felt warm from the wine, warmer still from Sam's proximity, and . . . safe.

And that was it. When he opened his eyes and looked back to the left, he was surprised to see that the sun had hardly moved. Still pressed against him, Sam took a shuddery breath. "That's . . . What just happened?"

"We got married," Ulysses said, and Sam started to giggle.

"Oh my god, we actually did." He stepped back, then sat heavily on the bench, looking down at his hand with the ring on it. "Do you think our friends will be pissed they didn't get to come and throw flower petals at us?"

"I think they'll understand." Ulysses sat down next to him and put his arm around Sam's shoulders. "Eventually, anyway." Sam snorted, and Ulysses added, "We could always have a more traditional ceremony sometime, if you wanted. Mariah would probably offer to officiate."

"No," Sam said immediately, and Ulysses grinned. "I can't go through that again. Anyway, rule three, right? This isn't for them."

"That's rule two."

"I'm renumbering them. The old system was unintuitive." He pressed his face against the side of Ulysses's for a moment. "We should head back. It's going to be dark before we get to the parking lot."

"Yeah." Ulysses took his hand and got up, pulling Sam to his feet as well. "Moon's rising, though."

"Should we bring the wine?" Sam asked, picking up the bottle.

"It'd be nice to leave it as an offering, but I think that constitutes littering." He retrieved the cork from his satchel and tossed it to Sam.

"I think the gods are satisfied."

"You'd know."

"I really wouldn't." Sam shoved the cork in and shouldered the satchel. "Dinner? Did you say something about a new French restaurant?"

Ulysses followed him up the steps, pausing at the top to look out at the sunset once more. "Twelve thousand years or more of human habitation," he said, mostly to himself. "And now we're a part of that." They already had been, but this visit felt more significant. Which was funny, because at the time of their last visit, he would never have thought anything could outweigh that.

"We're just a blip," Sam said, taking his hand. "It's kind of reassuring, in a way. People come and go, and someday they'll keep doing it all without us."

"You find that comforting?"

"Believe it or not, it's nice to be one more event in an endless chain for once." He smiled a little uncertainly. "Almost everything else in my life is ringed with the phrases, 'Oh, we have no idea, that hasn't happened before.' Even my relationship with you. *Especially* my relationship with you, maybe."

"That's the price you pay for being remarkable," Ulysses said. Impulsively, he pulled Sam back and kissed him again, because he could. "All right, come on. It's getting cold."

"Can I be there when you see Laz next?" Sam asked. "I want to see his face when he notices the rings." And he followed Ulysses into the gathering darkness.

Acknowledgments

Although the bombing of Sterling Hall happened over fifty years ago, there are still many Madisonians who remember it. I've been fortunate to chat with a few of them over the years. I also had an office in the (rebuilt) basement myself back when I was a grad student and remember walking past the plaque to the man who died as a result of the bombing. His name was Dr. Robert Fassnacht. Three others (Paul Quin, David Schuster, and Norbert Sutler) were injured. It didn't feel appropriate to tie their names to the actual text of this novel, but I do want to acknowledge that this was an event with huge repercussions, both for these people's families and for the community.

Incidentally, in an early draft of *Old Time Religion*, Ulysses thinks about how the Red Gym had been firebombed in January 1970. (This line didn't make it through to the final draft, but it's an actual thing that happened; Sam alludes to this in chapter 6 of *Troth*, too.) That bombing was carried out by one of the same men who bombed Sterling Hall eight months

366

later—Karl Armstrong. After serving some time in prison, he returned to Madison where he operated a food cart called Loose Juice and later opened a deli called the Radical Rye. I once went there on a very unsuccessful date.

There has been a lot of writing, scholarly and not, about the protest movement and the bombing. For those interested in an in-depth look, I recommend Andrea Rochelle Bimling's 2004 senior thesis, "Blood on the Third Coast: Causes and Consequences of Madison's 1970 Sterling Hall Bombing," which is available at https://lux.lawrence.edu/luhp/130.

Finally, I have a lot of people to thank for their assistance, as always. Rowan the book doula, Bryan my alpha reader, the Middle Lion Critique Group (Justin, Monique, Wendy, and Alice), Katy, and Blaine all read various drafts of this and offered feedback, some on tight deadlines. Eliot West edited it and did an excellent job. Sara was my sensitivity reader for Laz's PTSD and answered my questions about the military. Dr. Jesse provided Latin translations. Ben proofread the manuscript incredibly quickly. I am profoundly grateful that so many people believe so deeply in this project. You are all the absolute cat's pajamas.

If you enjoyed this book, you might want to check out the Wisconsin Gothic extras, which include the free short story, "Dous," available on my website (http://ehlupton.com/extras/). It's a modern day alternative universe of *Dionysus in*

Wisconsin with a lot more philosophy and only a few ghosts. You can also join my mailing list at https://winnowingfanpress.eo.page/luptonomicon or find me on social media—@pretense_soup on Instagram and Threads, or @pretensesoup on Bluesky and Mastodon (@pretensesoup@romancelandia.club). Book 4, *Lazarus, Home from the War*, will be out in the first half of 2025. The Sam and Ulysses saga will conclude in book 5, toward the end of the year.

About the Author

E. H. Lupton (she/they) lives in Madison, WI with her husband and children. Her novel *Dionysus in Wisconsin* (Winnowing Fan Press, 2023) was shortlisted for the Lambda Literary Award and was a runner-up at the Midwest Book Awards. Her poems have been published in a number of journals, including *Utopia Science Fiction*, *Paranoid Tree*, and *House of Zolo's Journal of Speculative Literature*. She is also one half of the duo behind the hit podcast *Ask a Medievalist*. In her free time, she enjoys running long distances and painting.

More From E. H. Lupton

The Joy of Fishes (Vagabondage Press, 2013)

Wisconsin Gothic series (Winnowing Fan Press):
Book 1: *Dionysus in Wisconsin* (2023)
Book 2: *Old Time Religion* (2024)
Book 3: *Troth* (2024)
Book 4: *Lazarus, Home from the War* (2025)

Made in the USA
Columbia, SC
30 October 2024

45357487R00224